A Scarecrow Wins an Award

The Misadventures of a Paranormal Post-Relationship Personal Effects Repossession Specialist, Book Two

Scott Burtness

FREE Short Story

Get *Five Stars,* a FREE demonic horror comedy short story, when you sign up for **The Paranomedy Pint**, Scott's once-a-month email featuring a great book to read, a fun show to watch, something terrific to drink, and a little paranormal weirdness to enjoy!!

For Liz.
May you always haunt my dreams.

Contents

Somewhere in Minnesota...

Why did the scarecrow win an award?

It was outstanding in its field.

CHAPTER 1

"A good farmer is nothing more nor less than a handy man with a sense of humus."
– E.B. White

S O THERE I WAS, running for my life.

Some might call that an exaggeration. An embellishment. A colorful overstating of events for dramatic effect. I was probably running, sure, but for my life? Really? Would I actually die if what I was fleeing caught me, or was I maybe—just maybe—telling an above-average-height tale? Stretching a minnow into a northern pike? Whipping up a good, old-fashioned Minnesotan whopper? Folks might be of the opinion that I was upping the stakes a smidge for the sake of a good story. Here's the thing, though. Opinions are like assholes. Everybody has one. It doesn't change the fact that I was running for my life.

My legs and arms pumped like flesh and bone pistons while my lungs struggled to keep up. Each inhale filled them with manure-scented air, and each exhale promised to be my last. While my feet sped me down the dirt road as quickly as they could, my mind pinballed around a myriad of possibilities. I could look back to see how close my pursuer was. Interesting to know, but it would also risk slowing me down, or worse, tripping me up. Might as well slit my own throat with a meat cleaver. I could duck into the stalks of corn lining the road. Maybe my pursuer would run right past. Or maybe not. I could shift into something with four legs. That would mean running a lot faster, but only after getting free of my clothes. Also, even if I stayed one step ahead, I wouldn't have my nifty hand with its opposable thumb. I needed that to carry the reason I was running in the first place. So, yeah. There were options, and the best one was to keep running for my life.

I spared a thought for the object clutched in my fist. A small thing to cause such a fuss. Had I known how upset the guy would be about the trinket, I would've never taken the job. I'm used to folks being a bit ruffled when I show up. As a post-relationship personal effects repossession specialist, I didn't have the luxury of meeting people at their best. Breakups are almost never easy. When I'm hired to get that special whatever back from someone's ex, I get to swan dive into a messy pile of post-relationship crap. What can I say? Someone's gotta do it, so it might as well be me. What seemed excessive was how often the jobs put my life on the line.

And there's no way in hell I'm dying in Vermillion-frickin-Minnesota, I decided.

Not for the first time—and likely not the last—I cursed myself for taking a job so far from home. Minneapolis, Minnesota wasn't where I'd been born, but I'd lived there long enough to know it like the back of my hand. Every street and alley. Every building with an unlocked back door. Every business where someone wouldn't mind if I hid in a closet or under a desk. Straying from my backyard meant I didn't have those advantages. Not such a big deal for the easier jobs, maybe. When you're being chased by a goblin, though...

I heard a guttural curse behind me—way too close behind me—and felt the tip of a blade graze the back of my jacket. Knowing my pursuer was close enough to damn near cut me with his cleaver sent a fresh jolt of adrenaline to my tiring legs. What really kicked me into high gear, though, was the thought of someone hurting my Schott Perfecto motorcycle jacket. It was my most favorite thing. Feeling the cleaver's blade whisper down its back sent my pissed-o-meter from 'red' to 'fuck that,' and a fresh burst of speed followed.

"Not the jacket, asshole!" I screamed, risking a lungful of air to let my pursuer know how not-okay it was to hurt my baby.

"Drop the hafada ring!" an angry voice barked back.

Hafada ring? I thought.

My pounding feet knocked clumps of memories around until one shook loose. A few years back, I'd had a couple of dates with a tattooist and piercer. She'd told me about some of the more unusual piercings she'd done. Eyelids and septums and stretched labrets and rhinos and... hafada piercings.

"This was in your scrotum?" I cried. Then I tripped, and then I was falling, and then I was eating what must have been a mile of dirt and gravel. It gave me plenty of time to consider how I'd gotten myself into this particular mess.

It had surprised me when a goblin walked into my office a few days prior. Jay, my friend and de facto landlord, had been more than surprised. He'd screamed his bloody head off and had run for the hills, the jerk. After I'd apologized for his rudeness, I'd invited what I'd assumed was a lady to pull up a chair and tell me her particular tale of woe. I should clarify, though. It didn't surprise me to see a goblin. Minnesota was brimming with paranormal whatnots. We called ourselves PNs—pronounced 'pins'—for short, but that tiny acronym encompassed a wide variety of not-human things, goblins included. Anywhere there was dirty drudgery to be done, you could easily find one of the hunched, ornery buggers. So, yeah. Seeing a goblin? Just another day. What had surprised me was learning a goblin had been in a relationship. I mean, sure. There's someone for everyone, right? It's just hard to imagine that holding true for goblins, and the lady's appearance—for me, at least—demonstrated why. She had lurched in, looking like a rag doll from hell. Torn leather shift and mismatched boots. Leathery skin stretched over wiry muscles. Indecipherable tattoos under layers of dirt and grime. Piercings through pretty much every pierceable thing. Coarse hair cut with what must've been a dull knife wielded by a blind person. Fingernails so dirty they were practically black, including the one she'd used to scratch the inside of a wide, wet nostril. When the goblin had told me her name was Snarchurraga and that she'd been in a relationship, her words had crawled through yellowed teeth and shoved their way past cracked lips, punctuated by a green tongue that poked out like the head of an angry snapping turtle. My brain had chugged on the 'been in a relationship' part. From that moment on, I knew I'd be able to picture goblins doing relationship stuff and cursed my thrice-damned luck.

Snarchurraga had heard about my exploits from earlier in the summer: how I'd bested a vampire, a warlock, and a troll without even breaking a sweat, and all in the name of getting someone's special thing back from their atrocious ex. I'd swallowed a laugh and kept a serious look plastered to my face. The local free paper had the only official account of that evening; a story about some freak weather and an earthquake—which Minnesota never gets, by the way—wreaking havoc on a river island park and event pavilion. Someone had said something, though, and rumors did what rumors do. The tale of my exploits had spread faster than crabgrass and grown taller than Jack's proverbial beanstalk. I had told her my version, where the warlock bested the vampire, the troll bested the warlock, and my chief contribution had been turning into a goat. It was a noble effort, but my words had fallen on deaf ears.

The heartbroken goblin had traveled up from a small farming town to request my help. A trinket, she'd said. A small thing, but it was hers. She wanted it back, and her ex wasn't making it easy. We'd haggled, then settled on a favor to be repaid. I'd been surprised. A favor was worth more than my standard rate. Money was useful. Favors? Invaluable. She had spit on my desk. I'd added my own gob to the gooey spot while my stomach sank at the prospect of cleaning it later. Just like that, I'd committed to dragging my ass to Vermillion, Minnesota, sneaking into a goblin's hovel, and reclaiming Snarchurraga's trinket.

I'd made the trip down to farm country and followed her directions. The me that had rolled my old Moto Guzzi to a stop had been human. The me that had walked down a winding dirt road to a lonely, leaning shack had been human. The me that had crawled through an open window, however, had been a Maine Coon cat. Why? Well, humans are kind-of okay at the sneaky stuff. Cats are masterclass.

My furry paws had padded silently around the detritus only a goblin could collect. Cat eyes built to see in the dark discerned the edges and shapes of things, but weren't able to decipher much of what they were seeing. The tiny part of my brain that was still human could, though. What it couldn't suss out by sight alone, the cat's delicate nose revealed. Added together, it was a sensory mosaic of grossness. Piles of discarded work clothes soaked through with sweat and grime. Mostly empty pizza boxes and tin cans with their lids torn open. Bottles still smelling of cheap booze. Bones with bits of flesh and fur still attached. I had assumed they'd been squirrels or maybe racoons, and fervently hoped they weren't cats. Lazy flies had startled, then settled back to their late-night snacks as I crept past. I didn't judge the goblin for his questionable diet. You know, stones and glass houses and all. His complete disregard for hygiene? That, I was judging. Seriously judging.

Garbage cans, I complained. *Has this guy seriously never learned about garbage cans?*

It wasn't a fair question, though. Expecting a goblin to be tidy was like expecting a fish to ride a bike. If there was one thing I'd learned over the years, it was the importance of having the right expectations. I lowered mine and considered the goblin's home. It had a roof and its windows still had glass. There was furniture, too. An armchair with stuffing pushing through a multitude of rips in its fabric, a battered T.V. tray, and a large rock that might've served as an ottoman. After reframing my perspective a bit, I'd decided the place was actually pretty nice.

It hadn't taken long to find the source of the mess. Nevermind that the shack was tiny. I could have found him in the dark during a thunderstorm by following his snores. My client had said her ex was a heavy sleeper. She didn't mention he suffered from a deviated septum as well. The wheezes, coughs, and sputters had sounded like my bike's gearbox when I didn't squeeze the clutch hard enough. With a mental note to always use the clutch, I padded toward where a hanging horse blanket pretended to be a wall. Beyond it, draped across a stained mattress on the floor, was the source of the ear-splitting noise: Snarchurraga's ex.

So, anyway. There I'd been in the goblin's makeshift bedroom. It was not where I wanted to be when he woke up. I'd shifted, then crouched—naked and afraid—while waiting to see if he would wake. He hadn't, so I'd taken a step. A floorboard had creaked, the snores had stopped, and I'd damned near added some literal crap to the various proverbial piles on the floor. After a tense few moments, the log-sawing had resumed. I'd timed my steps across the traitorous floorboards with the goblin's snorts and snuffles, and finally reached a wooden pig trough turned on its end. There, in a hand-carved bowl, was the curved trinket my client had described. While the goblin had sawed another log, I'd nabbed the reason for being there and bolted. Humans don't fit easily through windows, so I'd used the back door and sealed my fate. I could have tiptoed carefully and quietly to freedom. Instead, I'd hauled my naked ass into the night and didn't think to gently close the door.

An interrupted snore had followed the slam, then a loud goblin curse. I'd barely pulled on my second boot when a mostly naked and completely upset goblin burst through the back door like pissed-off puss from a boil. His eyes held murderous intent, and his hand held a meat cleaver. Which brings me back to running for my life, learning I had grabbed a goblin's sack flair, tripping, and eating a mile of dirt and gravel.

The pain of fresh bruises and road rash momentarily blinded me. When I opened my eyes, tears blurred the contours of the slender trinket I'd managed to not drop. It was bone colored and would have made a complete circle had a gap not separated its ends. One of those ends tapered to a needle sharp point. It was a trinket, though. The goblin's ex had said it was a trinket, and trinkets looked like all sorts of things, even carved bone rings. That didn't mean they belonged in a goblin's nut bucket. The hafada ring fell from my disgusted fingers, and I wiped my palm on my jeans. Meanwhile, the goblin had stopped a few feet away and doubled over. His hands—one still holding the goddamned meat cleaver—rested on his knees while he gulped air.

"Of course it was in my scrotum," he growled between heaving gasps. "During coupling. For fertility. Where else would it go?"

During coupling? And... there goes my brain, I thought as a torrent of horrible images seared the backs of my eyelids. *Great. Just great.*

I muscled myself up from the pavement, shook out my battered elbows and knees, and gingerly wiped my bloody cheek with the back of a hand. After making it to my feet, I bent and gingerly picked up the curved sliver of bone.

"I'll tell you where it's going," I proclaimed after depositing it in my jacket pocket. "Back to Snarchurraga."

The goblin stretched his crooked spine. His cleaver caught the moon's glow as he rolled a wrist. I watched the blade warily, ready to bolt at the first sign of an impending chop. When it fell from his suddenly limp fingers, I let out a tightly held breath and tried to act like I hadn't just been terrified.

"That's right," I said with as much self-importance as I could muster. "She's engaged my services as her post-relationship personal effects repossession specialist. All I care about is returning the special... whatever... to my client. You wanted to keep the ring? You should've thought twice before coupling with that saucy little orcette, you cheating bastard."

The goblin gasped. "Snarchurraga told you about her?"

I curled my fingers into a fist, swung it out to my side, and flicked my pinky out. It was a particular goblin gesture which, loosely translated, meant, "Of course, and go fuck yourself." What can I say? When it comes to being offensive, I'm multilingual. It had been an impulsive reaction. Could you blame me? The guy had tried to slice my favorite jacket with a meat cleaver. Some things are simply unforgivable. Even so, I shouldn't have been surprised when his yellow eyes went wide, nor when he lunged for my neck with outstretched hands. The goblin's assault knocked me onto my back. He climbed on top of me and curled his fingers around my throat. The goblin was smaller than me, but those hands were strong and he seemed immune to the battering of my fists. I had a notion that shifting could help, but in my panicked state, I couldn't decide what to shift into. Spots swam at the edges of my sight. The scuffle was definitely not going well, and I knew I was going to die. I only wished I'd been able to wash my hands first after carrying his hafada ring. My arm weakly dragged my palm across the ground, then a voice cut through the night.

"Get off my lawn," it complained, full of age and irritability. "You're crushing my weeds."

The goblin's fingers relaxed. A moment later, I'd recovered enough to shove him hard and send him tumbling to the side. It dawned on my oxygen deprived brain that we were on a lawn and not in the cornfield. I hadn't noticed the house when I'd arrived. To be fair, my mind had been occupied with thoughts of sneaking into a goblin's hovel. That tends to narrow one's awareness a bit, so I'd walked right past the place without registering its existence. The low, long structure had probably housed farm hands back in the day. Now, it looked like it only housed mice and spiders.

"He started it," I croaked into the night.

"Did not!" the goblin cried, clearly affronted.

"I don't care," the ancient voice replied tartly. "You're trespassing."

My eyes blinked away pained tears as I tried to find the sour voice's owner. A shadow moved near the back corner of the house, and there she was. I wondered at why the goblin had fallen backward and was crab-walking away. I mean, sure, old ladies in dingy housecoats are scary, but seriously? Snarchurraga's ex was acting like he was being stared down by a seventh-circle demon.

Unless maybe she is, I realized. Demons came in all shapes and sizes, after all.

"I know you, goblin. Know you well. Now scat," the old lady demanded with a wave of a gnarled hand, "or I'll pay you a visit and suck you dry."

The goblin gave me one last murderous glare, then vanished into the night.

"Thanks and all," I managed. "That guy was an asshole, but let's get one thing straight, demon. I didn't ask for your help, so there's no bargain or whatever."

The old lady rocked back on the heels of her thick-soled geriatric shoes.

"A demon? I should suck you dry for saying such a thing. A demon? Pah," she spat. "Youngsters. Stupid. Rude. Every last one of you."

"A vampire, then?" I hazarded. I mean, she'd been talking about sucking, so it seemed possible. But probable? Not really. There aren't many old, ugly vamps. As a rule, they liked to turn the young, pretty people. It was annoying because they all ended up being insufferable little pricks. Too cool for school, so hot it hurt, and—baring the usual stuff like sun and stakes—practically immortal, so they could torture generation after generation with their pretension. My brain bent when I tried to imagine a vampire turning what had to have been an octogenarian spinster in...

Where am I, again?

Vermillion. Yeah, I was in Vermillion. Small farm town south of Minneapolis. So yeah. A vampire in Vermillion turning a gnarled and gap-toothed lady into one of their own? Inviting her to join the ranks of their elite club? Actually wanting the old biddy hanging around for centuries to come? Unlikely didn't even start to cover it.

"Not a vampire," I decided. "Okay, then."

"Oh, shut up," the old lady said dismissively.

She waddled over and reached out a bent arm. I skeptically took the offered hand and was more than a bit surprised when it returned my grip with a strength its sagging skin belied.

"Thanks," I croaked, after finding my feet and massaging my bruised throat. "What are you, anyway?"

Asking was rude, but me and politesse had gone our separate ways long ago.

"Stupid shifter," she muttered. "I should suck you dry to spare you another minute of being so stupid."

Again with the sucking, I thought, and then the dots connected.

"You're a hag!"

"And you're an idiot."

She wasn't wrong. I blamed being strangled by a goblin for being a little slow on the uptake. How many clues did I need? She was old, ugly, and irritable. She had scared off a goblin like it had been a roach caught in the open after flicking on a light. Add in all the stuff about sucking and the obvious became painfully obvious. My unlikely savior was a goddamned hag. Just my luck.

"I suppose I am," I answered. "Thanks anyway. That goblin would've killed me."

"And why's that?" she asked with a note of genuine curiosity.

I showed her the hafada ring while stifling a disgusted shudder.

"I get stuff back for people after messy breakups," I explained. "A goblin lady kicked his goblin ass to the curb when she found out he was messing around, and she wanted her, you know, this thing back. I didn't know it was a scrotum ring. Gross, right?"

The old lady closed the distance and peered at the off-white circle in my palm with interest, then lifted her ancient face to glower at me.

"Are all shifters as squeamish as you, or are you just a wussy?"

I glared. Having never met a hag, I didn't want to rush to judgment. That said, I'd never heard good things, so rushing to judgment seemed reasonable.

"Wussy. I've had hemorrhoids that were tougher than you. I should suck you dry to spare you the shame of being such a wussy."

My fingers curled around the bone ring and pushed it back into my pocket.

"Screw you, lady. My night's already been plenty shitty. I don't need you piling on."

Something akin to guilt crossed her weathered and wrinkled face. She sniffed, and I impulsively held my breath and leaned back.

"Shifters," she sneered. "I've known my fair share, you know. Not many of you. No, of course not. Still, there's been a few, and I've known 'em. I'd wager you're no better than the rest, but maybe not as bad as some." Eyes clouded with the perpetual promise of cataracts peered at me. "You said you get stuff back after people split up?"

"Yeah," I agreed. "Why? Wait...You don't. I mean, you weren't..." When those eyes narrowed, I laughed. "Really? You and Father Time have a falling out? Need your denture glue back? Or those monogrammed adult diapers?"

I wasn't an expert on old people. Even so, I knew enough to know they aren't supposed to be all that strong or nimble. The lady hadn't gotten that particular memo, I guess, because she bent, lurched, twisted... and once again, I was flat on my back and gasping for breath. It seemed a bit much. Seriously. How many times does someone need to painfully hit the ground in one night?

"I need my spoon back," the hag said after placing a foot on either side of my waist and leaning down. "Maybe you're the one to get it," she murmured as her crooked and warty nose touched the tip of mine. Sour breath washed over me as she whispered, "Ah, yes. Maybe you're the one, indeed."

Jay was about to fall out of his camping chair, he'd scooted so close to its edge. Despite knowing the story obviously didn't end with me dying or even getting hurt too badly, he was hanging from the proverbial cliff.

"And then what happened?" he asked breathlessly.

I took a pull from my can of beer and leaned back in my chair. Its familiar creak echoed in the confined space of my office until I found just the right tilt. One boot landed on the top of my desk, and the other crossed its ankle.

"The hag let me up. I had her describe the spoon. She didn't have a picture, but I'm pretty sure I could pick it out of a line-up. I walked back to my bike, saddled up, and swung by Snarchurraga's new hovel to return her, ahem, trinket. When I gave her back the ring, she patted her—I don't know. Whatever she was wearing—in search of a pocket, didn't find one, then shoved the ring's pointy end through her upper lip. I almost threw up, then reminded her she owed me a favor. I rode home, patched myself up," I said with a tap on the gauze pad taped to my cheek, "and passed out. Getting chased by a murderous goblin and body-slammed by a hag is exhausting."

"Damn it, August," my friend complained. "You need to get better at finishing stories."

My shoulders moved in an easy shrug. "And you need to get better at keeping the beer fridge full. This was the last one," I chided, while waggling my empty can. "Want to take a walk to Philo's?"

The walk was probably a bad idea. The previous night's debacle had left my knee the size of a grapefruit. I could barely bend it, which meant I had to hop down the stairs from Jay's art studio and limp away from the converted old casket factory it occupied. After a half block or so, the tendons loosened a bit, and I picked up the pace. The late summer's heat wasn't pulling any punches, and I didn't want to be out any longer than necessary. The janitor's closet in Jay's studio that I used as an office didn't have air conditioning, but it was a damn sight better than being outside.

"You didn't tell me who her ex is," Jay said, his long legs easily pacing my awkward limp. "A hag's ex? That's gotta be a story. Who would date a hag? I don't know anything about hags, and I know that nobody would date one, right? I mean, they must be even harder to match someone up with than you. Hey, spare me the indignant routine. Am I wrong?"

I swallowed a retort. He wasn't wrong. Me and romantical escapades weren't exactly compatible. My most recent ex was an oracle who had lost her second sight and chosen a blind sabbatical over hanging around with me. Before that, I'd tried to hook up with a hot succubus bartender and ended up puking—actually puking—down the front of her sweatshirt.

"You aren't wrong," I conceded. "And to answer your question, her 'ex' is her sister. Another hag."

I'd limped a few more steps before I realized Jay had stopped. When I turned back, he'd pushed his fingers up into his thick dreadlocks in dismay.

"I thought that sort of thing was illegal," he said. "I mean, it is for humans. PNs don't, you know, date their sisters, do they?"

"Some do. But usually no," I hastily added when his face screwed up, "most paranormals don't date their sisters. Fannie wasn't dating Elouise. I guess they were really close. Then something about that spoon drove a wedge. A big one. Fannie used some pretty choice words to describe her sister. Made me cringe, and that's saying something. Anyway, Fannie says she found the spoon at a rummage sale, and now Elouise won't give it back. Enter one post-relationship personal effects repossession specialist."

We'd reached Philo's before Jay could pepper me with more questions. We'd also passed two other liquor stores on the way, but they weren't Philo's Liquors, so we didn't stop. You wouldn't understand why until you met the proprietor and namesake of the place: Philo himself.

"August! Jay! My two pavorite fatrons. Uh," the satyr tried and then hiccuped. He languished on a flat bench against the liquor store's outer wall: elbow on the bench, side of his head resting on a fist, fawn legs stretched out along the wooden planks. A mostly empty wine bottle rested comfortably against his potbelly. His free hand raised up just enough to waggle its plump little fingers, then resumed its ceaseless caressing of the thick, curly hair that flowed like waves down his chest.

"Moses wept, Philo," I complained as I covered my eyes. "Didn't the city say you had to wear pants?"

"They did," he agreed solemnly. "Fined me, too. I would, I really would, but pants are so..." he let the thought dangle, not unlike the particular bit of anatomy his languid pose left on full display, "unnecessary."

"Hey, Philo," Jay offered, nonplussed. "Good to see you. Well, most of you. Didn't need to see all of you, if we're being honest."

The satyr's laugh was grapes ripening on the vine, wine flowing from the pitcher. My ever-present curmudgeonliness couldn't hold against that laugh, and I smiled a genuine smile.

"Maybe you've got a sheet or a tablecloth inside?" I asked. "Let's meet halfway and get you into a toga. Deal?"

Philo sighed and hiccuped again. "As you wish. But August," he tacked on with the wink of a twinkling eye, "it'd best be a king-sized sheet, else what's the point?"

I chuckled at the randy goat's innuendo and followed his bare and furry behind into the air-conditioned store. Philo was always a kick. The satyr was a flagrant hedonist and never missed an opportunity to remind folks of that fact. Why, after his long years and many travels, he'd decided to settle in Minnesota and open a liquor store, I couldn't imagine.

I suppose the chance to get a bunch of Scandinavian prudes' undies in a bundle was too good to pass up. That, or he knew how much us 'Sotans loved to drink. While he headed for the storeroom, I headed for the coolers along the far wall. I didn't even have to think about where to look. Third door down, second shelf from the bottom. My fingers slid through the handle of a cardboard case, and a gentle tug pulled the box of beery goodness free. After the store's proprietor had returned, I slid a few bills across the counter, then Jay and I waved goodbye to Philo and his improvised toga.

We shared the load, but my tee-shirt was still clinging to my back by the time we'd climbed the stairs to Jay's studio and got the sweating cans into the fridge. Even though we were closer to September than July, the dog days of summer had refused to move on. I passed a cold beer to my friend, grabbed another for myself, and made a comment about how it's not the heat, it's the humidity that really gets you. He agreed, and we opted to stay in the open studio rather than my cramped office. Jay peeled back a tinfoil blanket from a window and cranked it open. My conspiracy-crazed friend must've been feeling the heat, too, if he was willing to risk those government ne'er-do-wells being able to snoop on him with their secret spy gizmos. The breeze wasn't cool, but it still felt good to have some air moving around.

"Much better," I proclaimed as I settled into my customary beanbag. "So? I shared my adventures. You gonna spill the beans about your new project or what?"

Jay glanced at the window, then rose, closed it, and carefully taped the tinfoil back in place. Apparently satisfied with his reestablished defenses, he gave me a devilish grin.

"I'm doing seed art."

I waited for the punchline. And waited.

"Seed art," Jay repeated. "You know. Pictures made with seeds?"

My head shook to show I was coming up with nothing.

"The State Fair? Big contest? People make crop art? Mosaics with seeds. Scarecrows. Corn stalk sculptures. Millions of people see it?"

The reason for my cluelessness became abundantly clear. The "Great Minnesota Get-Together," also known as the Minnesota State Fair, was not on my list of reasons to love my adopted state. Hundreds of thousands of sweating, jostling, fanny pack wearing, deep fried grease on a stick chomping, crap buying 'Sotans in one place was definitely not my thing. Jay must've read that thought as it crossed my mind, because he took a deep breath, then puffed out his cheeks with a frustrated exhale.

"Right. Not your thing. Well, maybe this year, you'll feel differently. Maybe this year, you'll go. Because this year," he said with growing intensity, "I'm going to steal the show."

"You're going to steal pictures people made with seeds?" I asked with a crooked grin.

That got me a friendly, "Asshole," and then we settled into one of our usual routines; discussing his conspiracy du jour. Jay was a fervent believer in all things conspiratorial. The moon landing? Fake. Elvis and Tupac? Alive. World leaders? Puppets. Government agencies? Nefarious enablers of illuminati machinations. An afternoon chat with him was like binge-watching three seasons of *The X Files*. I'd barely made a dent in my beer when he launched into a lengthy diatribe about genetically modified seeds. How they affect our physiology, and how the Department of Agriculture was in cahoots—yes, cahoots—with the Big Ag chemical industry. He'd even found a few nuggets about ties to undercover—wait for it—aliens. Yep. Aliens. Jay being Jay, he'd decided it was his mission to blow the lid off of a deep state conspiracy by making mosaics of seeds glued to plywood. I was about to suggest that glue was probably worse for the planet than GMOs when my phone rang.

"Duty calls," I apologized as I untangled myself from the conversation and headed for my office.

My old rotary phone had rung three more times before I got there. While I was hobbling to my office, Jay reminded me—again—that I could answer calls from anywhere with a smartphone. I reminded him—again—that I wanted my technology to be as dumb as its owner. On the next ring, I answered with an almost-friendly hello. In response, I got an earful of soft static and then a voice said my name.

"You again?" I groused. "C'mon, man. I'm sick of this shit. Just tell me who you are."

Like every other time the strange caller had rung me up, he left my question unanswered, then disconnected the call. I dropped the receiver back into its cradle and muttered a few unkind words. The caller hadn't heard them, but venting felt good, regardless.

"Again?" Jay asked from my office doorway. "How many is that now?"

Over the previous week, I'd had more than a few prank calls. Same thing every time. A voice I almost recognized would say my name, then the caller would hang up.

"Lost count," I replied, hoping to project a nonchalance I didn't feel. "They'll eventually get bored with the game and move on. Now, I think you were talking about how those hotdogs I love to eat are disrupting my endocrines..."

I half-listened to Jay as he unraveled more of his worldview's twisted and tangled threads, but more of my brain kept circling back to the odd phone calls. Shadow governments and aliens and all the rest were about as important to me as which side of the toast got buttered. That mysterious voice I almost recognized, though. That had me worried.

CHAPTER 2

"If choose I must between a soggy hat and an empty stomach, I'll suffer a little rain on my head. The field's needs surpass those of fashion."
- Huggledee Porlwyn

IN TYPICAL MINNESOTA FASHION, the previous day's sun had given way to a soaking rain. My cafe racer had a lot of perks. It was easy on gas. Easy in traffic. Easy to park, even with the sidecar. Easy to insure, too, mainly because I didn't have insurance. Despite all of those upsides, it had one teensy weensy problem: weather. A gentle rain was no sweat. A soaker the likes of which was lashing my apartment window? That kind of rain normally kept me on my couch with a trashy horror novel, or in my office with a case of pilsner. I'm dumb, not stupid.

Unfortunately, I had work to do. With a forlorn sigh, I pulled on my rain gear and headed into the downpour. As my yellow rain pants squeaked on the bike's saddle and I squeegeed my helmet's snap-on faceplate with a finger, I decided Fannie and her precious spoon would have to wait. A trip to Vermillion wasn't worth the misery. Luckily, I had a stack of stuff to repo closer to home. I'd still be soaked, but at least my waterlogged wallet would be a little thicker.

A quick stop at the office was first on my docket. I'd left a list of names, addresses, and crap the recently heartbroken couldn't live without on my desk. Jay offered a distracted wave when I stomped in and shook the rainwater off. One look, and I knew not to engage. When the guy was into his art, he was decidedly not into anything else. Leaving the artist to wield his formidable forces of creation—or glue seeds to squares of plywood or whatever—I unlocked my office door and stepped inside, the rubber soles of my boots squorking on the concrete floor. The room's only light, a naked bulb dangling from the ceiling high above, revealed a simple life: a chair to sit in. A desk to rest my heels on. A floor sink in the corner to dump the dregs of yesterday's beer in. Four safes to keep things, you know, safe. It was simple. Nice and simple.

And sad, a too-honest part of my brain added.

Better sad than dead, a much more realistic part of my brain replied.

Dead would be sadder, that first part of my brain grudgingly admitted.

That was the crux of the matter. My life wasn't glamorous, but I was alive. Staying alive meant keeping things simple. I'd broken that rule earlier in the summer. Things had definitely not been simple, and the world almost ended. If that wasn't reason enough to keep things simple, I didn't know what was. Simple was good. Simple was safe.

With my simple mantra firmly in mind, I shoved my professional life around the desktop until I found a torn sheet of paper and my laminated map of the Twin Cities metro. Yeah, smartphones and their whizbang navigation. You can have 'em. Sure, they might make it easy to find where you're going. They also make you easy to find. Being findable meant complications. Complications were, by definition, complicated. Complicated, by definition, was not simple. One look at Jay proved that point. The guy loved complicated. He'd recently upgraded the art studio's security. Unlocking the door now required three separate keys and the combination for a padlock. I didn't want to be that guy. I wanted things to be simple. My job. Some hotdogs. Beer.

That's all I want, I decided. Sadly, no one ever cared what I wanted.

"Gonna repo some shit," I called out as I killed the light and closed my office door. "Need anything?"

"I need Big Ag to stop forcing us to eat physiology-modifying science experiments so their CEOs can buy twelve more yachts, and the government to actually do its job and stop them instead of dumping tons of proverbial fertilizer on their nefarious profiteering plans, and aliens to stop trying to turn us into baby factories for little alien hybrid babies."

Alien hybrid babies, I thought. *That's new.*

"So, you don't need anything," I replied.

"Nah, I'm good," he called back. "Now, stop bugging me. I'm working."

With a few choice words for the crummy weather, I kicked my bike to reluctant life and squirmed uncomfortably. Rain gear keeps you dry enough, but that's about all it has to offer. Hunching over, I unfolded my list of exes. The rain was turning my scrawling handwriting into one of Jay's impressionist art things, so I memorized what I could. My day was going to take me from Minneapolis to Saint Paul to the 'burbs and back. The weather meant it would be miserable, but the variety would make it entertaining.

My first stop was in Uptown—Minneapolis' post-college landing zone—to drop in on a hungover werecat.

"Lillian wants her iPad back."

Then over to Saint Paul's Frogtown neighborhood to break into a bathroom and nab some bath bombs and a loofa on a stick. Neither held much value, sentimental or otherwise for my selkie client. She simply didn't want her ex to have even a moment's enjoyment. As instructed, I left a note. Not the one she had asked me to, though. I'm a jerk, not an asshole.

Down to the richie rich streets of Edina, a nearby suburb, to severely disappoint a Druid while rainwater soaked his hooded cloak.

"Fiadh wants the macramé Celtic Knot hot pad her mom made last solstice."

Back across town to Brooklyn Park. It was another suburb, but one with a vibrant West African neighborhood. I found the restaurant where my client had worked, then carefully and politely requested the return of one immersion stick blender from an obayifo. Per my client's instructions, I made sure to avoid all mention of food and to not turn my back on the woman in the sleeveless gown with faintly glowing armpits. I didn't relax until I'd put a solid couple of miles between me and the food crazed witchy vampire.

Each item that I repo'd went into a garbage bag in the bike's sidecar to keep it dry. A twinge of jealousy for the bag's contents creased my forehead and curled my lip. A surprising amount of rain had snuck down the collar of my rain gear and mingled with the sweat of spending a warm day encased in plastic. I was soaked from the waist up and felt a good ten pounds heavier. Sick of the weather, I decided the remaining items on my list could wait. With a twist of the throttle, I pointed my Guzzi toward good old Nord'east and my favorite neighborhood bar. I just hoped Betty's schedule hadn't changed.

I cracked open the bar's door and scanned the dingy space. A handful of humans in pairs and trios, a sullen vampire, and two coblynau standing on their stools to reach the bar all turned a variety of disinterested looks my way.

"No succubus," I confirmed, and headed inside.

After stripping off my gear and rolling it into a soggy bundle, I tugged my shirt a little straighter, wiped my damp palms on my jeans, and pushed my hair around to make it a bit less helmet hair and a bit more messy-by-choice. I grabbed an open stool and raised a hand to the bartender. He slid a pint my way, and I settled into my usual pastime of drinking and brooding.

I'd studiously avoided the bar when Betty the bartender was working. The way things had worked out between us was a pity. I'd been crushing on the succubus pretty hard earlier that year. I might've had a shot, too, had her on-again, off-again warlock ex-boyfriend not tried to kill me. Okay, fine. There might have been some other things at play. My general unlikeableness, for example, or that time I threw up in her sweatshirt while she was wearing it. I mostly blamed the warlock, though. Well, him and the lefse-baking huldra Betty had latched onto. The ill-fated dinner party where her ex-boyfriend had tried to end the world had done more than wreck half of Nicollet Island. It had brought Betty and Vilde, the Lefse Queen of Minnesota, together.

"I hope you're enjoying your shared sexy narcissism," I toasted as I raised my pint up and clinked an imaginary glass.

"Who you calling a sexy narcissist?"

I startled, unaware that there'd been anyone to see my impromptu air-toast. The reason quickly became apparent. I'd been looking up, not down. While I watched, a hairy coblyn hoisted his foot-and-a-half tall frame up onto a barstool. Once perched safely on top, he held out a small fist, which I gently bumped.

"No one," I replied, embarrassed that he'd noticed my air-toast. "Just drinking to my past and what might have been."

"Yesterday is behind you. Learn from it. Tomorrow is ahead. Prepare for it. Today is here. Drink it," the coblyn advised from behind a bristly beard.

The short sage's words wormed their way into my brain as I sipped on the cold pilsner. I'd had quite the 'yesterday' earlier that summer. Meeting a bona fide oracle. Knocking on death's door too many times. Learning I was more than some schlub floating in a cosmic soup, and that maybe—just maybe—I could shape my own destiny. Heavy stuff. Was there something to learn? Something to maybe help me become better than I was? Thinking about it was exhausting, so I turned my thoughts to tomorrow. What was over that not-too-distant horizon? Was I ready for what my future held? After getting drawn into Clarissa Steyer's future-scrying world, I wasn't sure I could handle spending any more brain space on tomorrow. Which left today. All things considered, it was the same as any other.

That'll have to do, I decided with another swig.

"Thanks, Ted. Good advice. What brings you in?"

Tedendunderalmagustor Havestorial Rundendunderobesk—a.k.a. Ted—tilted his head to the other coblynau at the bar. One noticed and offered a quick wave, then returned to his project. In the brief span between me walking into the bar and Ted hopping up on the stool next to mine, the two cobs had been working industriously. Pint glasses were a bit unwieldy for their small hands, so they'd cobbled together a crane to lift a shot glass, dunk it in the beer, then swing it back down to the bar for easy drinking. Amazing what you could do with a couple of empty glasses, a bunch of stir straws, two emptied lemon wedge trays, a shoelace, some gum, and a stolen wine key. How did I know it was stolen? While the coblynau used their improvised crane to transport beer from the pint to their waiting mouths, the bartender was holding an uncorked bottle of wine and looking rather befuddled.

"It's Mouse Trap night," Ted replied. "Regionals are coming up. Gotta stay sharp."

Mouse Trap, that iconic board game from the 60s where players competed to build the best Rube Goldberg machine, was a hit with the coblynau. They had tournaments and everything. Ted had won regionals the prior year and being the statewide champion was on his over-engineered bucket list. I shuddered to think of what the trophy would look like.

"And you?" he asked. "Things good?"

My shoulders lifted and fell, and a worn smile found its way onto my face. "Good enough."

It was funny, seeing the coblynau after having so recently crossed paths with a goblin. Cobs and gobs were branches of the same weird tree, albeit very distant branches. Where goblins were bigger, cruder, more ill-tempered, and not overly bright, coblynau were quick and clever. You had to be careful with them, and never be fooled by their size. As likely to hurt as help, cobs always worked with their own ends in mind. In my limited experience, they weren't wicked per se. It was more that when a coblyn wanted something, they got it. The rest of us were either grease for their gears or obstacles to be cleared. Cobs proper traced their lineage back to Wales. Once upon a time, they were best known for helping—or tormenting—coal and silver miners. These days? A few like Ted preferred the hustle and bustle of the big city. More stuck to the mining towns. I knew there was a sizeable community up in the Minnesotan iron range and plenty crawling around the state's various quarries. Minnesota was full of limestone, granite, gravel, and silica sand. If there was something to dig up, there were coblynau. Besides mining, they had a knack for engineering complex solutions to simple problems. They were also fond of hoarding their secrets. That's where Ted was a bit of a rarity for his kind. While other cobs would mine the deep seams and keep the location tightly under wraps, he mined wise words and shared them liberally.

I'd helped him out a year or so back, and we'd been friendly ever since. He'd wanted a particular contraption back. It would toast, butter, and cut the crust off of bread with the pull of a lever. No wonder his ex had wanted to keep it. Ted had been an entertaining client. He simply couldn't believe my plan was to knock on his ex's door and politely ask for his super toaster back. If we'd done things his way, we'd have spent months putting his Mouse Trap skills to unnecessary use. He'd even shown me his plans. The 'super toaster retrieval device' would have started with the flipping of a simple switch. A bowling ball would've rolled down a winding track, clipping the handles of three garden shovels along the way. Each of the shovels would have fallen backward onto three bass drum pedals, and each pedal would have knocked another proverbial domino on his super toaster retrieval machine. Lights would have flashed, pulleys would have pulled, bags of sand would have spilled, and cantilevered scales would have risen. Gears would have whirred, wind vanes would have spun, and finally, a toilet plunger's handle would have poked a rooster in a wire cage. While the fowl cried foul and distracted his ex, I would have snuck in the back door and gathered up his personal effects. Yep. That was Ted's plan. The really funny part? It wasn't even that outlandish... by coblyn standards.

"Don't let me keep you, though," I said when I noticed his eager twitching. "Go build that better mousetrap."

"Sooner begun, sooner done!" Ted announced.

We bumped fists again, then off he went while I resumed my brooding. Once again, the cob's words sunk their little barbs. I'd put off paying a visit to Fannie's sister because of the rain. An excellent reason, but...

"I'm sure it won't be too bad," I reasoned, "and I'm already wet. Might as well get it over with."

Decision made, I finished my beer and went in search of a spoon.

The next day's sunrise painted the sky magenta and gold. A light dusting of clouds, remnants of the prior day's rain, caught the light and folded it into their soft contours. Trees rustled in a gentle breeze, and bird song accompanied the city's waking. It was as fine a morning as Minnesota had to offer. At least, I assumed that had been the case. I didn't know because I'd slept in. Since I'd missed the real sunrise, I let my imagination languidly fill in the details. There was nothing that needed doing. Picturing a beautiful sunrise seemed like a fine way to spend my time. It didn't take much effort, either. Minnesota could certainly dole out its fair share of gorgeous weather. My sunny disposition, however, was more of a rarity. Letting my gaze slide from the window to my cracked ceiling, I wondered at the lightness I felt. Optimism of any sort was not my thing, but the sunny kind? Nope.

No sooner had the thought crossed my mind than the light falling through my window dimmed. Maybe a heavy cloud riding a summer breeze? That seemed like a nice thing. A nice and normal thing. The window, wall, and ceiling disappearing? Not normal.

Confusion and surprise joined forces and tried to yank me up, but I couldn't move. Heavy restraints squeezed my wrists and ankles, and thick straps anchored me to the rails of a hospital bed. Another strap chaffed my forehead and pressed the back of my skull down hard against a thin pillow. I saw harsh fluorescent lights in a drop ceiling. Stainless steel articulated arms bristling with needles and drills. A plasma bag with a translucent tube that snaked to my wrist. Serious boxes with glowing screens perched on rolling carts, their screens a mystery of lines and bars and numbers. While my eyes rolled, electronic beeps and mechanical whirrs pounded my eardrums. The sounds threatened to drive me mad. A door opened, and a huge and horrible face eclipsed the lights above. Its bent and warty nose drew closer and closer to my own, and its cracked lips parted.

"Get up, you stupid shifter. Get up!"

My eyes opened. The hospital room was gone, but the horrible face remained. I tried to scream, but my lungs were empty. I tried to flail, but my limbs were frozen.

"Bah. Wussy. I've had fungal creams made of stronger stuff than you."

Her dig was definitely directed at me. The next bit seemed to be for someone else.

"You're a right monster, and that's a fact."

Another voice, as awful as the first, laughed in response.

"Ignore her," the first voice said. "Now, let's get you out of here. Off we go, then."

Fingers like steel cables wrapped around my ankles, and then I was sliding on my back. My arms drifted out to either side and ended in a Y above my head, and my jacket and shirt bunched up around my shoulders. Whoever was pulling me muttered a stream of curses. Hell if I knew why. They weren't the one getting friction burn on their back. It didn't take long to discover that everything is relative, though. When I was dragged over a door's threshold, it caught on every single vertebra in my spine. Compared to that, a little friction burn was nothing. Then we got to the stairs.

"Fuck-uck-uh-uh-uck-uck!" I exclaimed as my tailbone, spine, shoulder blades, and skull went down that first step.

"Oh, quit it," the voice chided. "You act like no one's ever dragged you down a few steps before."

I wanted to point out that no one had ever dragged me down a few steps before. However, I was too busy being dragged down a few steps—splintered wooden ones, to boot—to make that particular point. A final thunk of my head added a few more stars to the night sky above, but the dragging didn't stop. There was a brick landing at the bottom of the stairway, and those bricks were crumbled, broken, and full of jagged edges. A long groan lurched its way out of my lips, and tears streamed from my eyes.

"Wussy. Just a bit farther," the voice chuffed. "You might want to try one of those fancy diets from the magazines. Drop a few pounds. Not exactly a feather, are you?"

The floor had been bad. The door's threshold, worse. The steps and their brick landing? Horrible. Then we got to the hard packed dirt. By that point, everything above my belt was road rash, and the back of my skull felt like it had an inch-wide gash running its length. Now those wounds were being stuffed with grit and gravel. I heard myself whimper something that might have been, "Please, stop." Still, whoever was heaving me along kept tugging and chuffing, chuffing and tugging, and my poor body slid inch after agonizing inch.

"Almost there, shifter."

Fresh tears broke free, but there were a few relieved ones mixed in. Then I went over a big rock.

"Fuck!" I cried out again.

"Wussy," I got in response. "I've had bunions that complained less than you."

There were a few more grunts and a slow turn, and then, finally, a cool, soft respite from the hard pain. The smell of wet clover filled my nostrils. My head lolled, and I saw cornstalks. There were a few more tugs, and I passed through the doors of an old work shed. Whoever had been holding my ankles let them fall to the ground. Blood rushed to my feet, bringing along a thousand pins and needles and forcing a last whimper from my lips.

"Oh, quit with your sputtering, you big baby," the voice said.

I opened my eyes and there was a face, an awful face. Muscles that a moment before couldn't move bucked as I reflexively tried to flee.

"Wussy," the face chided. "I should suck you dry and be done with it. Spare you the misery of being such a wussy."

Something akin to a rational thought crossed my mind, and my panic subsided. The face was awful, sure, but it was one that I knew. One that belonged to...

"Fannie."

The hag nodded. "Good. That's good," she said as soothingly as her creaking voice could manage.

With all the grace of a drunk after a bender, I used my elbows to lever myself up. Once I'd gotten to about a forty-five degree angle, I looked around. The first surprise was the darkness. The sunrise I'd imagined had faded with the rest of the nightmare. The next surprise was that I wasn't at home. For a groggy moment or two, I puzzled out where I was.

Vermillion. I was in Vermillion. I knew because the shed was definitely not my apartment, there was a wall of corn beyond its open doors, it smelled like manure, and Fannie lived in the small farming town. I flexed my powers of deduction and added the clincher; I'd planned to go to Vermillion to get Fannie's spoon. So yeah, Vermillion. That realization knocked loose a slew of memories. A soggy drive down. The rain letting up at the end of my trip as night was falling. Finding the decrepit house that shared a dirt road with a goblin's hovel. Knocking on Elouise's front door. Suppressing the desire to run when the hag opened it. Explaining that her sister had hired me to take possession of one very specific spoon. Being told to wait.

"This spoon, I suppose," Fannie's sister had said when she'd returned a moment later.

She'd held it up, and I'd leaned in to confirm it was the one I wanted. It hadn't occurred to me to wonder what the old lady's other hand was holding behind her back.

"Your sister brained me!" I blurted out. "With a frying pan!"

"Yeah, that sounds like her," Fannie acknowledged. "Damn near sucked you dry, too. Stupid shifter. I've had rashes with more sense than you. It's a good thing I was keeping an eye on you. I thought you knew how to do your job."

The memory of the frying pan lit a fire in the side of my skull. My strength gave out, and I lurched to the side.

"I'm a professional," I muttered through clenched teeth.

Fannie clucked her tongue. "And I'm a lingerie model."

She seemed ready to say more, but an eerily similar voice cut through the night.

"Nice try, sister! What happened? All the clowns were busy, so you had to send that?"

The shed sat across a wide side yard from the ramshackle house I'd recently visited. Elouise stood at the edge of her porch, fists on her hips. Fannie opted to only put one fist on a hip. The other, she shook irritably.

"The spoon's mine, Elouise. You know you can't be keeping it from me. You know what it means to me."

I squinted at Elouise and decided seeing her from a distance was no better than seeing her up close. I could be on top of a skyscraper and would still shudder if Elouise was a speck on the sidewalk far below. She was that ugly. Of the two, though, she was the better dresser. While Fannie clearly favored her decades-old housecoat, Elouise tried to look elegant. An ankle length gown with long sleeves, a high collar, and lacy frills. Large pearl earnings and a matching string around her neck. A brooch that winked in the moonlight. On literally anyone—or anything—else, the outfit would have looked fancy.

"You always thought you were the clever one," Fannie spat at her better-dressed sibling. "So smart. So full of ideas. But this is different, Elouise, and you know it. You know it!" she repeated with an angry stomp.

And then there was a new woman's voice, different from the other two but equally irate.

"Would you both please shut up? Your bickering is driving me crazy. Every night? Seriously? Go to therapy. Or not. I don't care. Just please stop screaming at each other all the damned time. Or else."

Fannie had the good grace to look at least a little chagrined. Elouise extended a middle finger, then stepped curtly into her house and slammed her front door. It took a few attempts thanks to the house being in such ill repair, but each attempt was another opportunity to express her indignation. While the hag was repeatedly slamming her door, I turned to see who was crazy enough to yell at the sisters.

Surprisingly, she didn't look crazy. Given my clientele, I felt like I had a pretty good bead on what crazy looked like. I'd dealt with enough nutsos to know a thing or two. Call me judgmental if you want. All I'm saying is with enough experience you can see someone, and—boom—you know they're a whackadoodle. This lady? Crazy was definitely not the right word. That said, she certainly looked... eccentric.

Where to start? Maybe with her clothes. Definitely not run-of-the-mill for a farming town. Standard attire in those parts started with durable shirts, extended to functional jeans, and ended with dirt-crusted work boots. This woman had exactly none of those on her—okay, this might be gratuitous, but c'mon, I'm a guy—very shapely person. She wasn't dressed practically at all, unless you defined 'practical' as gracing the cover of a hot rod magazine. Bright pink satin short-shorts with snappy white racing stripes. Fishnet stockings over creamy thighs guaranteed to drive the mosquitos crazy. White tube socks with bright green bands at the top. The shoes those socks disappeared into? Definitely a minus-two on a scale of one to practical. On the plus side, they were boots: thick-soled Doc Martens that laced up high above her ankles. On the downside, they had white leather uppers. When I thought of how much work it must've taken to keep those kicks gleaming and pristine, my eye twitched. Heading the other direction from those roller girl shorts was roughly half of a mechanic's work shirt. The part covering her shoulders and about half of her torso was blue with white pinstripes. I assumed the rest had looked the same before being hacked off. A big patch with crossed corncobs rested comfortably above one breast, and a tattoo peeked out where the top few buttons were undone. It was large and obviously elaborate, and I really wanted to see the parts that were hidden beneath the shirt. When I convinced my eyes to move on from their contemplation of those great big, um... that tattoo on her chest, I saw a pixie face that was heavy on the lipstick and mascara, and a mohawk dyed to match her shorts.

"Hi," I offered, but to no avail. Those black-lined eyes were too busy sending daggers at Fannie and Elouise to notice a schlub like me.

"Or. Else!" she repeated, and then spun on a white boot's heel and stomped back into the corn.

Fannie flapped a dismissive hand in the woman's general direction, then grabbed my wrist and hoisted me to my feet.

"Never mind that one, and get up," she instructed. "We need to talk about how you're gonna get my spoon, and this time I'll do the planning."

A short while later, Fannie and I had wrapped up our strategizing, and I was back on my bike motoring north. The sun had long since set, so all I had to look at was the cone of my headlamp's light. With nothing else to do, I ruminated on the old hag's plan, turning it this way and that and inspecting it for flaws. Near as I could tell, there weren't any. I'd come back down the next night, park the bike a ways up the dirt road, and sneak over to Elouise's place. Fannie would meet me and keep an eye out for her sister. When the hag went out to feed, Fannie would give me a sign. My client had assured me her sister had a voracious appetite, giving me at least an hour to work with, maybe even two. Plenty of time to slip in, get the spoon, and return it to Fannie. After that, I'd decided, I would never, ever set foot in farm country again.

"Why can't you do it yourself?" I'd asked. It wasn't that I'd been trying to be difficult. I had simply been exploring options that wouldn't get me brained with a frying pan again. It had seemed like a reasonable question, but Fannie had bristled at the suggestion.

"Steal? From my own sister? Are you wicked or just daft? You don't steal from your own kin."

"... But the spoon is yours," I'd protested, shocked by the outburst.

"That it is, and no question," Fannie had agreed, "but breaking into her house? Taking it? With her none the wiser? I should suck you dry for even suggesting such a thing. She might be a rotten, no-good so-and-so, but she's family. You don't do that to family."

I'd leveled a cool stare at the old hag. "But it's okay to hire someone else to do it."

"You aren't just someone. This is what you do. You said so. I have your card."

She did, in fact, have my card, and she had waved it under my nose to prove it. Why she needed to prove it, I couldn't say. I'd given it to her, after all.

"Someone doing their job isn't a problem," she'd snipped. "I could send in a plumber to fix her pipes. A cleaner to dust her hutch. Sending in a," she squinted at my card with old eyes, "post-relationship personal effects repossession specialist is the same thing. Tell me I'm wrong," she'd finished with crossed arms and a glower.

She hadn't been wrong, so we'd agreed on the plan, and she'd sent me on my way.

The miles slipped under my bike's tires, and the wind tugged at my head and shoulders. Eventually, the city's skyline lit the evening horizon with a growing radiance. I exited off the highway and wound through the side streets with every intention of heading home. Betty's bar was on the way, though, and temptation got the better of me. I gave a nod to the Plymouth Avenue Bridge and the troll I assumed still lived underneath. Canute and I had saved the world together. While I liked to think we had built up some camaraderie along the way, I was smart enough to know that trolls and camaraderie lived in separate universes. It was a shame. Once you got past Canute's looks, smell, negative IQ, and endless appetite, he wasn't all bad. Well, okay, he was, but still. We'd saved the world.

That's something, right? I asked myself.

Sadly, myself had nothing to say back.

Chapter 3

"Weeding is as necessary to agriculture as sowing."
- Mahatma Gandhi

THE BAR WAS SLOW, which was fine by me. Busy would've meant jostling, and I—with my assortment of bumps, bruises, and scrapes—was not in a jostling mood. I took one of the many open stools, settled into a comfortable slouch, and raised a hand to signal a pint of the usual. It hadn't occurred to me to think about what night it was. When I looked up in eager anticipation of a much-needed beer, my face fell.

"Aw, crap," I blurted out.

"Geez, August," the succubus replied, her tone dryer than a martini with no vermouth. "Don't hold back. Tell me how you really feel."

She knew damn well how I felt. It was the same as any person with a pulse would feel after seeing the succubus. Betty fully embraced her namesake of Betty Page. Her black hair flowed over the creamy skin of bare shoulders and long bangs curled above a gorgeous face. The outfit of choice was a black leather bustier on top, and skin tight low rider pants below. I forced my eyes to not look at the inviting cleavage—which was tough because there was so damned much of it—and scrunched my face into something close to chagrin.

"Hey. Sorry. I just. I thought the other guy was working."

Betty glided down the bar, propped her elbow and that amazing cleavage across from me, and rested her chin on her fist.

"Steve, huh? Never would've thought he'd be your type, but life is full of surprises. What is it? Those broad shoulders? Chiseled jaw? Or maybe the foot long beard hanging off it? That is a damn sexy beard."

I laughed. When the bartender laughed in response, my head swam, and I realized how much I'd needed that. Between Elouise braining me with a frying pan and Fannie dragging me like a block of cheese across a cheese grater, I'd been wound a bit tighter than normal. All that, and I'd genuinely missed the succubus.

"I'll take your word for it," I replied. "You're the expert on those things."

"Beards?"

"Sexy stuff."

The succubus smiled her irresistible smile. "Ah, those things," she purred.

The hair on my arms stood on end, my mouth went dry, and all the blood in my brain went... somewhere else. The sultry vixen batted those crazy eyelashes, and her lips curled up in a knowing smile. I felt her fingers touch mine, and an eager sigh found its way out from somewhere deep inside me. I leaned over the bar, transfixed. The succubus moved closer. Those electric fingertips slid over the back of my hand and up my forearm, and those inviting lips parted. At the last possible moment, she lifted her chin and planted a big, wet smack in the middle of my forehead.

"Yeah, I know a bit about those things," she said with another laugh. "God. You should see your face right now. And your forehead. One sec, I'll get a napkin."

When she turned away, a shiver raced from the crown of my head to my toes. My tormentor returned with a white paper square, and I rubbed it across my forehead. It came back smudged with what had to have been half of her dark red lipstick.

"You deserved that, you know," she remarked. When I glared in confusion, she added, "For avoiding me. Which you've totally been doing. I haven't seen you since... all that stuff at Nicollet Island."

A shadow crossed between us. That dinner party, the one where her warlock ex almost ended the world, had been a hell of a thing. Small wonder I hadn't felt up to crossing paths with the succubus afterward, but explaining that was harder than I would've imagined.

"So, um. You and Vilde? Things still, you know, good?" I finally asked.

Her smile seemed confused. "Good? I suppose that's one way of describing it. I mean, sure, we're happy enough. She's just so... you know."

Something about the way she said 'you know' made me think of poor Leonard. He'd been a crucial ally when I'd repo'd a particular book for a huldra named Vilde Tanck from her vampire ex, and we'd become something like friends along the way. The guy had worked for Tanck without issue until the day when he foolishly ate store-bought lefse instead of the Lefse Queen of Minnesota's speciality. The mercurial elf had pushed him into a woodchipper for his transgression. Afterward, she'd had her vampire necromancer boyfriend stitch and staple Leonard's body back together, then use the dark arts to smoosh his soul back into the reassembled flesh. That wasn't what made me shudder, though. It was the other thing. The thing where just looking at the surreally beautiful elf inspired a near-fanatical adoration. That was creepy as fuck.

"Uh, yeah. I think I know," I agreed cautiously. "But you're at least, you know. Okay?"

The succubus pushed a strand of dark hair behind her ear and looked at the bar's flecked laminate.

"I guess so," she finally said. "One thing's for sure. I haven't eaten this well in years," she finished with a laugh and a pat on her belly. "That lady is an all-you-can-eat buffet."

The double entendre sent a wave of red up my neck and over my cheeks. I knew in a distracted sort of way that succubi fed off of the energy created when two people had sex. I hadn't really considered it before, though. The whole eating energy thing. It wasn't just succubi. Vampires did it more literally when they drank your blood. Other PNs sustained themselves with less tangible life force. Like...

"Hags. You eat like a hag!" I blurted, and was reminded why my inner monologue really needed to stay inside.

"Did you seriously just compare me to a hag?" the bartender asked.

I hadn't. Not exactly. I'd compared how she ate to how hags eat. In my opinion, that wasn't nearly as bad, but no one ever cared what I thought.

"... No?" I finally said.

The succubus had finished filling a pint for another patron. The guy was going to have to wait a bit longer for his drink, though, because that first one ended up all over my face.

"Hey!" I sputtered. "Why?"

Ignoring me, the succubus refilled the pint, slid it to the guy who was now laughing at my misfortune, and then sauntered back to my end of the bar. With a smile sweet enough to stop your heart, she handed me a bar rag.

"Why would you ever put me and 'hag' in the same sentence?" she asked. "Did you get another concussion? Have you been possessed by a very rude spirit? Or are you just incredibly stupid?"

"I'm dumb, not stupid," I growled as I finished transferring as much beer as I could from me to the rag. "I'm not possessed by a spirit, but since you mentioned it, I got knocked out with a frying pan."

The succubus snort-laughed. "Of course you did."

It might have been funny in a time-plus-tragedy-equals-comedy kind of way. Not much time had passed, though, and I was struggling to find the humor Betty found so apparent.

"A couple of hag sisters had a falling out, and now one wants something back from the other, and I'm stuck in the middle. When I tried to get the thing from one hag for the other, I got brained."

The succubus attempted to pout at my misfortune, but couldn't sustain it.

"You really should start wearing your helmet 'round the clock," she laughed as she lightly rapped her knuckles on the top of my head.

She wasn't wrong, and I said as much. It seemed like the situation had been diffused—funny stories about head trauma will do that, I guess—so I steered the conversation back to my original question.

"Seriously, though," I said. "The whole eating energy thing. How does that work?"

In response, I got one of those 'what in the hell are you talking about?' looks.

"Humor me," I growled. "The hag that knocked me out. She started to... eat me... while I was out. But you don't need someone to be asleep or unconscious or whatever to, you know, eat. So how does it work? What's the difference? I mean, when I'm hungry, I eat a hotdog. When you're hungry, though..."

"I could also eat a hotdog," she interrupted tartly, "but I'm not a disgusting slob who puts whatever is within arm's reach into my mouth. If I'm going to eat regular food, it sure as hell won't be a hotdog."

The ever-smoldering sparks in her eyes had flashed again. When she'd decided that I would never, ever accuse her of stooping to my culinary level, she continued with her explanation.

"Regular food is nice and all, but it doesn't sustain me. Like, if I just ate food food, I'd eventually starve."

That was a thought I couldn't wrap my mind around, and my face must have conveyed as much. Betty sighed and held up a finger to pause the conversation. She worked the bar, filled a few more pints, popped the caps off a few more bottles, and set my libido spinning when she shook a martini shaker. When the next lull presented itself, she leaned a hip against the beer cooler and crossed her arms.

"The same is true for lots of PNs. I consider myself lucky. At least I can eat human food. Vampires? If they try, yuck. Barforama."

I nodded sympathetically. I'd once had a newly turned vampire as a client. While I'd been enjoying some chips, she'd asked if she could have one. Just one. It had taken me an hour to clean my desk after that particular whoopsy.

"I guess you could say hags and I have that in common," she grudgingly admitted, "but nothing else. We can eat human food, but we get our true sustenance from life force. And that is it. Full stop. There is literally nothing else that I have in common with a hag. Clear?"

"Crystal," I replied while my mind ran down a list of things they had in common, starting with their temperaments and ending with a general dislike of me.

"Even so, it's different," Betty continued. "I eat the energy that's created when two people have sexual chemistry. A little flirting is a sip," she said in a voice gone low and throaty.

The succubus leaned in, batted her long eyelashes, and traced a single finger across the back of my hand. I shuddered, and she smiled.

"See? Like that. A tasty little sip. And you are pretty tasty, you know. Not like humans. Honestly, you're not like anything else I've ever tasted."

I didn't know what to say to that, so I went with, "If flirting is like a sip, is sex like a keg stand?"

The succubus convulsed with another snort-laugh. "Sure, August. Sex is like a keg stand. God, you're something else."

"Yeah, yeah," I grumbled with a dismissive wave. "So, what about hags? What's it like for them?"

Betty's lips pursed in thought. "Darker," she decided. "My kind feeds on pleasure. Hags feed on nightmares. To get to those, your meal has to be asleep—or unconscious, I guess—so they can draw out those nightmares."

My face squelched up in disgust, but if I'd expected sympathy, I wasn't getting it.

"What? They have to eat, just like anyone else," she snapped. "They can't help that they need nightmares to live."

She had a point. I'd known plenty of PNs, and some of their dietary habits were pretty out there. Setting that aside for future contemplation, I asked the next question that popped into my mind.

"And if a hag says, 'I should suck you dry,' what's that about?"

Betty pulled back and wrapped her arms around herself. "Did someone say that to you? Oh, August. That's awful. If the Northern Quorum knew someone was doing that to people, there'd be hell to pay."

Her words rocked me back on my barstool. "The Northern Quorum?" I repeated in shock. "Seriously?"

"Don't be an ass. You know the rules as well as I do. PNs don't kill humans or other PNs for food or sport. Self-defense, sure. Anything else is a definite no-no. If a hag were to suck you dry, you'd be as good as dead. You might still have a pulse, but that's it. There'd be nothing else left in you. You'd just be a drooling idiot. August, do not—and I mean this—do not let a hag suck you dry. If there's one out there doing that to people, the Quorum needs to know."

The gravity of what she'd said caught me off guard. Everyone knew the Quorum existed. They were the PN's equivalent of the Supreme Court, except the human's Supreme Court didn't execute people. I'd never met a member of the Quorum. Nor had anyone I knew, or if they had, they hadn't shared. Which made a certain amount of sense. You didn't want to meet a member of the Quorum. If you did, it was likely to end badly.

While I was ruminating on that invisible and influential body, Betty was staring at me from under her long lashes. It took me a minute to notice, but when I did, I squirmed under the intensity of her glare.

"August? Is there a hag sucking people dry?" she asked.

"No..." I muttered. "Maybe. I don't know. The one I'm working for keeps making that threat, but in a crabby old lady kinda way. I don't think she's serious. She scared off a goblin when she said it once, though."

The succubus rolled her eyes and turned to fill a pint for another patron. "Hags and goblins, huh? You really have to stop getting mixed up with the wrong people, August," she called over her shoulder. "Whatever happened to getting sweaters and cheap jewelry back for broken-hearted saps? Why do you keep diving in over your head? Didn't you learn anything this summer?"

"You started it," I shot back. "If I hadn't gotten your herbs back from Tony, I wouldn't have been in his crosshairs."

And then there was more beer. I sputtered in shock while the guy whose drink I was wearing guffawed.

"My fault? You think what happened was my fault? Unbelievable," Betty spat. "You should leave, August. You're making me waste perfectly good beer."

She extended an arm and a slender finger. I shoved myself off of my barstool, and moved my boots in the direction she was pointing. My hand slammed into the door, and I was in the street. Beer dripped from my eyebrows and ran down the front of my shirt. Still, I counted my blessings. At least I'd left the bar of my own volition. It definitely beat being carried out by a warlock's magic wind.

CHAPTER 4

"The farmer hopes for rain, the walker hopes for sunshine, and the gods hesitate."
- Chinese Proverb

I'D JUST ARRIVED IN Vermillion, and what a difference a day made. The drive in better weather had been surprisingly pleasant. A grudging respect for farm country had taken root as Minneapolis dwindled behind me. Verdant fields stretched as far as the eye could see. Some were soybeans, but more were tall stalks of corn with tassels waving in the breeze. Here and there, I saw farmhouses. Some were elaborate old Victorians with beautiful spires and graceful awnings. Others were more pragmatic, a testament to the no-nonsense hardiness of the locals. I got stuck behind the occasional tractor, but used those moments to appreciate the view. Since the odds of getting whacked with a frying pan were good, I'd made it a point to enjoy the drive.

I didn't go directly to Fannie's place. Fannie's place was Elouise's place, or close enough. After their spat, Fannie had moved from the decrepit main house to the decrepit shed. From an emotional perspective, there was a gulf between the two sisters. From a linear feet perspective, there were only thirty or forty. Since rolling up their front drive wasn't the sneakiest way to start our sneaky endeavor, Fannie and I had agreed to meet by a particular sprawling oak near the property at dusk. I wanted to arrive early so I could find the spot. Looking for a particular tree in the dark is hard, and this particular job had been hard enough already.

A glance at my watch confirmed I was earlier than planned. After folding my clothes into a small pile beside the corn that stood like troops waiting for an inspirational speech from the commanding oak tree, I shifted to give my legs a stretch. The safe bet was the bloodhound. No one would look twice at some local farmer's pooch running around. That, and the damned thing's nose was awesome. The pervasive manure smell was off-putting for a city dweller like me. For the dog, though? It was going to be a treat.

I trotted into the field. My nose plugged me into an extraordinary array of scents, and my long ears flapped with a *whap-whap* sound as I ran. Soon, the human bit of my brain was giggling like a kid with a sugar high. I didn't worry about the job at all. It was just the dog, the smells, and me. Life is all about the simple moments. Unfortunately, they never last. I heard a voice and recognized it instantly. Its icy edge made me sympathize with whoever she was talking to. An image of eyes flashing from within deep pools of mascara and the spikes of a bright pink mohawk wavering like reeds in a stiff breeze filled my mind. My short legs locked up and left four skid marks in the dirt. My head tilted, and my long ears pulled words from the air.

"This is serious," she snapped.

I lowered my belly and moved my legs. A few rows of corn slid by before I could see her. Dogs don't see colors quite like humans do, but the woman's bright shorts and technicolor hair still made an impression. She had her hands on those shapely hips, and every line of her body showed how not-happy she was. Why she was pissed at a tattered scarecrow, though, I hadn't a clue.

"You know how serious it is," she said. "You've seen what's happening. The old ways are gone. If we're going to survive, I need it."

Something answered with a horrible voice. If rotting carrion could speak as it spoiled under a midday sun, if the psycho's ax could give voice to its intention a moment before splitting your skull, if the darkness of being trapped by an avalanche could whisper its madness, it would sound like that voice. A low whine started in the back of my throat, and the woman uttered a sharp, "Shush!"

The horrible voice stopped, but its effect on me was just getting started. Terror took root somewhere way down in my bowels. That terror spread and reached my legs, and they all kicked into high gear. Cornstalks whizzed by as I darted a jagged path through the field. I didn't know where I was going. My dog brain had the wheel, and it was beyond piddly concerns like getting lost. All my spark of humaness could do was hold on for the ride.

Stop! I begged. *Please stop! Heel! Sit! Stay!*

Finally, my legs got the message. The fear had abated, and I struggled to understand what had happened. It wasn't like I'd seen or heard something that raised the poor dog's hackles. The fear hadn't been 'out there.' It hadn't been some external threat. More, it had felt like the fear was inside me. Something that was always there, lurking just under the surface of my awareness. Something that was bearable only because—most of the time—it was locked away in my subconscious. The voice had changed that. It had unearthed my fears while shoving aside everything else at the same time, so the only thing left in my world was a terror that dwelled deep inside. I knew I'd never be able to fully explain it. I also knew that I never wanted to experience it again.

The dog gave itself a good shake, then looked around. I had no clue where I was, other than still being in the cornfield. My nostrils twitched and parsed a myriad of smells until

I found the ones I was hoping to find: my own. It took a while to find my way, since my scent was ebbing and flowing on the summer breeze. Finally, the dog burst through the last row of corn and shoved its nose into my pile of clothes. I was enjoying my shirt's armpit when a woman's voice caught me by surprise.

"You again?" she asked. "Didn't think I'd see you around these parts."

She stepped out from the corn a few yards away, resplendent in her punky glory. My tail gave an impulsive wag, and my tongue lolled. She'd obviously pegged me as more than just a dog. Likewise, I had that hard-to-explain sense that she wasn't human. What kind of PN she might be, though, I didn't care. I simply knew that I liked what I saw.

"Hi," I said, but not actually. Dogs don't speak English. Regardless, she must've spoken at least a little barkese.

"Hi, yourself. Why were you in my cornfield?"

"Woof?" I requested, then pushed my nose into the clothes beside me.

"Take your time," she muttered as she turned her back.

A quick shift left all of my bare skin exposed to the swarming mosquitos. After hastily pulling on my clothes, I gruffly told her I was decent.

"Decent? Really? With the company you keep?"

"What the hell is that supposed to mean?" I shot back.

"Your girlfriend," she replied with a pointed look over my shoulder.

My girlfriend? I wondered, and then the breeze shifted. I smelled mildew and throat lozenge.

"She is not my girlfriend."

The hag coughed out a laugh. "Damned right, I'm not. You couldn't handle me."

That left me and the punky lady gaping until Fannie asked if there was any particular reason the other woman was there.

"If no one's bothered your precious corn, you got no need to be bothering us," she spat.

The mohawk's spikes lowered threateningly.

"Mind your tongue, hag. Don't forget your house is on my field. I've kept that little kernel to myself. Learn some manners, or rumors might spread about two nasty old ladies feeding on the folks in town. Probably not your idea of a good time, unless you like torches and pitchforks."

Fannie wagged a recriminating finger. "We pay. Who are you to be making threats when your purse is full?"

The two women traded glares. One full of youthful disdain, the other full of experienced ire. The tension was killing me, so I cleared my throat.

"I'm August," I said with a wave.

On the upside, I got her attention. On the downside, her response was a narrowing of her eyes and an extended middle finger. My kind of girl.

The hag hawked a phlegmy glob into the dirt and smacked her cracked lips. "If you two are done with your flirting, we've got business to attend to."

The mohawked woman put the full weight of her ire on me. "Whatever that business is, stay out of my field. If you don't, the Strach na wróble will be the least of your concerns."

"What's a stracknawobble?" I asked.

In response, she stared at me. In response to her response, I stared at her. After our match went a few rounds, she turned and stomped off through the corn. Soon, even the pink tips of her spiky hair were gone.

"Worthless slip of a girl," Fannie spat. "Good riddance."

I wanted to ask about that worthless slip of a girl. Where she lived. What she did for fun. Were those, um, tattoos real? Did she have a name? Was she into unlikeable shifters with basement apartments and unreliable transportation? Unfortunately, Fannie's demeanor made it clear that, despite being human again, I'd still be barking up the wrong tree. The hag had only one thing on her ancient mind.

"You'd best not muck this up, shifter," she scolded. "My sister's frying pan was bad. What I'll do to you is worse. Do you follow?"

"Happy Everyone Threaten August Day," I groused as we walked the dirt road. "Just do your part, and I'll take care of the rest."

The plan was simple. Fannie and I would creep close to Elouise's house and wait. Hags normally slipped out to feed after dark. Back when we'd put the plan together, I'd mentioned that I was perfectly capable of seeing when someone left a house. Fannie had offered a gruff chortle in response.

"We're hags, you dolt. You see me because the sun's cruel rays don't let me hide. Night, though. Ah, she's a kinder mistress. Approves of the sort that sneak about. You'll see naught but shadows. I'll see my sister," she'd finished with conviction.

I hadn't been convinced, but also hadn't been in the mood to argue. If she wanted to be on hag spotting duty, that was fine by me.

Now, we walked in silence until the house came into view. I was about to slip into the cornstalks when her hand gripped my arm.

"You'll not want to be doing that," the hag advised. "No telling why, but Dagmara's taken a shine to you. You go trampling about in her field, that shine'll fade faster than the gleam in a dying man's eye. Crouch near the corn if you must, but don't go in."

"Dagmara? That's her name?"

"Stupid shifter."

"Right. Dagmara."

As was common in the late summer, the sun took its own sweet time to set. I squatted on my heels and let my imagination run wild. I'd bump into Dagmara, maybe at a bar in town. By the jukebox. She'd be punching in some punk classics. I'd follow with my favorite grunge numbers. She'd nod approvingly at my choices, and I'd acknowledge punk's influence on Seattle's signature 90s sound. I'd buy her a drink, and we'd share a table. I'd say I liked her hair, and she'd remark in an offhand way how attracted she was to mediocre middle-aged guys.

Yeah, I'm sure you're totally her type, a snarky part of my brain snarked.

Shut up and let me have this.

A couple of feet away, Fannie sat with her legs crossed. Boney elbows rested on knobby knees, and a warty chin rested on the swollen joints of interlaced fingers. A moment passed, then two, and then I heard a soft snore.

"Seriously?" I complained.

"Hush," came the immediate and tart reply. "If you want to feel the frying pan again, run up there. If you don't, shut your trap and wait."

I grit my teeth and locked a nasty retort behind them, then drew a slow breath in through my nostrils. After holding it for a moment, I relaxed my jaw and let a long sigh slip out. I hated waiting, but as places to wait went, the edge of a cornfield on a pleasant summer night wasn't bad. Crickets chirruped. The wind whispered. The sky had that magical quality where the sun was going but not gone, and the stars were polishing themselves up for a big night ahead. When I considered some alternatives, like the castle of a spray-tanned vampire I'd visited earlier that year, waiting by a cornfield wasn't too shabby. My mind wandered back to the absurdly opulent home of Dieter Saint James.

Elouise better not have a dungeon under her house, I thought.

The sun finally said its goodbyes, but still we waited. It had been full dark for about fifteen minutes when I heard the hag suck in a breath.

"There," she whispered, soft as old paper sliding across a wooden desk. "Do ya see?"

I rocked onto the balls of my feet and braced myself with fingers splayed in the dirt. At first, I didn't see a thing, but that was because I'd been watching the front door. Something at the edge of my vision caught my eye. I looked up in time to see a blot of darkness ooze and jerk its way out of a side window. A moment later, the shadow had disappeared.

"And there she goes," Fannie chuckled. "That sister o'mine has always been a hungry one. The beater barely rings the dinner bell, and she's already headed for the buffet."

The hag gained her feet in a remarkably ungainly way, then faced me.

"Well? You gonna earn what I'm paying you, or just sit there in the dirt like a dummy?"

"Yeah, yeah," I complained with a dismissive way. "I'll see you at the oak tree when I'm done."

I crouch-ran across patches of weeds and dirt and up the front steps to the door. A quick tug on the knob confirmed it was locked. Despite the rest of the house's disrepair, the hag had recently invested in some new hardware. I walked along the home's front porch and nudged a window. Also locked. Reason dictated any other doors or windows would be secured as well.

"Why is nothing ever smooth?" I muttered.

The skills I brought to my esoteric profession were a willingness to tolerate uncomfortable situations and a certain sympathy for the furtively inclined. I didn't mind the sob stories, the tantrums, or even the occasional tussle. I just rolled with the punches—some figurative, others not—until they gave up the goods. As for those 'on the sly' jobs, I was good at finding things. Although, to be fair, people were pretty bad at hiding stuff. So, yeah. Those made up my extensive list of qualifications to be a post-relationship personal effects repossession specialist.

Well, that and a willingness to break and enter.

Squinting in the dark, I pulled my lock pick kit from my jacket's pocket and set to work. As it turned out, picking the lock was easier than getting the poorly fitted door open. The damned thing was stuck in its jamb like a troll's foot in a faerie's slipper. With a lowering of my shoulder, bracing of my legs, and a Herculean shove, I was inside.

The house was dark, so I slipped out a penlight and flipped it on. Its narrow beam swept the small home's living room, and I considered what I was seeing. The home had likely been abandoned many years prior. It was also obvious someone had overlooked that fact and tried to spruce the place up. Elouise's taste seemed firmly rooted in years gone by, about a hundred or so from the looks of things. None of the furniture matched, but everything looked built to last. Old stuff was like that. Rural Minnesota had plenty of antique malls and flea markets, and Elouise obviously knew where to shop. The eclectic collection went together really well. The flashlight's cone didn't do it justice, but I could tell that in the light of day, it would look pretty nice in there. I found my very reasonable dislike of the old hag softening. I still really disliked her, but maybe a smidge less than I had before I'd broken into her house.

Just so we're clear, though. I still really disliked her.

After getting my bearings, I mustered up my other skill: my sympathy for the furtively inclined. I was good at my job. I had a gift for finding things that didn't want to be found. To be honest, it wasn't that hard. You just had to know where to look.

The first rule of finding stuff is that a lot of it isn't hidden. If what you're looking for is something they'd use day-to-day, it'll be right in front of your nose. That expensive espresso machine? It won't be stashed under frozen burger patties in the basement chest freezer. It'll be on the counter in the kitchen. Need to get some classic vinyl? Don't waste time looking under the toaster oven's crumb tray. Try the record player. When people don't expect you to be in their home uninvited, they usually won't go to great lengths to hide things, even things that aren't theirs.

The second rule of finding stuff is that people aren't very creative when they do hide something. Forget about the movies. You don't need to find a loose floorboard or check behind vent grates, and no one hides something in a plastic bag inside of a toilet tank. If what you're looking for is small, check their underwear drawer. Guaranteed, it'll be in the back rolled up in a pair of unmentionables. Bigger than a breadbox? Garage under a tarp damn near every time. I'm not kidding. People—human or otherwise—are terrible at hiding stuff.

With my two rules of finding stuff firmly in mind, I headed for the kitchen. It was a no-brainer. Houses were carved up by function. Sleepytime stuff went in the bedroom. Bathroomy stuff went in the bathroom. Kitcheny stuff? You guessed it. I swept the flashlight's beam through an archway to the connected dining room and trained it on a swinging door that had to lead to the kitchen.

I knew Fannie's silver spoon wouldn't be in a drawer with the other utensils. It was decorative. Something you'd have on a spoon rack on the wall, if you were the kind of weirdo that enjoyed collecting spoons and hanging them on the wall. After pushing through the door, I took in a smallish galley kitchen with an old farm sink, some counter space, and a small wooden table with a couple of old spindle chairs. The walls were bare except for the thing I knew I'd find: a wooden rack specifically designed for weirdos that liked to collect and display spoons. It had notches for twelve or maybe fifteen, but only one hung on the whole thing.

"Bingo," I said with a smile.

I reached out to pinch the spoon's bowl between my finger and thumb, but froze when I heard the whisper. My ears strained for another few seconds. Nothing. No floorboard creaks or footsteps. No voices. With a dismissive grunt, I lifted the spoon from the rack and slipped it into a pocket. Mission accomplished, I paused. Experience had taught me that giving my intuition a little time to do its thing could pay dividends. I gave the kitchen another hard look. Above the stove, a too-familiar frying pan hung from a hook. A butcher block on the counter held a few large knives. I crossed to the cabinets and pulled open a couple of drawers. One had a spatula. The other was empty. I gave a satisfied nod. Nothing of interest, which meant it was time to leave. Except it wasn't. Not quite.

My moment of contemplation had included the kitchen table. Large sheets of paper covered its top. My curiosity traded blows with my caution, and—as was usually the case—curiosity won the match handily. It didn't take an architect to know the sheets ofpapers were architectural drawings. I leaned over for a closer look and saw a rendering of a large Victorian-era house. I lifted the top page to look at the next in the pile and saw a cutaway reminiscent of opening a doll house. The page was labeled 'East: Bedrooms, upper and lower floor.' It showed a point of view of each room akin to looking at a set on a stage. The illustrations were nicely done. Cozy chairs, side tables, beds, wardrobes, and chest of drawers had been carefully brought to life. Measurements and dimensions covered the white space between.

The next few pages were similar in style but looked in on the house from different directions. I saw more details on the bedrooms, a spacious kitchen and large dining room, and a sitting room on the main floor. Then I flipped to the illustration that convinced me I wasn't looking at a simple Victorian-style house. The front door opened to a small foyer off the sitting room. Past the foyer, there was a high desk with a large, open book depicted, and an old-fashioned key holder on the wall behind it. The more I studied the drawing, the more it felt like I was looking at an old-timey boarding house or hotel.

I checked in with my intuition and agreed with its suggested course of action. I took a page at random, rolled it into a tube, then folded it twice until it was small enough to fit in my pocket.

"What is a hag doing with these?" I wondered out loud.

When I heard the creak of hinges in need of oil, it was almost like the house had answered my question. I frantically looked around for a place to hide and came up short. Not as short as the person who pushed through the kitchen door, though.

"Who the hell are you?" the coblyn asked. "And where the hell is that hag?"

My mind churned. Bad enough that I was in a classic breaking and entering situation. Worse, that it was the residence of a very unpleasant hag. Those two facts were enough to ramp up the old nerves a bit. This recent addition, though, really set the panic lights flashing. Looking up at me from a height of just under two feet was a too-familiar face. Not one I knew personally, but also not one I wanted to know personally. It belonged to Tordundanragnorfolsteck Mastiwallerick Blundergibalfronalbesk, more commonly known as Blunder. Don't laugh. Not at the name, and not at my sudden wariness. When it comes to PNs, size doesn't matter. Don't believe me? Spend an afternoon with the likes of Blunder. I only had second-hand accounts, but one was from a gnome who was missing his second hand. He'd borrowed money from Blunder and hadn't paid the vig. Of all the things I knew about Blunder, the most important one was that I didn't want to be anywhere near him.

"And where is the spoon?" Blunder asked as his caterpillar eyebrows crawled into a suspicious V above the dark pits of his eyes. "The one that should be up there?"

"Ran away with the dish," I said.

"Is that so?" the cob replied while taking a menacing step forward.

"Ah, yup," I agreed with a careful step back.

When he leaped, I pivoted and lunged. The kitchen had a back door. I hoped it led to a mudroom and not a pantry. The cob caught my ankle as we passed, and I tumbled hard into a counter's edge. A flailing hand knocked over the butcher block, and a clatter mingled with my curses. With a shove, I was back on my feet a split-second before the little guy landed on my back. I felt small hands scrabble for a grip and gave a panicked yelp. Reversing my steps, I lurched back against the fridge and heard a pained squeak as I slammed against it. Having gotten Blunder off my back, I yanked on the kitchen's back door and thanked every god I didn't actually believe in that it wasn't a pantry, then cursed those gods as I fled to a root cellar. My flashlight still in my hand, I ducked between hanging gourds and clumps of strange weeds, then saw my escape: two wooden doors angling down from the ceiling with a couple of wooden steps leading up to them. I begged those same gods to please let the doors be unlocked and then cursed when they gave me the finger. A sliding barrel bolt held the doors shut. On the upside, the barrel plate and its catch were screwed into wood that had softened with age and weather. The sound of small, pounding feet behind me lent my shove an extra boost. The screws holding the bolt lock in place ripped free, the doors flopped open, and I clambered into the night.

The backyard was small. Besides the old shed that Fannie had moved into, there was nowhere to hide. Nowhere except the corn that encroached on the yard's edges, that is. I flicked off the flashlight, then pushed through the stalks and fled blindly into the field. My race through the cornstalks wasn't a quiet one. Between the rustling and my repeated curses—at the coblyn, at the hag sisters, at myself and my own stupid luck—I was making a hell of a ruckus. It was no surprise that Blunder followed me so easily.

"Stop!" the coblyn commanded. "You can't run forever."

He wasn't wrong. I'd never aspired to be part of the 'in' crowd, and that included being in shape. Coblynau, in comparison, were legendary for their stamina. They were small, sure, but also built to delve into the earth's crust and dig out whatever they found down there. I might have been able to cover more than twice the ground with each step compared to my pursuer, but I'd also tire long before him. It was a classic case of the tortoise and the hare. If I didn't give him the slip fast, I'd drop from exhaustion, leaving Blunder to amble up and do his worst.

I forced myself to stop running and tried to slow my gasping lungs and pounding heart. For a long moment, all I could hear was the blood rushing through my veins. Finally, though, other sounds became more discernible. Like the heavy breathing right behind me. I cocked my head to the side and considered the sound. It wasn't the gulping of air through a coblyn's open mouth. That would have come up to my ears from closer to the ground. This breathing sounded like the breather's mouth was more on the level of my shoulder. It also sounded like how a person might breathe if they were really, really angry. In through the nose, out through tightly clenched teeth. A seething sort of breathing. That wasn't auspicious. Guardedly, I turned around and saw Dagmara.

"What are you doing here?" I blurted out in an urgent whisper. "You can't be here. It isn't safe."

"This is my field," she replied, each syllable sharp as the harvester's scythe, "and no. It isn't safe."

I nodded my head and stepped forward with every intent to grab her by the shoulders and push her away. It was a good plan, too. Nice and chivalrous and all. Saving the cute girl from the nasty old coblyn. Except it didn't happen. Dagmara's eyes narrowed and my back muscles seized up. I raised an arm and my shoulder screamed in pained protest. A charley horse spasmed in my calf and caused me to stumble. My vision swam and lightning crackled behind my eyeballs. Someone turned my temples into timpani drums and set to beating on them. That step I'd planned to take before my calf cramped up left me kneeling in the dirt as a myriad of pains consumed every inch of me. Then I heard Blunder.

"Ah! Got you now. Whoever you are, lady, you don't want to be watching this."

I couldn't see the coblyn, but knew he had to be looking over my hunched back at the punky woman standing a few feet away. I lifted my head on a creaking neck and saw her black-lined eyes go wide.

"Is that a knife?" she whispered. "In my field?"

Blunder made a sound. It might have been the start of a word. What word in particular, we'll never know. All that came out were a couple of disjointed syllables: a sort of *buh* followed by a long *uurk*. I'd been tased before. My entire body had tensed up, including my jaw muscles. I'd wanted to scream at the literal shock, but all that had come out was a very similar *buh* followed by a very pained *uurk*.

The next thing I heard was the sound of a small, sturdy body falling to the ground.

"Why is he chasing you?" the woman asked.

I wanted to reply. Possibly with an answer, possibly with a snarky 'go fuck yourself.' The jury was still out. What mattered was that I couldn't reply. An unbearable fatigue was smothering me, and every muscle in my body felt like it had been aggressively pulled. Talking wasn't an option. Dying, sure, but talking? Nope.

"Ugh," a disgusted voice complained. "Get up."

The pain and fatigue faded enough to make moving possible, albeit still painful. I found my feet, then stumbled as a head rush threatened to send me back to the ground. Before I could fall, a steadying hand grabbed my shoulder.

"Come on," she instructed.

After a quick glance back at the huddled and moaning shape behind me, I followed her through the corn. Where my earlier passage had been one of chaos and calamity, Dagmara barely disturbed a single leaf on any of the tall stalks. I tried to follow her lead, but it was impossible. I was the proverbial bull in a China shop by comparison, and I could tell it was bugging the crap out of her. Every time my boot turned on a clump of dirt and my shoulder pressed into a nearby stalk, her fingers would twitch, or her shoulders would hitch up, or her back would kink. It was like every time I bumped up against the corn, a ball peen hammer rapped her on the knee.

"Sorry?" I offered, but got no response.

I tried my best to be more careful, but had little luck. By the time we emerged onto a grassy expanse of lawn, I was exhausted from trying to be careful, and she was exhausted by my failure to do so.

"You were a lot less of a pain when you were a dog," she remarked as she turned to face me.

The lady had saved me, so I swallowed an angry retort. You know, manners and whatnot. My self-control must've been worth something because she scratched her chin, then asked if I wanted a drink. I want to drink in the best of circumstances. Being asked if I wanted one after some very unpleasant ones yielded a mirthless chuckle.

"I'd love one," I replied. "Honestly, I'd love as many as you can spare."

CHAPTER 5

"Farming looks mighty easy when your plow is a pencil and you're a thousand miles from the cornfield."
- Dwight D. Eisenhower

AFTER SAVING ME—OR TORTURING me, depending on how you looked at it—Dagmara had led me to a farmhouse. The clearing it occupied was an island in the endless sea of corn. Its front drive wound off through the stalks, and I realized it would connect with the dirt road. Like the hags' house further down, it was easily a century old. A copse of mature trees huddled near its side like whispering old men. Past them, a grain silo and a large barn stood stoically. Closer to the house, an old Ford pickup brought Norman Rockwell to mind. The whole place oozed Americana. You could practically smell the apple pie in the oven. A vague understanding formed in my mind. The farmhouse before me was where old Farmer John, or whoever, had lived with his family many decades ago. The long, low house down the way must've housed seasonal farm workers back before industrial combines had made them obsolete. That hovel the goblin called home was likely a convenient place to store whatever it was they used back when people harvested corn by hand. I wasn't looking at old buildings. I was looking at a piece of American history. A monument to a different past. There was something beneath that, though. Something sadder. The house's paint, once likely a crisp and clean white, was weathered and cracked. Wood grain showed through like the first spots of leprosy. That pickup? Closer inspection showed rust working its inexorable way through the body's metal. The barn's silhouette had a tired sag that spoke to its age and lack of repair. It felt like a dream that had slipped through fingers too weak to hold on. A fading echo of what once was.

I followed my savior as she mounted the creaking steps to the porch. When I followed, I felt a board sag beneath my foot. She slid off her still-immaculate white boots after stepping inside the house's front door. I churlishly kicked off my dirty boots and tried not to think about the mismatched socks they'd concealed. Together, we passed through a small hallway into the living room. I sat on the sofa and waited for her to return with something alcoholic. A moment later, Dagmara pushed a chipped porcelain coffee mug into my hand. I took an eager sip and almost spit it out in surprise.

"Water?"

"You were expecting something else?"

I had been, and I said so. My sore head, back, and legs made it come out a little sharper than intended. Well, that and my disappointment. I'd really wanted to find booze in the cup.

"Getting hydrated will help," she replied tersely. "Drink your water."

Churlish defiance made me drain half the cup. A couple of moments later, the headache dialed back a smidge. I kept an irate expression on my face, regardless. No need to let her know she'd been right. We studied each other over the rims of our respective cups. I didn't know what she was thinking, but her expression was less homicidal than before. I was thinking she really was attractive. Beneath the punky clothes and heavy makeup was a woman in her mid-thirties. She had the pale skin, high cheekbones, and narrow chin common to eastern Europeans, and the hair that wasn't either shaved down or dyed pink was a straw-colored blond. Her eyes were a dark blue that I already knew went a darker gray when she was angry. Speaking of eyes, I let my own surreptitiously drift down. The mechanic's shirt was gone. Today's outfit was a Dead Milkmen band shirt with the sleeves cut off and the collar cut out to make a ragged V. The tattoo on her chest was mostly hidden, but I glimpsed flowers. Small blue flowers.

"They're corn flowers," she remarked dryly.

Oops. Not as surreptitious as I'd thought.

"Nice, uh. Nice ink."

"No one says that."

I frowned. "People don't like your tattoo?"

"No one says, 'Nice ink.' It's cheugy," she clarified.

"I don't know what that means."

Dagmara rolled her eyes. "I'm not surprised."

She took another sip of water. I finished what was left in my cup with a big gulp.

"So, you're from Vermillion, huh?" I asked in a banal attempt at small talk.

"No."

I waited for more, but waited in vain. When the silence had long since passed uncomfortable, I asked where she was from.

"Originally? Poland."

"You don't sound Polish."

"You don't sound well-traveled enough to know what people should sound like."

This is going swimmingly, I thought with a mental scowl.

"Yeah..." I agreed.

She took another sip. I lifted my cup to my mouth, then pretended to drink when I realized it was empty. She raised an eyebrow. I set the cup down and picked something off my jeans.

"So," she said.

"So?" I asked in response.

"Why were you and that coblyn trampling my field?"

It wasn't a question I'd expected. Phrased the way she had, it made it sound like me and Blunder had nothing else on our minds but offending the corn.

"He was chasing me. I was trying to get away. Sorry that meant running through your field. To be fair, pretty much anywhere you run in these parts ends up being through a field."

I saw her eye twitch in irritation. "Sure, but you were in my field. Not just any field. You were in mine."

Why I felt so sheepish, I couldn't say, but my shoulders lifted in an apologetic shrug.

"Why was the coblyn chasing you?" she asked.

"I asked it too many questions," I quipped. I had meant it as a joke. She didn't laugh. "Uh. I don't know, really. I needed to get something from the hag that lives there,"

"Elouise."

"Right. And then give that thing to her sister,"

"Fannie."

"Right. And when I went to get the thing while Elouise was gone, Blunder showed up. He was the coblyn."

"Obviously."

"Uh huh. I don't know why he was there. I do know he's not the kind of cob you want around. Most coblynau are no problem. Blunder and his buddies? Bad news bears. I ran, then ran into you, then you did... whatever it was you did to us, and here we are."

"And here we are," she agreed. "So, that's what you do? You get stuff back for people?"

I nodded, and she relaxed a bit into her chair.

"What kind of stuff, and from what kind of people?" she asked.

"Special stuff. Sentimental stuff. I'm a post-relationship personal effects repossession specialist." When she raised a skeptical eyebrow, I pushed on. "You know. Love happens, and love ends. When it does, most folks usually just want two things: their special whatever back, and to never see their ex again. That's what I do."

Both of her eyebrows raised up when she said, "You get their stuff and kill their ex?"

"What? No! I get their stuff so they don't have to see their ex. Geez. That got dark quick."

Dagmara pursed her lips, then almost smiled. "Sorry. So Elouise and Fannie were dating? That's a disturbing image."

I chuckled in agreement. "Yeah, no. They weren't dating. They were together for like, I don't know, maybe decades, maybe centuries. How long do hags live?"

Dagmara lifted a shoulder and let it fall. I noticed how the cutoff sleeve of her shirt slid across the smooth skin, then mentally kicked myself under the table and told myself to behave.

"Anyway," I continued after clearing my throat, "they recently had a falling out. Fannie had this silver baby spoon. Weird, I know, but I don't judge. Something about it came between the two sisters, and it got serious. I guess when Elouise kicked Fannie to the shed, she didn't let her take the spoon. Fannie hired me to get it back, and I did," I said with a smidge of pride. "It took getting brained with a frying pan and chased by a knife-wielding coblyn through your cornfield, but some jobs are like that."

"Dangerous line of work."

"Uh huh," I agreed. "Sometimes. Other times, it's just knock, knock, who's there, the guy that needs the thing."

When she chuckled, my heart did a somersault and a goofy smile tripped and stumbled its way onto my face. Things were going well and getting better. I knew—just knew—that she had something better to drink and was about to offer me some. We'd chat a bit longer. Get to know each other a little better. Then...

"Well, I have a long day tomorrow, um..."

"August," I supplied as my brief fantasy shattered.

"August," she agreed. "Thanks for visiting, but I need to call it a night. You understand."

I muttered that I did. We walked together to the porch. There was a moment when we tried to go through the door at the same time. We brushed against one another, then stepped back, then tried again.

This will be a great story for the grandkids, a part of my brain that I hadn't known existed said.

Grandkids? every other part of my brain yelped in shock.

"... down the drive. It'll curve through the field until it hits the road," she was saying when I was able to pay attention again. "Maybe a five-minute walk. Stay on the drive, though. Do not go into my field again."

"Yeah, yeah," I grumbled. "Lesson learned. So. Anyway, uh."

There went that eyebrow again. "Have a pleasant night, August," she drolled.

I said the same to her, thanked her again for helping with the cob, told her the water at her place was pretty good, better than expected. I clarified the directions she'd given me, remarked on the low humidity, made a lame joke about mosquitoes, and basically acted like a complete buffoon. Then, unexpectedly, she asked if I had a card.

"Sure," I replied as I fished one from my jacket's inner pocket. "Why?"

She chewed her lip. Whatever she was thinking, she was considering it carefully.

"I was in a relationship, and they have something of mine that I want back. I'll call you and we can talk about it."

As my feet trod the worn ruts of the dirt lane, I considered my recent trend of new business. As marketing strategies went, getting chased by angry PNs wielding sharp objects seemed like an ill-advised way to find new customers. It was cheaper than T.V. ads, though, and this customer in particular was one I'd been happy to meet.

After walking to my motorcycle, I headed back to the oak tree to deliver the spoon. The hag was more than irate when I rolled up.

"And where have you been?" she asked. "I'm out here, my poor bones aching, bugs trying to do their worst, about to die of hunger. And you?"

"Job was a bit more involved than expected," I apologized.

She continued to glower until I'd produced the spoon. She whispered something—at least, I think she did—then plucked it nimbly from my hand. There was a flash of silver, then it disappeared into a pocket of her housecoat.

"Welp," I'd said, extending an open palm, "I guess that's that. Pleasure doing business."

Fannie glowered and sucked on her gums. "Money," she finally spat. "It's all about money. It's always about money."

Crooked fingers shoved their way through this pocket and that. Every thrust of a hand into a new pocket was a disgusted commentary on the free market.

"Money," she said again, making the word into a curse.

Handfuls of coins and crumpled bills were slowly unearthed from the mine of her dingy clothing. With each find, she slapped it in my hand, then resumed her digging. All the while, she continued her complaining.

"Was a time when me and Elouise didn't worry about such things. We were fine with a dark hovel to huddle in and folks close enough by to keep ourselves fed. When the feeding got scarce, off we'd go. We didn't need any finery. We didn't need things. Was Elouise who got the itch for that nonsense. Not me. She's the one that wanted money."

More bills emerged, and Fannie shoved them at me like grenades about to go off.

"It wasn't enough to sneak in and get a taste of the sleepers," she continued. "Oh no! She turned us into petty thieves. Rummaging through pocketbooks. Digging for coins in the cushions. Pah! Shameful. I said so, too. And then she got her big idea."

"Is that what this is?" I asked. "Her big idea to make money?"

I pulled the folded sheet from my pocket. The page I'd grabbed from Elouise's kitchen was one of the dollhouse-style cutaways. Fannie snatched it from my hand and opened it wide. Her eyes narrowed when she looked at it, and then she pointedly turned her nose up.

"So, now she's got pretty drawings of it? Pah. Stupid. We don't need such a thing, I told her."

I shoved the most recent wad of bills into a pocket, then reached out to flick the paper.

"What is that, Fannie? I think I know, but I don't believe it."

The hag sniffed and pressed her thin lips together. I leveled a cool stare at the hag and waited. She might've thought she was stubborn. She knew nothing about being stubborn.

"Oh, fine!" she finally snapped. "Not that it's any of your business, but yeah. That's Elouise's grand idea. A bed-and-breakfast, she'd said. No more scraping and scrounging to pay rent. No more climbing through windows or sliding down chimneys to get our sup. People coming to us—right to our door, if you can believe it—and paying us good money to stay. Them sleeping under our roof, rolled up like little pigs in blankets. Never a hungry night again, and all those fools would expect is some dry toast and burnt coffee come morning."

The ridiculousness of the idea poked my funny bone, and I laughed. Fannie's disapproving glower pressed her eyebrows down so far I could barely see her eyes. It made her look cartoonishly irate, which I also found funny, so I laughed harder.

"Oh, yeah. Laugh all you want, shifter. I laughed, too. The likes of me and Elouise running a place like that. Might as well have that goblin down the way open up a beauty salon. No one would be stupid enough to set foot in a hag's house. Not for all the burnt coffee and dry toast in the world."

The hag found one more collection of coins and dropped them in my hand.

"You'll need to count it, I suppose."

"I suppose," I agreed with a dose of churl to match her own.

I started with the coins, retrieving them from one jacket pocket, counting, and then depositing them in a different pocket. Next, I worked on the bills. While counting up what she'd paid occupied my hands—no easy task given the dark night and randomness of the currency—I asked about the spoon.

"Found it at a salvage store," came Fannie's tart reply.

I'd finished counting the bills and handed her back a few bent fives and a couple of ones. "Here. It was a bit more than you needed. What's so special about the spoon, then? I mean, if you just found it."

Fannie eyed the bills I was holding out, then snatched them up and shoved them into her housecoat's pocket. "None of your business, shifter. Now, we're settled, are we not? Off you go."

Chapter 6

"The ultimate goal of farming is not the growing of crops, but the cultivation and perfection of human beings."
- Masanobu Fukuoka

Dagmara hadn't called.

I'd made the mistake of getting my hopes up, something I knew I should never do. Me and the opposite sex were more than opposites. We were damn near antithetical. My recent track record was a poignant reminder of that inalienable truth. In my very recent past, I'd twice attempted to be boyfriend material. Both attempts had failed. The one thing they had in common was me. It wasn't the kind of realization that put you in the best of moods.

"It's only been two days," Jay complained. "Would you relax? Geez, you're annoying."

I accepted the beer Jay was holding out and dropped to the beanbag. While I shifted around to get comfy—and produced a symphony of farty sounds—he put the final few seeds in place for his crop art creation. Like everything the conspiracy-obsessed artist put his creative mind to, it was impressive. Weird, but impressive. He'd covered a four-by-eight sheet of plywood with a multitude of panels, so it almost read like a comic book. Each picture was made entirely of corn kernels and grains. The level of depth and detail was astounding, and the story that unfolded as my eyes worked their way across the tableau was a shocking one.

If Jay's visual narrative was to be believed, it started with proto-humans hopping down from the trees. They progressed from hunting and gathering to agriculture. Civilizations rose, but progress plateaued. Then the aliens came. Spoiler alert: they never left. Not for want of trying. Apparently, the ship they arrived in burned up on entry. The survivors of that fiery crash were exceptionally long-lived and now occupied key positions of authority in government and other institutions. Their goal was to shape the course of evolution until humankind's reproductive whatnots became more alien than otherwise. The main device of their nefarious plot? Genetically Modified Organisms. Each bite of GMO food that we eat inserts tiny fragments of alien DNA into ours. According to Jay's tableau, it will only be a matter of time before humans start popping out aliens instead of more humans.

"Huh," I commented when my eyes reached the end of the story. It wasn't a nice ending, either. Scores of humans were shackled and collared in breeding pens while the aliens looked down from atop high walls.

"Right?" Jay agreed. "I was shocked, too. But the more I researched it, the more it made sense."

I gave what I hoped was a reassuring nod and told myself not to worry about the guy. He'd always been a little out there.

"What happens now?" I asked.

"Obviously, you need to stop eating the crap you eat. Never mind being like ninety percent high fructose corn syrup and sodium benzoate. You're probably twelve percent alien by now."

I laughed. When Jay scowled, I tried to move the conversation past the part where I was an alien.

"I meant, what happens now with that?"

The artist's indignation evaporated, and Jay's eyes actually twinkled. "Now, I art-bomb the State Fair's Crop Art Contest."

I didn't enjoy hearing Jay put the word bomb in any sentence. He'd always been on the fringe—honestly, it was a big part of the artist's appeal—but had never seemed like the violent type.

"That sounds fun…" I started hesitantly.

He opened his mouth to share more, but my phone chose that moment to ring. I hauled myself off of the beanbag, hoping against hope it was a certain punky chick from Vermillion.

"Hello? August Shade. Post-relationship personal effects repossession specialist. How can I help you?"

I held my breath in anticipation, certain that it would be Dagmara. It wasn't.

"August Shade."

"Again? C'mon, man. This got old after the first time. Now, it's farting cobwebs."

The prank calls had become part of my daily life. They were never at regular intervals, but were always the same. A voice I almost recognized would say my name and then hang up. I waited again for the inevitable click of a disconnected call, but something new happened. The guy said one more word:

"Soon."

The call ended after that, leaving me more than a little rattled.

"Who was that? Was it her?" Jay asked from my office doorway. "If it was her, she didn't talk much. What'd you do? Try being yourself again? I keep telling you not to do that."

"Not her," I said when my brain restarted. I gingerly set the receiver back in the old rotary phone's cradle. "Just that prank caller again."

Jay huffed. "Again? Wow. That's lame. Still no clue who it is?"

I shook my head. "Nope. I swear I recognize the voice, but can't for the life of me figure out how."

"It'll come to you. Try not to think about it," Jay advised. "The harder you try to think of it, the harder it will be to remember. You need to distract yourself."

"With what?" I asked.

"With helping me," he replied with a wide smile. "It's State Fair season, and we've got work to do."

The Minnesota State Fair was going to start that Thursday. I knew a handful of useless facts about the event, the result of stumbling into a round of bar trivia a few years back. The grounds covered three hundred and twenty-two acres, or roughly half a square mile. Around two-hundred animals, mostly of the farm variety, were born in its barns during the twelve-day event. Five U.S. presidents had visited the Fair in their lifetime, but don't ask me which ones. The Midway held over thirty different rides run by who knew how many scary carnies. There were over three-hundred food vendors, including some offering interesting twists on hotdogs. That particular fact was intriguing. Unfortunately, the Fair drew millions of people through its gates. I wasn't a people person, much less a millions of people person, and I made that point to Jay. He promised I wouldn't have to see any of those people, because we wouldn't be there during regular hours. We were going to go during irregular hours, as in the hours when people aren't supposed to go.

"We'll break in. I'll cause a distraction and then you'll sneak in with the board. I've got it all figured out," he promised.

I followed him back to his studio space where a few two-by-fours braced up his art. I'd already seen the front, but Jay wanted to show me its back.

"See how it's designed to look like an acoustic panel? The Agriculture Building is full of them. The entire building is concrete blocks. Acoustic panels dampen the noise. Once you get it into the building, you're going to mount it on the wall above the main seed art display."

"Okay..."

"See how I've got these hinges at the bottom and this eye-hole screw at the top? That's for the latch. After the judges come round with their stupid ribbons, I'll trip the latch. The board will swing down right on top of the other stuff. Boom! Right in front of everyone's eyes. It's going to be epic."

I made a mental note to discuss the definition of the word 'epic' with Jay. He didn't seem to fully understand its meaning.

"You've obviously put a lot of thought into this," I admitted, "but there are, I don't know. I guess a few details I'm curious about. You know, since I'm helping and all."

Jay was all business. "Shoot."

"The distraction?"

"Better if you don't know."

I silently debated that assumption, but moved on to my next question.

"How am I going to carry it?"

"Go-go-gorilla."

This plan is getting better and better, I thought.

"And to mount—is that the right word?—sure, mount it on the wall, you'll need what? A hammer drill? Probably some self-tapping concrete screws?"

"Yup. Got 'em."

"And who do you know that's strong enough to drill the damned things into the wall?"

It was an important detail. Jay wasn't a stranger to using a variety of tools. Some of his project got pretty big and used a variety of materials. The guy was only a buck-seventy soaking wet, though. Not exactly the drill-stuff-into-concrete type of build.

"Go-go-gorilla."

"Ah. So, you're going to distract the security guards. I'm going to carry this thing in, and then hold it up on the wall by myself while I drill in the screws."

"And the clasp up top. You got to make sure you get the clasp in right."

"While I'm a gorilla."

"Yup."

"Jay…" I chided, but we both already knew I'd do it.

Why not? I decided.

That whizz-bang plan of his rolled around inside my head. I had just enough social deviant in me to be excited. And honestly, there wasn't anything I could think of that I wouldn't do for Jay. He was my best—and only—friend. If it hadn't been for him, who knew how my life would have ended up? The debt I owed the guy was one I'd never be able to repay, but I was determined to try. If that meant running around the State Fair at night as a gorilla and doing some odd interior decorating, so be it.

"So, meet you here at about eleven?" he said.

"Wait, tonight? We're doing this tonight?"

"Of course," he replied. "Might as well get it over with. Unless you have something better to do."

I didn't, and he knew it. The jerk.

My bike didn't have a roof. Jay's car did, so we tied the seed art on top. Beyond that, there wasn't much of a difference between our respective rides. With my sidecar, he only had one more wheel than I did. That extra wheel was a donut, though, so I wasn't sure it counted. Sure, he had a windshield, but my half shell had a snap-on faceplate. He technically had windows, but only two of them worked reliably. Since the heater didn't blow warm air and the A/C didn't blow cold air, we were both at the whims of the weather. Only in the rain did he truly have a leg up. My bike was way cooler, though, so I still felt like it was a tie.

The plastic tarp over the board snapped in the wind. Each crack convinced me the endeavor was going to end up as a pile of seeds and broken plywood on the road behind us. I could see that Jay was nervous, too. Both hands gripped the steering wheel as he slowly chugged along and tried to avoid bumps and potholes. On the upside, we were far from the downtowns of Minneapolis and Saint Paul, so there was no bar traffic to contend with. There were people out and about, but not many. I saw the occasional sparkly eyed vampire and a couple of ghouls. I even spotted a large and misshapen shadow that was likely a restless troll. One alley we passed revealed some goblins emptying a restaurant's dumpster. There were some humans, but they were few and far between. The night was for the PNs.

As we motored east, I tried not to worry. I wasn't above the occasional act of vandalism. I'd never aspired to be an upstanding citizen or a productive member of society, but I also didn't try to be a scoundrel. It was more that I wasn't one to make trouble because trouble-makers drew attention. A very important detail of my adopted Midwestern life was keeping a low profile. I'd done a pretty piss-poor job of that earlier in the summer, and kicked myself for knowing I was about to make a similar mistake. Breaking into the Minnesota State Fair smacked of stupidity.

"And yet, here we are," I mused out loud.

"Not quite," Jay replied, obviously thinking I'd been talking to him.

There wasn't any sense in correcting the guy. I'd already agreed to help. Upstanding citizen or scoundrel, I was someone that kept my promises.

Jay maneuvered his car off the main road and down a bus-only street. Despite knowing that there wouldn't be any buses running its length late at night, he killed the headlights. We were on the Fairgrounds' western edge. To one side, a tall fence ran alongside dirt parking lots. The other side had a narrow band of grass and a decent number of trees. I had to give it to Jay. When he pulled up over the curb and in between a few wide trunks, I realized we would definitely be out of sight. As long as we were gone before the morning buses started their routes, we'd be golden. Parking on the Fair's western edge meant we'd have to carry the crop art about a half a mile, but it would be through the part that held the farm animal barns. Jay's reasoning was that the barn side would likely have the lightest security. Knowing how a lot of Minnesotan's felt about their livestock, I wasn't so sure, but that wasn't the concern I gave voice to.

"Please tell me you remembered the cart," I said.

The sheet of plywood weighed close to fifty pounds by itself. With all the conspiracy-shattering stuff Jay had stuck on it, the damned thing had to be closer to a hundred. After silencing the engine, we stepped into the night. Jay had remembered to bring the cart, and it wasn't too hard to assemble. Next, we muscled the board off the car and rested its long edge on the wheeled contraption. I gave it an experimental shove and nodded in approval when the tires rolled easily across the asphalt. After crossing the road and getting the cart up over the other curb, Jay jogged back to his car and returned with a boombox and a rugged pair of wire cutters. It didn't surprise me he had the cutters. Jay's projects used an array of stuff, and heavy-gauge wire was definitely in the realm of creative raw material. Even so, it was disconcerting to watch him expertly snip through the fence's metal diamonds. While he wasn't making much noise, I couldn't stop myself from wincing at each snip. Soon, he'd finished a vertical and horizontal line of cuts. After slipping on a pair of thick work gloves, he grabbed the vertical edge and pulled a section of fence back. After I'd gotten the board rolled through to the dirt lot on the other side, Jay ran the wire clippers back to the car and returned with a backpack holding the drill and screws. He rejoined me inside the fence and pulled the loose section back into place.

"Little help?" he asked.

While I held the fence, he zip-tied the section he'd cut away back into place. In less than a minute, the fence looked whole. While not perfect, it would certainly pass a casual inspection.

"You've really thought this through," I observed. "So when exactly did you go from subversive artist to criminal mastermind?"

Jay scowled. "I'm hardly the criminal here," he scoffed. "They're turning us into unwilling alien baby factories."

"That presupposes there are people who, if given the choice, would willingly become alien baby factories."

"Now isn't the time to discuss how gross some people are," he replied. "Can you remember this spot? Find it in the dark?"

I gave the surrounding area a good look. There were a couple of tall sodium lights that illuminated the expanse of dirt. The lot's entrance was directly opposite us, opening onto a street called Judson Avenue. It ran between the large animal barns and straight to our destination: the Agriculture and Horticulture Building.

"In the dark? Um, sure. I guess. If I come straight down Judson, it should be easy enough."

"Good," he replied. "Stay here for five minutes, then head over to the Ag Building. There are a couple of roll-up garage doors. They'll be locked. I put a pry bar in the bag. Think that'll be good enough?"

I snorted. Human doors with human locks did a good job of keeping humans out. Gorillas, on the other hand… I gave a confident thumbs up, and tried to feel better about the whole thing when Jay smiled. He was obviously excited. Despite myself, I realized I was excited too.

"Let's do this," I said, then bumped fists with my friend.

Jay produced a dark bandana and tied it around his face like an old-school bank robber.

"Want one?" he asked.

I considered the offer. "Do you have one big enough for a gorilla's head? Then, no. I think I'm good."

My friend winked, grabbed the boombox's handle, and slipped off in a crouched run. He headed north along the fence, staying under the canopy of small trees that were planted along its inside. We knew there were likely cameras, but were banking on the fact that they weren't being closely monitored. Jay had said he'd cause a distraction, but had stubbornly refused to share what that distraction would be. All I could do was hunker down beside his latest art project and wait. I saw his silhouette cross the lot and disappear behind a distant building. After five minutes, I was worried. At the ten-minute mark, I began to sweat. When fifteen had passed, I'd convinced myself he'd been pinched and tugged nervously at a zip-tie in the fence.

Then the distraction happened.

Two of the Fair's permanent attractions were the SkyRide and the SkyGlider. Each was a string of gondolas that glided above the grounds in an endless loop. One traveled east-west and the other north-south. Hell if I could remember which was which, but I could definitely tell that Jay had chosen the north-south one. How he'd started it, I had no clue. I was too far away to see the ride itself, but I could see the electric glow over the buildings and trees, and I could hear the low hum of the engines. A moment later, I could also see the beam of a halogen flashlight cutting through the night sky like a toy version of a Batman skylight. I could also hear what sounded like heavy metal. The distraction Jay had decided on was a one-man dance party in the sky, and it was working. Sirens wailed, and red and blue flashing lights added a little more zazzle to Jay's light show.

"That definitely qualifies as a distraction," I muttered. "But damn it, Jay, there are cameras everywhere."

No sooner had I thought that particular thought than the power went out, and with it, the lights. All of them. The streetlights. The security lights. The lights on the buildings. It made the red and blue flashes near the park's north end and Jay's halogen flashlight beam that much brighter.

I had no idea how Jay planned to avoid arrest or how he would pay the fines he was going to incur when he got caught. Mine was not to wonder why, though. I gave the cart a shove to get it rolling, then got up to a light jog. The board bounced and wobbled as the cart traversed the dirt lot. Once I hit the street, it rolled like a dream. I could hear the cattle, horses, and pigs stir and settle as I rolled past their barns. More structures passed on my left and right, and then the Agriculture and Horticulture building rose up where Judson curved north. A glance showed that Jay was still defying arrest. His halogen light cut through the night sky like the world's biggest light saber. With an awestruck shake of my head, I ducked around the building's far side. My clothes came off and went into a pile under a decorative bush. For a moment, there was a naked middle-aged guy crouched in the night, and then there was a gorilla.

A U-bolt and padlock secured the garage door to the ground. I shoved three of my gorilla-sized fingers through a door handle and yanked. The handle tore free, but the door itself didn't budge.

"Chugh," I cursed with a puff of my cheeks.

Opening a backpack's zipper with gorilla fingers was a chore. I persevered, then shoved the pry bar's edge under the door. My shoulders flexed, and I heard the satisfying sound of a U-bolt snapping. The garage door rattled noisily on old rollers, but there was no one around to hear it. So far, so good.

I grasped the cart with its epic—again, Jay's word, not mine—art and rolled it through the door. The Fair-wide power outage had triggered some emergency lights. It gave me a surreal look at the space inside. The octagon-shaped building made for a wagon-wheel floor plan inside. As I trudged along, I noted the vendor booths lining the wide circular hallway. Ones with signs advertising better seeds, better fertilizer, better pesticides bumped up against impressive displays of pumpkins, applies, corn, flowers, and more. I saw homemade ice cream, jars of honey, flowers by the truckload, and a large space that housed the Minnesota Craft Brewers Guild. Longing swelled in my breast, but I managed to stay on task. Besides, the beer wasn't distracting the gorilla. All the other smells? That was a different story.

Focus. Focus, August, I reminded my gorilla brain sternly, and kept my gigantic feet moving.

When I got to the stretch of hallway housing the crop art display, I gave a slow whistle. Well, a mental one. If I could've made the gorilla to whistle, I could've run off to join the circus and given up my life of crime.

The cart gave a low squeak as it rolled to a stop, and I considered the best spot to do my nefarious deed. Jay had been specific in his instructions. His panel had to be mounted horizontally over an existing acoustic panel so it could swing down to cover a high concentration of art. Fortunately, it didn't take long to find a spot. Time was short. I couldn't hear any sirens outside the building, and had no way of knowing if Jay was prolonging his hijinks or already in handcuffs.

My big gorilla mitt swiped for the backpack and upended it. A drill and a box of screws fell to the concrete with a clatter, and I got to work. Lifting the board into place was easy. Holding it in place with one hand while trying to set the screws and use a human-sized drill was not. It didn't help that DIY wasn't really my thing. I was more of a SECDI—Someone Else Can Do It—kind of guy. Unfortunately, I was on my own. I picked up a screw with my fat fingers and convinced my gorilla hands that, yes, they could use the drill. With a good shove, the screw chewed its way into the wall. After repeating that three more times, I let the board swing down. Jay was going to be happy. It instantly became the most prominent thing on the wall, and I'd even gotten it mostly level. All I had to do was get the latch mounted up top and I'd be good to go.

One of the nearby stalls had an old whisky barrel as a display table. The steel-banded wood looked sturdy enough. My assumption proved out when I balanced on it and it didn't collapse into splinters. I pushed more screws into the wall, then swung the board up to its concealed position. After hopping down, I gave it another good look, then galloped in a tight circle and thunked my chest in celebration. It looked like an acoustic panel high up the wall, just like Jay had planned.

My happy dance ended abruptly when I heard a transformer hum. The fluorescent lights flickered and warmed, so I took off at a four-limbed run. I'd just made it to the garage door when they fully lit up. Once outside, I shifted, doubled over to let the nausea pass, then dressed as quickly as I could manage.

"August? August! Get over here."

Jay was huddled behind a park bench across the street. When I rounded the bench's back and crouched down, he grabbed my shoulders and shoved his bandana-clad face in mine.

"Did you do it? Is it done?"

"Done as a turkey the day after Thanksgiving."

"Awesome," he whooped. "Come on. We have to get out of here."

We snuck behind buildings, scuttled across streets, and eventually reached the Midway. None of the rides were powered up, but more than a few had their own emergency lights. It created a mosaic of light and shadow. As we wove past the Tilt-A-Whirl and through the carnival game booths, I found myself appreciating Jay's tactics. The Midway offered plenty of spots to crouch and hide, and we needed more than a few. At one point, we huddled beneath the gunny sack slide, and memories of Clarissa Steyer talking about entropy filled my brain. In his way, Jay was fighting the same inexorable forces she was. The realization made my head spin a bit. He was creation. He was negentropy.

And me? I wondered. *What am I?*

I set that unpleasant thought aside to focus on more immediate concerns. If we made it out of our current mess, I could wax philosophic 'til the Fair's cows came home.

When we reached the fairground's northern edge, Jay climbed the fence, and I followed. Safely on the other side, he adopted a perfectly nonchalant stroll. How, I did not know. I hadn't done a fraction of what he'd done, yet I was pumped so full of adrenaline that my steps were more akin to a jig. When we reached the car, I collapsed against its side and offered Jay a shocked smile.

We'd pulled it off. I wasn't sure how and had a lot of questions for my friend. For the moment, though, I let myself bask in the realization that we'd done it.

Back at the studio, Jay took his usual spot in the camping chair and cracked his beer. After grabbing my own from the fridge, I dropped into the beanbag, popped the tab, and took a long, satisfying drink.

"So?" I asked. "You going to share any details about that distraction?"

The artist's chin tucked down to hide an embarrassed smile. "Oh, it doesn't really matter, does it? We're here now. We did it."

"Sure, but seriously. How did you do it? Getting up to the gondola. The power. And how did you get away?"

They were all reasonable questions. Jay had a lot of strengths, but strength wasn't exactly one of them. Those gondolas were high above the ground, and—as far as I knew—didn't have rope ladders hanging down from each one. I tried to image him swinging Tarzan-style along the steel cable from the ride's boarding pad to a gondola halfway along its circuit and failed. I tried to imagine him leaping thirty feet into the air, catching a gondola's lip, and pulling himself up. Again, I failed. Every attempt I made at sussing out how he'd gotten up to the sky ride failed. Then there was the power outage. Jay was talented, but those talents didn't include electrical engineering. Once, he'd plugged in an art project and blown out the studio's microwave.

While I waited for an answer to my questions, Jay worried the hem of his conspiracy tee-shirt. It was one of many, and each was pithy as hell. Where he'd found the current one, I had no idea, but I had to chuckle at the 'Tinfoil Hats are Sexy' emblazoned across its front.

"I know a guy who got me a key for the electrical room," he finally said without meeting my eyes, "and getting up to the gondola wasn't that hard. Getting away? Um, I just. Well, you know cops. Too many donuts, not enough cardio."

I tipped my head to the side and regarded my best and only friend. The only person in my world I trusted completely. Sure, he was human, but that didn't matter. Some PNs might be finicky that way. Not me. I didn't care what was under a person's skin. I judged people by their actions, and Jay had proven again and again that he was solid. Honest to a fault. One of the few good people in the world. My cheeks pulled my lips into a confused smile as I tried to sort out an unexpected feeling. The feeling I had wasn't just unfamiliar. It was unprecedented, and I wasn't sure how to process it. I took another sip of my beer and tried to set my worry aside, or at least hide it well enough that Jay wouldn't notice. On the inside, though, my mind was reeling as it tried to figure out why Jay was lying to me.

CHAPTER 7

"The master's eye is the best fertilizer."
- Pliny The Elder

"S ERIOUSLY. STOP CALLING," I snapped into the phone's receiver. I'd had two more prank calls and was beyond surly.

"Why do people hire you?" a voice asked. "I mean, I've met you, so I know why most people probably wouldn't. I just figured you'd try to keep new clients in the dark for a bit. You know. Fake it 'til you make it, or whatever."

"Dagmara?" I said. At least, I think I did. It was hard to hear over the sudden pounding of my heart.

"August," she replied coolly.

I rubbed a sweaty palm on my jeans and took a breath. "Sorry about that. I've been getting prank calls. Some guy that doesn't know when to quit."

"Well, let's hope you two have that in common. I need your help."

"Really?"

"I'm starting to change my mind."

"No. Don't do that. I think that's great. Really great."

"Great."

"Yeah. I mean, of course. I can absolutely help. It's great that you called so I can help. That's what I do. I'm, uh. Helpful."

"So you've said."

"Yup." I agreed, astounded at what a complete idiot I was being. "I did."

There was a long stretch where neither of us spoke. My excuse was that I'd locked my jaw shut to prevent another stupid syllable from making it past my lips. Hers was likely because she was too busy regretting calling me to talk. When panic got the best of me, I blurted out that I didn't know she'd been seeing someone.

"You didn't ask."

"No. That's true. But you were, right? I mean, obviously. And they dumped you? That was dumb. So dumb. Unless you dumped them, in which case they deserved it. Total asshole. You're better off without them."

The torrent of stupidity gushing from my mouth finally slowed, and I planted my forehead on my desk.

"It's complicated," she said with a hitch in her voice, "but sure. I dumped them. They have something of mine, and they won't give it back. This is where you do your helpful thing, right?"

I'm not sure how, but I managed to hogtie and gag my inner teenaged buffoon.

"Absolutely. I return people's rightful property to its owner after a relationship ends. So, miss... um, Dagmara. What is the personal effect that you need repossessed?"

There we go. Cool. Collected. Totally professional, I congratulated myself.

"A corn dolly."

A cool, collected professional that repo's dolls, I amended with a mental shrug.

"Got it. And can you describe the doll?"

"Dolly. It's made from corn. The husk, not the cob."

"Uh huh. How big is it?"

"Doll-sized."

"Okey doke. So, family heirloom? Or just your favorite doll?"

"Dolly. And no, it's not a family heirloom, and it's not my favorite doll. It's more important than that."

"Of great personal significance," I said, as I wrote on a notepad. "And your ex?"

Again, that slight hitch, and then she said, "The Strach na wróble."

I'd heard that word before. Back in her cornfield. "A strach... what?" I asked. "Could you spell that?"

Dagmara spelled it out for me and then added, "And it's the Strach na wróble, not a strach na wróble."

"... okay."

She sighed. "Like a scarecrow, but the real deal. Not some stuffy-guy on a stick in Farmer John's used overalls and a beat-up flannel."

"You were dating a scarecrow?" I asked.

"Does the judgmental bullshit cost extra, or do I get that for free?"

"I'll give you the friends and family discount," I replied. "I just. Wow. You're taking that punky thing to a whole new level, aren't you?"

She barked out a surprised laugh. "And that discount better be pretty damned steep. Keep this up, and you'll be paying me to get my corn dolly back."

I reminded myself that not being an asshole was an option, too. After I'd gotten my nature under control, I mentioned my standard hundred-dollar rate. There was a brief pause, so I knocked twenty-five bucks off. Another pause, and I cut it to fifty. As negotiations went, I was bleeding money, but she was still on the phone. Seemed like a win in my book. We settled on fifty dollars, and I asked where the strach-thing lived.

"In the cornfield."

"Uh, could you be more specific?"

"My cornfield."

I jotted down a note, glad that she couldn't see the sarcasm leaping off the notepad.

"No problem. I can swing down there tomorrow, talk to the strachy-thing."

"Strach na wróble."

"That's what I said. I'll get your doll back."

"Dolly."

"Yep, and then. Um. I could meet you at a bar or even at your place, and I can give it to you. Back to you. Give it back to you."

And this is why I don't get dates, I sighed inwardly.

"There's a bar on Park and Main. What time?"

"That's okay. No worries. I didn't mean... What?"

"Time. What time do you want to meet me?"

"At a bar?"

"Yes, at a bar. What time?"

The concept of time was meaningless, along with pretty much everything else in creation. All that mattered, the only thing of importance, was that she wanted to meet me.

"At a bar," I repeated. "We'll meet there. Holy shit. I mean, nine. How does nine sound? Does nine sound good?"

"Nine o'clock at the bar on Park and Main. You'll be there with my corn dolly."

I nodded vigorously, then added out loud for her benefit, "Damn right, I will."

"I hope so," she said, then hung up.

Jay clapped my shoulder in surprised appreciation. I'd shared the details of the Dagmara's call. He was every bit as shocked by the outcome as me.

"Maybe you're not a lost cause," he suggested. Not convincingly, but it was nice of him to say.

When I asked what he had lined up for his day, the artist replied he was heading to the State Fair.

"I want to scope the place out. Get a feel for things. Make sure everything is ready for the big reveal."

I hadn't pressed him on the details of that 'big reveal.' I was curious, though. The panel had a clasp on top. In its current position, the explosive—Jay's word, not mine—art project was pressed against the wall. The board's back, disguised to look like an acoustic panel, was facing out. When that latch on top was tripped, gravity would swing the board down on those hinges mounted along its bottom edge. The bottom edge would become the top edge, and Jay's seed-spiracy exposé would be on full display. What I couldn't figure out was how it would get tripped. There wasn't a string or remote electric doodad, and the clasp was a good twelve feet up the wall. Jay wasn't going to waltz in with a ladder, flip the latch, and yell, "Ta da!" The whole thing was supposed to be clandestine. Secret.

One could even say guerilla, I thought with a chuckle.

"What's so funny?" Jay asked.

"Guerilla art. Gorilla art."

The artist snorted. "I hadn't thought of that. Anyway, I know you won't want to come along, so I won't ask. What's your day look like?"

It didn't look like anything, and I said as much. Just a typical day of getting stuff from unhappy people and returning it to unhappy people. That, and grabbing a hotdog in between. I figured I'd head down to Vermillion around six, find the strachy-thing, get Dagmara's doll, and have time for a few pints before she showed up. Beer didn't make me better company per se, but it did make me less aware of being bad company.

Jay reminded me to lock up and headed for the door. I grabbed my list of the day's jobs, spun the dials on my safes for good measure, and headed down to the building's parking lot. Thoughts of the punky farm girl filled my head. I speculated on what her ex would be like, wondered if I should go with my usual tee-shirt look or find a shirt with buttons, pondered what she liked to drink—beer, whiskey, something foo-foo?—and realized that I'd likely have to pay because chivalry just won't die. I suppose that's why I didn't notice three short figures converging on me until it was too late. One coblyn buckled my legs from behind with a small club. The moment my knees hit the pavement, a second pulled a canvas bag over my head and then yanked my arms back and zip-tied my wrists. The third turned out to be Blunder. I couldn't see him, but his voice was unmistakable.

"I warned you, you bastard."

Riding in a trunk sucks. A car's shocks give you a smooth ride when you're sitting inside, but don't do a damned thing when you're in the trunk. Average, everyday potholes and cracks in the city streets felt like craters and sent me bouncing around the confined space. We'd hit a bump, I'd have just enough time to curse, and then another pothole would do it again. Fortunately, it wasn't a long ride. Brakes squeaked, the transmission thunked, and the engine cut off with a sputter. There was an enjoyable moment of not playing a rock in a rock tumbler, then the trunk opened.

"Get him inside," Blunder said, "and be careful. Shifters like to shift. The second you see anything on him change, put a bullet in him. Hell, for the trouble he's caused me, make it three."

The salty thought, *Well, there goes Plan A,* crossed my mind. Sadly, I didn't have a Plan B.

Rough hands tied a rope around my ankles. I heard a loud creak, then the rope went taut. Another creak, and I was roughly dragged from the car. I landed hard and gave my bagged head a shake to clear the fireworks from behind my eyes. Small but surprisingly strong hands muscled me onto my side, and I felt a hard board press up against my back. Those same hands pushed me flat again, then one pair shoved on my shoulders while the other pulled the rope around my ankles. They rolled me across an indeterminate distance. I only knew I'd crossed from 'outside' to 'inside' when the faint light filtering through my head sack dimmed a little more.

The place they'd brought me into echoed with the sound of their boots rapping on bare concrete. Somewhere in the not-too-distant background, I heard screeches and clangs, the chug of diesel engines, and the clang of warning bells. I could feel the space around me, so I figured it was a warehouse hear a railyard. My brief moment of deductive reasoning proved out when one cob shove me off the cart and pulled the sack off my head while the other untied the rope from my ankles. I sat up and looked around.

Yep. Warehouse. Knew it, I thought. *Can't fool old August.*

I returned my attention to the bearded cob that stood before me. With his diminutive frame, dusty gray herringbone suit, and newsboy cap, he could've been mistaken for a newsboy from the 1920s, assuming that kids in the '20s were able to grow brown and bristly beards. Blunder looked irate, but it could have also just been his face. The other two coblynau flanked him. They didn't look annoyed. If anything, they looked excited, and that made me nervous. Very nervous.

"You. Chair. Now," the one to Blunder's left said.

I craned my neck around and saw what Lefty had called a chair. Pipes and beams framed in three sides of a simple, straight-backed wooden chair like scaffolding around a post-modern sculpture. Gears, pulleys, ropes, and levers covered the framework, and metal arms jutted out at weird angles from weird heights. Each arm ended in a bright red boxing glove.

"I'm good here, thanks," I said when I turned back to Blunder and his buddies.

Boss cob gave his head a tilt, and the one to his right pulled out a gun. In a human hand, it would've looked like a pea shooter. In Righty's hand, the damned thing looked like a cannon. An image of the little guy pulling the trigger and sailing backward almost made me laugh. The image of a bullet ripping its way through me was a poignant reminder that none of this was funny.

"Fine," I grumbled with a beleaguered sigh.

Once I'd scooted my bony butt onto the chair's seat, I asked what they wanted me to do next. In response, Lefty pulled a lever. There was a whirring of gears. One of the many arms swung, and a boxing glove that was obviously stuffed with some heavy shit slammed into my kidney and knocked me back to the floor.

When I was able to speak, I angrily grumbled, "To hell with you and your thrice-damned contraptions." Then, after another pained breath, I asked, "Why'd you put me in a chair if your plan was to knock me off of it?"

"I figured you'd appreciate getting a fist or two. You know. Help you understand the seriousness of this moment. Give you a chance to make this easy. If you want to skip ahead to the part where your fingers get cut off one by one, though, just say the word."

I kept my mouth shut. I liked my fingers where they were. In what he probably thought was a considerate gesture, Blunder waved his goons over to help me back up to the chair. I looked at the funny mechanical arms and their corresponding mitts, and my shoulders hunched in anticipation. When none swung in my direction, I let my shoulders drop.

And then Lefty tugged a lever, and a glove crossed my jaw.

"Oh, come on!" I roared over the pain of my slugged cheek. "That was mean."

"Mean?" Blunder spat. "Mean is when someone puts up a not inconsiderable amount of money and a lot of hard work for a business venture, and the lynchpin of that venture is rudely stolen by some interloper. Mean is when you're forced to waste time trying to get it back, and every day that passes is a day the dollars aren't flowing. That, you big oaf, is mean."

My mind tried to connect the dots he was throwing around like feed for pigeons in the park. Given that I'd been abducted and twice-slugged, it wasn't doing a good job. Blunder had been at Elouise's place. He'd been looking for her. He'd chased me through the field. Now, he was talking about money and business ventures.

Why, though? I wondered. *Unless... He put up the funds for the bed-and-breakfast.*

I turned the guess around in my brain. It made sense. Elouise would have a hard time getting a small business loan from the local credit union. That meant turning to shadier sources for funding. Sources like a loan sharking little coblyn.

What was the lynchpin he'd been on about, though? I wondered. *What could be so damned important to bother with all of this?*

"The drawing?" I asked, trying to follow. "The house drawings? I only took one page."

I saw Lefty tug another lever, and then a glove hit me in the kidney again.

"The spoon, you idiot," Blunder growled. "You. Took. The. Spoon."

That didn't make a lick of sense. When I said as much—and I actually said, "That doesn't make a lick of sense." Don't judge. I'd just been punched for a third time—Blunder leaped onto my lap, grabbed the front of my shirt, and yanked me forward until his beard tickled my chin.

"Tell me where it is. Do that, and I'll let you go with all of your fingers. The longer it takes for you to tell me, the fewer fingers you'll have. If it isn't where you say it is, I'll be back to remove your teeth."

When I didn't say anything, Righty shoved his gun into his waistband and grabbed my arm. Lefty produced a wicked little switchblade, and I felt its edge press against my pinkie.

"Wait! Just hold on a second!" I cried. "Look at my face. Confused shock! I'm not not telling you anything. This is me in confused shock!"

Blunder gave a minute shake of his head, and the knife's cold steel lifted from my finger. He hopped to the floor, then produced a pipe and a pouch of tobacco. After filling its bowl, he tucked away the tobacco pouch and retrieved a box of wooden matches. Scraping one across the box's side, it flared and briefly lit his craggy visage with demonic light. The coblyn puffed a few times and sent thick clouds wafting up toward the ceiling high above.

"Confused shock, is it?" Blunder asked conversationally. "You must think this whole situation is some sort of mix-up."

"That's exactly what I think," I agreed hurriedly. "I gave the spoon back to Elouise's sister. I don't have it. Why in the hell would I want a baby spoon?"

The coblyn's dark eyes shifted over my shoulder to one of his goons, and an eyebrow lifted.

"I think he's telling the truth," Righty said.

Twin plumes of smoke spilled from wide nostrils as Blunder exhaled and considered me thoughtfully.

"Horace there has a knack for knowing when someone's lying," he explained.

"He what?" I asked. My face was full of confused shock again, but for a different reason. "You threw me in a trunk, dragged me to this warehouse, and tenderized me like a hunk of meat when you could've just had that one call me on the fucking phone and ask if I had the spoon?"

Blunder shrugged. "One has to maintain one's reputation. I'm sure you understand."

I shook my head in wonder. Ted was nice. His Mouse Trap-playing buddies seemed nice. From what I could tell, most of the coblynau that called Minnesota home were nice. Sure, some were probably prone to the occasional mean streak. Who wasn't? But Blunder?

Wow, I thought. *What an asshole.*

"You're an asshole," I remarked.

I hadn't meant it as an insult. It was more of an observation, but Lefty pulled a lever, and a heavy glove walloped my gut. While I writhed and cursed, Blunder puffed a few more times on his pipe. He flipped it over, tapped its stem against an extended finger, then smothered the still-smoldering wad of tobacco with the toe of his tiny boot.

"New plan," he said heartily after returning his pipe to its pocket. "You say you don't have the spoon. Fine. You are going to leave here with all of your fingers."

"And some blood in my frickin' stool," I added bitterly, but Blunder wasn't listening.

"You'll get the spoon back from that hag and bring it to me. I'll give you a few days. Bring it here. Use that phone. Then wait. Clear?"

I gave a reluctant nod. There were plenty of other things I would rather do, and even more things I wanted to say. A little bravado might've salvaged my bruised ego, but at the expense of having everything else bruised. Not worth it.

The coblyn walked toward a far-off door in the warehouse's corner. When he was about halfway there, he twirled a finger, and Lefty and Righty hurried to fall in behind him.

"Best get to work, shifter," Blunder called back over his shoulder. A moment later, he and the punchy pair that followed him around were gone.

I leaned back in the hard chair, careful not to put pressure on my bruised lower back, and considered my particular predicament. My job was to return property to its rightful owner after a break-up. I didn't just steal shit. It might sound like splitting hairs, but to me, it was an important distinction. The spoon had been Fannie's. I'd returned it to her. I couldn't steal it from her.

She'll suck ya dry if you do, I thought with a wry smile.

Blunder will take your fingers and teeth if you don't, I thought, and that smile was gone.

I leaned forward with my hands on my knees and took a slow breath before pushing myself off the chair. My legs were wobbly, and I felt—surprisingly enough—like I had just been punched, but I made it to the door. Once I was outside, I looked around and confirmed what I'd expected to see: train tracks. They branched and branched again into multiple parallel lines so engines and cars could be loaded, emptied, and rearranged as needed. Trucks and forklifts criss-crossed the open space beyond the warehouse's lot. There were humans, and there were PNs. None paid me any mind, confirming my suspicion that Blunder had a lot of sway down here. Since no one seemed inclined to help the battered guy that had stumbled out of a warehouse, I shoved my hands in my pockets and started walking.

The railyard was on the northern edge of Nord'east Minneapolis. It would have been a short drive back to my office if I'd had my bike. Instead, it was a long walk. I considered catching a bus, but opted to stick with my feet. I knew it'd be about forty-five minutes or so in the midday heat, but I needed the time to clear my head. I also wasn't in a hurry. There'd be no repo'ing after what I'd just endured. No, sir. Just me and a beer or three.

And Dagmara.

"Crap," I grumbled.

I must've been more rattled than I'd realized. Blunder's muscle had slapped all thoughts of scarecrows and corn dolls and my impending date from my mind. I spent about half the walk wondering how I'd explain myself when I called her to cancel. When it occurred to me that I didn't have her phone number, I stopped, dropped my head, and just stood there cursing my rotten luck. A blaring car horn made me realize that I'd stopped mid-crosswalk at a busy intersection, so I skip-hopped the rest of the way, then settled back into my brooding pace. Not for the first time, I cursed my circumstances. Everyone else had smartphones. If they needed to get in touch with someone, it was a simple tap, tap, tap, and their message was sent. Sadly, smartphones were strictly off-limits for me. I didn't need Jay's intimate knowledge of deep-state conspiracies to know those little wonder-boxes collected and transmitted a ton of data about their users, and the companies collecting that data were happy to sell it to the highest bidder. The threat from Blunder was in the foreground of a panorama of ever-present danger. My life might not be great, but it was good enough. Keeping it that way meant keeping a low profile. Staying off radars. Being one of millions of unrecognizable schlubs.

"August? August Shade? You're him, aren't you?"

Oh, for fuck's sake.

"No."

The guy turned to walk alongside me. He had that slightly awkward gait that pegged him as a water dweller. Probably a nix. Selkies were rare in the Midwest since seals weren't overly fond of freshwater. Minnesota was the Land of Ten Thousand Lakes, which meant nixes were plentiful. Human enough when on dry land. Toss one in a puddle and there'd be a Great Northern Pike or a sturgeon or a muskie flopping around in seconds.

"Yeah, you're him. Dude, I can't believe I bumped into you. What happened to your face?"

I sighed, stopped walking, and finally looked at the guy.

"A stranger wouldn't leave me alone. It made me so angry that I ran into a wall in an attempt to knock myself unconscious so I wouldn't have to listen to him talk."

"Whoah. That guy must've been really annoying."

"He was."

"Yeah. I hate guys like that. But, dude. Seriously. If you've got a card or something, can I get one?"

Reflexively, I fished around inside my jacket and finally emerged with a small paper rectangle.

"August Shade. Post-Relationship Personal Effects Repossession Specialist. Some pets. No kids. Satisfaction not guaranteed, but at least you'll have that special whatever back," the guy read out loud after I handed it to him. "That is so cool. Do you have a pen?"

"Why?"

"So you can sign it. I can probably get fifty bucks for this."

"Go away."

I resumed my trek, but my steps had gone from a brooding slog to a determined march.

"A selfie, then? C'mon. Just one. Here, stop for a sec."

The guy had pulled a phone from his pocket. Before I could stop him, he'd stretched one arm out and thrown the other around my shoulder.

"Wazzup, peeps? I'm here with August Shade," he announced into his phone. "That's right! The shady shifter that trashed Nicollet Island and kicked some serious ass. Me and Auggie are just hangin' in the hood. Peace out, bitches!"

I angrily shrugged off his arm and spun to face him.

"What the hell was that?" I nearly screamed.

"Dude, relax. It's for my vlog."

If incredulity had a face, it'd be white, male, unshaven, a smidge over forty, and strikingly similar to what murderous might look like. I grabbed for the phone, but the guy was faster than me. He sidestepped my frantic swipes and had the nerve to look put out while doing it.

"Give me that damn phone," I growled after another unsuccessful swipe.

"You know, I'll bet you get a ton of business because of me. I'm not saying you owe me anything, but... I mean, you know."

"The phone!" I screamed, and damned if it didn't sound a bit like a gorilla's roar.

The guy gave me the finger and took off. I followed, but running after what I'd been through was tough. Before I could catch up, the guy slid like a runner toward home plate. He went straight toward a wide storm drain. I saw him stretch and shrink at the same time and caught a glimmer of scales. There was a far-off splash, then nothing.

"Well, fuck," I lamented.

There was nothing I could do but hope for the best. Sadly, 'the best' never seemed inclined to pay me a visit.

By the time I made it back to my office, my mood was as dark as the sweat stains under my pits. I checked the answering machine. Nothing. Checked the mail Jay had dropped on my desk. Nothing important. Checked the fridge for a beer. None. The only thing that could make my day worse would be driving to Vermillion and wandering a cornfield until I found a living scarecrow and took away its ex-girlfriend's doll.

You'll get to see Dagmara, an optimistic and little-used part of my brain offered.

And we know from experience how that's likely to go, the more realistic part of my brain replied.

Good point.

With a sigh as forlorn as sighs could be, I locked up my office, locked up the studio, and headed down to my bike. I barely saw the passing cars as I wove through traffic and blew through at least three stop signs. I was too busy looking for ambushing coblynau and imagining what would happen when my name and face hit the world wide web.

CHAPTER 8

"If you tickle the earth with a hoe, she laughs with a harvest."
- Douglas Jerrold

WHOEVER COMPLAINED ABOUT FINDING needles in haystacks had never tried finding something in a cornfield. On a good day—one where I'm not feeling too terrible about myself, where I'm carrying myself a bit straighter, holding my chin a bit higher, and wearing some thick-soled boots—I'm about five-foot ten. Corn stalks at the end of the growing season average around eight feet tall. Do the math, and it's easy to understand how I'd spent an hour wandering the field with nothing to show for my efforts. I wished I'd had something more useful in my repertoire. A giraffe would've been awesome, but such was my luck. More than that, I wished Dagmara had been a smidge more specific about where her ex might be. Finding him had gone from a task to a chore to a subtle form of torture.

"Dagmara?" I called out, stretching my neck in vain. She'd popped out of the corn before, so it didn't seem unreasonable for her to do so again. "You in here?"

I strained my ears for a snark-sprinkled response, strained my eyes for a glimpse of her hot pink hair. All I heard was the rustle of rough leaves. All I saw was the next row of corn. With a disgusted huff, I turned and walked through the stalks again.

"Here, strachy, strachy, strachy. Yoo-hoo. Scary scarecrow. Where you at?"

The only response was the endless sighing of the vast field.

Another hour passed. That, in and of itself, had me riled up. On top of that, I'd stopped looking for Dagmara's ex over half an hour prior. The rest of the time, I'd been trying to find my way out of the cornfield. I'd pick a direction, walk, walk some more, convince myself I'd walked too far, walk further, panic, turn, and repeat. My lower back hurt. My jaw hurt. My feet hurt. I stubbornly told myself I wasn't thirsty, about to die of heatstroke, or lost. The funny thing about facts, though, is that no amount of self-delusion will change them.

"Fine. Fine, fine, fine. Time for drastic measures."

I knew I'd never find my way from the ground. The damned field was the proverbial forest, and the damned cornstalks were the proverbial trees. I needed a bird's-eye view, and for that, I needed to be a bird. Decision made, my jacket slid from my shoulders, my tee-shirt came over my head, and my jeans slipped down around my ankles. A moment later, the only bird in my repertoire pushed off with its drumstick legs and flapped its wings. Turkey-me triumphantly cleared the tops of the cornstalks and kept rising. On a scale from penguins to eagles, turkeys were a few notches up from an ostrich. Not the best flyers of the avian world, but also not the worst. Once airborne, I resisted the urge to drift into a wide spiral. If I came down anywhere else in the field, I'd never find my clothes again. It was tough, though. Smooshing my consciousness into that weird turkey brain was an exercise in square pegs and round holes. The turkey wanted to do turkey things, whatever those were. It took some effort, but I persevered and kept myself limited to a few tight spirals.

Dagmara's, I thought with relief when I saw her house in the distance. With that to orient me, I continued my spiral.

There's the road, and my bike has to be right about there, I realized.

Seeing it from that vantage made the size of the cornfield hit home. It was immense. Finding the strachy-thing was a fool's errand. With a mental note to ask for better directions than 'cornfield,' I finished my slow circle and descended. I was still about ten or fifteen feet above the corn when I saw a thing, and it saw me, and I was literally scared to death.

The force of hitting the dirt was enough to kick-start my dead turkey heart. My eyes fluttered open, and I blurted out a terrified gobble. Flapping my uncoordinated wings, I found my feet and put them to good use. Turkeys can haul ass when the need arises. Their sturdy legs can hit over twenty miles per hour. I was likely doing less than that, given the need to maneuver through the corn stalks, but I was still moving my tail feathers at a damned good clip. I zigged, zagged, zigged again for good measure, and then went for one more zag just because. Unfortunately, my last zag sent me straight toward the scariest damned thing I'd ever seen in my life. My clawed toes left shallow ruts as I slammed on the brakes, and my snood—that ugly bit of flesh hanging over my beak—flapped as I whipped my head back. Instinct made me splay my tail feathers and spread my wings to look a hell of a lot bigger than I was, but that tiny, rational bit of bird brain knew the gesture was futile. The impossibly tall figure rising in front of me blotted out the world. It was the absolute worst of everything imaginable rolled up into one single, solitary figure, impossible in its awfulness.

Did it look scary? Not really. Long, thin legs in ragged, threadbare trousers rose from a cracked and weathered pair of work boots. A colorless twill shirt was buttoned to its collarless neck. A torn and patched jacket hung from its lanky frame. Arms stretched wide and ended in hands that looked like faded leather gloves, and a burlap sack started somewhere inside the shirt collar and sat in a shapeless mound above its bony shoulders. Thick, rough threads made two Xs where eyes might have gone, and a ragged slit gaped where a mouth might have been. Perched on that sack-like head was a weathered tiller wide brim hat that called to mind an Old West preacher. My tiny human awareness decided it shouldn't have been so scary. Human me might've even found it cool—in a rustic, days gone by sort of way—had turkey me not been so busy shitting myself. For the turkey, looking at the thing was like having my skull pulled open and stuffed full of horror. Visions piled up in my brain. I was trapped in a rusty wire pen, ankle-deep in my own bird crap, and surrounded by the terrified gobbling of a million more birds. A towering figure roughly dragged me out. Cruel fingers squeezed my neck as I was carried toward the low stump of a felled tree. Its rings were hidden beneath a wet and sticky puddle of brown-red blood, and an ax head was buried in its center, its handle jutting up at a threatening angle. That inescapable hand shoved my head down on the stump, and the blood of those that had gone before me soaked my feathers. Another hand grasped the ax handle and worked the head free. I saw the ax rise up, blood dripping from its edge.

Somewhere on the edges of my nightmare, the Strach na wróble loomed. Its crooked fingers splayed and slit-mouth gaped. The wider its mouth stretched, the more nightmares flowed into me. I wanted to flee—I needed to escape—but to my panicked bird brain, the rows of tall corn were an impenetrable wall pinning me in on all sides. The sky above was a no-go. I'd been up there a moment earlier, and I'd died. Fight-or-flight had kicked in, and flight was out. That left only one option. I raised a leg to show its spur; that wicked little claw on the back. Turkeys aren't nature's best fighters by a long shot, but they aren't the worst, either. If I was going to die, I'd at least give the nightmare incarnate a damned good scratch to remember me by.

That's stupid, a disparaging corner of my brain remarked. *You'd seriously bring a turkey to a bullfight?*

It had been years since I'd shifted into my Hereford bull. Many years. Basically, all the years since I'd escaped from the hospital. Once I'd found my freedom, I hadn't encountered a single situation where being a bull would have improved matters. If someone had asked me the day before if I'd like to shift into a shaggy, cud-chewing dolt, I'd have laughed. What a difference a day makes.

The Hereford didn't have those wickedly long and pointed horns you'd see on a Spanish fighting bull, but it had horns, plus a powerful neck and shoulders to push them into things I didn't like. That, and a skull that was as literally thick as my metaphorical one. I lowered that skull at the fright before me, and my stocky legs and powerful shoulders shoved it forward like a battering ram. Stalks of corn bent and snapped as I charged and caught the strachy-thing right in its gut. It was like diving headfirst into a pile of leaves, but it knocked the thing backward. The strange personification of pure terror let out a surprised "Oof!" and staggered back a few steps.

"That was uncalled for," a frightful voice whispered.

I shook my bull head, surprised to recognize the voice. It was the voice I'd heard when I'd taken my bloodhound for a stroll and had stumbled across Dagmara. Like before, it was dreadful. Having that voice directed at me was infinitely worse.

Had I been able to respond, I would have said it was abso-fucking-lutely called for. Since bulls can't talk, I went with an angry snort and a shake of my shaggy head, then scraped a hoof in the dirt. The scarecrow probably didn't speak bovinese, but I was sure that my ire transcended language. Burlapy skin folded down between those weird X-eyes. It straightened its wide-brimmed hat and bent its knobby knees. Those too-long arms splayed wide, and a tidal wave of fear broke hard against me.

I'll need to charge Dagmara for the fertilizer, I thought, once I had my wits back. The pile of manure behind me was substantial.

I wasn't a fighter by nature. I was disagreeable, though, and that inevitably got me into my fair share of scraps. Some got pretty weird, like when I'd turned into a gorilla and fought an air elemental at my favorite dive bar. I didn't know where this particular fight ranked in terms of weirdness, but a bull fighting a living scarecrow in the middle of a cornfield had to be in the top three, at least. The scarecrow would flap its arms and batter me with wave after wave of bowel quaking fear. I'd shake it off, lower my head, and charge. At the last possible moment, the damned thing would twist and arc, and my forehead would pound air. I clipped him once or twice, but with little effect. To make matters worse, I was tiring, physically and mentally, under its onslaught of nightmares. I was trapped in a narrow chute. A bolt of cold steel was about to plunge between my eyes and pulverize my brain. I was steak. I was hamburger. I was a collection of baseball gloves and designer knock-off purses waiting to happen. The endless deluge of nightmares was grinding me down. Even the white-hot anger of a pissed-off bull can't last forever. The fight paused, and my breath came out wet and hot. My muscles quivered and twitched. Was my adversary as wiped as I was? I doubted it. The damned thing spent long, hot days in the field. That lifestyle seemed likely to foster endurance. My usual routine of sitting inside and eating hotdogs? Not so much. If this contest didn't come to a decisive end soon, I was likely to just keel over and call it quits.

The Strach na wróble sent another wave of fear at me. I lowered my head and charged again. If the definition of insanity was doing the same thing over and over but expecting different results, I would've been certifiable. This time, though, inspiration struck. At the last possible second, I shifted into my gorilla. When Dagmara's ex tried to sidestep me, I grabbed the lapel of its sun-bleached coat and yanked hard. That rotting-carrion voice wailed in surprise, and its long arms beat down. They might as well have been willow boughs for all the damage they did. I lifted the Strach na wróble above my head, then body-slammed it to the ground. No sooner had its back hit the dirt than I shifted again. An elephant trumpeted, and wide feet stomped on the scarecrow's wrists. I bent my knees and let my weight settle down to flatten the thing. I squeezed my elephant eyes shut as terror ripped through me like buzz saws, pulled me apart like barbed hooks, pressed on me with glacial cold, and roasted me like napalm. My calf was dead and being eaten by lions. My herd had left me. I was being hunted. My tusks were being sawed off. I was shackled and bound with heavy chains in a cold, dark cell. There was only rotten cabbage to eat. My only freedom was when I was forced to perform for a screaming, jeering humans under a moldy tent.

A litany of horror tore through my elephant's mind, and I think I went insane. I know I blacked out. For how long, I don't know. What brought me out of it was a soft scrabbling. A prickling. A buzzing. A voice.

"Enough," it whispered. "Enough."

I got my feet under me and pushed my bulk up from the ground. That dementing fear wasn't gone, but it had ebbed. The elephant tripped and stumbled and came down on its front knees hard. The world tilted, and my trunk waved drunkenly, its flexible tip grasping at fallen cornstalks and split cobs. One clump of husks caught my eye. Grasping it as gently as I could with my trunk, I lifted the weightless thing and held it to where I could see it. Near as I could tell, it matched the description Dagmara had given me. Skillful hands had taken dried corn husks and woven them into a small, vaguely human-shaped doll. Some of the husks were fashioned into dress of sorts. Around where a waist would be, husks had been twisted and tied to delineate its lower half from a torso. Another was folded over a knot to give the impression of a hooded head. Corn silk fell in cascading waves like long, blond hair, and intricately braided husks bent hooplike from shoulders to waist like two arms with their hands clasped.

Corn dolly, my battered mind said without really understanding what the words meant.

Corn dolly. Dagmara's corn dolly, came the more complete thought, and then, *Shit. I gotta go.*

The elephant regained its feet right as a fresh tidal wave of fear was cresting. I ran through the corn, leaving a wide swath of trampled stalks in my wake. That voice, that terrible voice, screamed and wailed somewhere behind me as I fled. Maybe some small part of me remembered what the turkey had seen from high above the field. Maybe it was just dumb luck. All I knew was that I burst from the field into a grassy clearing. A house leaned, a copse of trees huddled beside it, and an old pickup counted its rust spots. I shifted mid-step, and a very naked and very scared human collapsed to the ground. Compared to elephant trunks, human noses aren't great for holding things, so the corn dolly dropped beside me. Terrified that I'd lose the only good thing to have come from my encounter with the scarecrow, I grabbed it and clutched it to my chest. Deep, ragged breaths slowed my heart rate a bit, but the fear had sunk its teeth deep. Foolishly, I cast a glance over my shoulder at the field behind me. The sun was setting red and angry over the waving stalks. All the nightmares I'd been forced to endure bucked and twisted, and that red sunlight turned to blood spilling over the corn. I used my feet and one arm to scrabble backward while my other hand squeezed the woven husk to my chest. There was a gap in the lattice skirting the home's porch that was too small for a human to squeeze through. Mustering the energy for one last shift, a coyote belly-crawled into the cobweb-filled shadows, dolly in its jaws. I tucked my nose under a hind leg and curled my tail around me. I wanted to stay awake, needed to stay awake. The strachy-thing was likely stalking me, relentlessly traversing the wide field in search of what had been taken. I had to be ready if it found me. I had to stay awake, but I couldn't. With a sigh, I melted into my human form, curled around the unusual personal effect I'd somehow repossessed, and slept.

Footsteps thudded above me. I woke to a host of discomforts, physical and mental. My mind was still reeling from the fear it had been soaked in. The madness scrabbled and scraped. It was a pale shadow of its former strength, though. When it finally subsided, it left me empty. I hadn't a clue as to where I was. It was pretty damned obvious that I was naked, dirty, and huddled in a dark crawlspace. Where, though, was a mystery. Honestly, I wasn't even sure who I was, and then I heard a voice mutter my name.

"Ghost me, will you, August Shade? Think you can just trample my field and then blow me off?"

Keys on a ring jangled, and then fell on the boards above my head. The sharp clatter caused me to flinch, and the sharp curse that followed caused me to flinch again.

Dagmara? I wondered, and the pieces clicked. I'd made it to her house, and it was her porch I was huddled under.

"Dagmara," I croaked. After a cough, I managed her name again with a bit more volume behind it. "Dagmara."

A foot lifted and fell, then another. Cautious steps crept down the porch stairs, then crunched over the grass until her white Doc Martens were just past the lattice.

"August?" she asked, unsure. "Is that you? Where are you?"

I shimmied forward and pressed my face against the thin slats of wood.

"Under here."

The woman squatted down and leaned until her tilted head was pointing her mohawk's spikes across the yard.

"You're under my porch."

"Yeah."

"You were supposed to meet me at the bar."

"Yeah."

"Are you naked?"

"Um. Yeah."

"Why?"

I slid her corn dolly through the lattice's gap in lieu of an explanation. She gasped and grabbed it up, then swung an anxious look over her shoulder. Clutching the woven corn husks to her breast, she leaned down closer to my face.

"You met the Strach na wróble," she said, tone making it clear it was a statement, not a question.

An involuntary shudder ran through me. "Yeah. Your ex is..."

"Scary," she supplied.

"I guess that's the word. Doesn't quite do it justice, though, does it?"

"No," she agreed. "It doesn't. Are you okay?"

A dry laugh kicked its way up from my chest and out through my clenched teeth. "I'm hiding naked under a porch, but besides that... Sure. Doing swell."

The look she gave me was sympathetic, but also touched with admiration.

"Come on," she said as she stood. "Let's get you inside. And I'm guessing a drink is in order."

"Not water."

"No," she agreed with a wry laugh. "Not water."

"I'm naked," I reminded her.

Her boots moved out of sight, and I heard her mount the steps to the porch. She paused and said, "I'll set out some clothes. They won't fit well."

"They never do," I agreed.

I waited until I heard her go inside, come back out again, then enter her home one last time. Escaping the crawl space meant shifting and for a moment, I wasn't sure I had the strength. After closing my eyes and gritting my teeth, a coyote squeezed through the gap. A moment later, I was staring at the clothes she'd set out. When she'd said they wouldn't fit well, she wasn't kidding.

At least they weren't a pair of satin short shorts, I decided after pulling on the borrowed outfit.

Dagmara was a lot shorter than me, which meant the elastic ankles of the joggers were up around my calves. The sweatshirt wasn't as bad since she seemed to like them oversized, but the 'NYC Punk' inside a red anarchy symbol didn't exactly mesh with my usual aesthetic. I was grunge, not punk. It might've seemed like a blurry line to some, but not me. There was a difference. Even so, I reminded myself that beggars can't be choosers and pulled on a pair of her tube socks. As dressed as I was going to be, I headed inside.

I made my way to the living room and dropped to the couch. My nap under the porch had done exactly nothing to ease my exhaustion, and my hands were shaking when I reached for the bottle of beer Dagmara was holding out.

"Want to tell me about it?" she asked after I'd managed a few sips.

I shared something between the CliffsNotes and Reader's Digest Abridged version. While I talked, she sipped her beer and watched me with inscrutable eyes. I made a mental note to never play poker with the woman, and ended my tale with a simple, "And then I got to your place, and then you came home."

The woman regarded me for a long time. Finally, she spoke.

"Thank you," she said seriously. "I'm sorry you had to go through that, but thank you."

"That doll must be pretty important," I muttered.

"Dolly, and yes. It is."

We'd finished our beers, and she rose to get two more. When she returned, I took mine eagerly. After a couple more swallows, I asked why.

"It holds the Spirit of the Corn," she replied.

That meant exactly nothing to me. When I said as much and pressed for details, she brushed my questions aside.

"Google it," she finally said.

"I don't Google," I replied.

"Of course, you don't."

Silence swelled between us.

"Sorry I missed our date," I said.

Her eyebrow raised like it always did whenever I said anything. "Date?"

Shit.

"Uh, meeting. I didn't mean to ghost you or whatever."

"You thought we were going on a date?"

"No. Yes. Maybe? I mean, if it had been one," I said awkwardly, "I don't know. Would that have been so bad?"

Her lips pursed in thought, then she said, "I'm going to take a quick shower. I won't be long."

I didn't point out that I couldn't leave. I didn't have my clothes, which also meant I didn't have my pants. That meant I didn't have the keys that were clipped to a belt loop with a carabiner. I used to think losing my pants was an impossibility. These days, it just seemed inevitable. Also, my bike was a long walk away, a walk by a cornfield that was harboring her terrifying ex. So, yeah. I couldn't leave, but I kept that to myself. I also didn't point out that I didn't want to leave. How to say that, though? How do you tell someone that their mystery has its own gravity? That the moon could just up and leave the earth's orbit more easily than I could willingly walk out of her door. The depth of emotion I'd discovered was surprising and rendered me speechless, so I simply nodded while my fingernail pulled at my beer bottle's label. She rose and left the room, and a long sigh slipped through my lips.

"What are you doing, August?" I asked myself.

As usual, I didn't have an answer.

She'd been telling the truth. It wasn't that long. Barely ten minutes had passed before I heard the water shut off, then heard footsteps upstairs as she moved about. When she returned to the downstairs living room, she'd traded her punk attire for a much more subdued pair of work coveralls. The dark blue fabric brought her pale face into sharp relief, but sans mascara and lipstick, her features were gentler. Softer. More stoic. Her hair hung down from a center part and framed the high bones of her cheeks in an energetic pink, an incongruity that made my heart trip. She patiently endured my regard as she sat back in her chair, but that patience had limits. Inevitably, her eyebrow lifted.

"Sorry," I muttered. "You just. You look different."

"So do you," she replied with a crooked smile.

I tugged at her borrowed sweats. "Yeah? You like? I think my calves are my finest feature."

Unbelievably, she laughed. Actually laughed. Emboldened, I asked about the coveralls.

"Wouldn't you rather wear those in the field?"

"Why?"

Feeling suddenly foolish, I said, "Don't people around here give you a hard time?"

The corners of her mouth turned down. "They'll do that no matter what I wear. I'm not what you might call popular."

"Oh. Well, what about dirt, or mosquitoes?"

"What about them?" she asked. "Those don't bother me."

"When you're farming? Seriously?"

Dagmara ran her fingers through her hair, then smoothed it back down again. "I don't farm."

My confusion showed, so she explained that others worked the land. Her job was different.

"Oh, so you own the place," I said.

Her stoicism cracked, and those eyes flashed. The fact that they weren't swimming in pools of mascara didn't make them any less fierce. If anything, the emotion I saw was deeper, more raw.

"I don't own the place," she whispered.

Something in the way she said those words brought a frost to the summer night's warm air. I wanted to ask more questions, try to see more of that iceberg whose tip I'd just glimpsed. Before I had the chance, though, Dagmara pierced me with those eyes again.

"You honestly thought we were going on a date tonight?"

Since she'd asked for honesty, I shrugged and nodded. "You seem surprised."

"I am," she admitted. "Why? Why did you ask me on a date?"

The directness of her question caught me off guard. Why wouldn't I have? She was gorgeous and radiated confidence like a furnace. She liked the Dead Milkmen. She was a study in contradictions that my contrarian nature found irresistible. I tried to put all those thoughts into words and came up with, "You're pretty cool."

Her eyes went wide. I hadn't known her long, but thought I'd learned enough to know that I'd never be able to surprise her. Annoy? Sure. Disappoint? Obviously. But surprise? Knowing that I had left us both reeling from that particular emotion.

"No one has ever told me that," she whispered. "Ever."

Her respose left me baffled. "But you are," I said, confused. "I mean, look at you."

She took my suggestion literally and looked down at her coveralls. Nervous fingers toyed with its zipper.

"I try," she said. "I try really hard. When I first came over from Poland, I spent some time in New York City before coming here. The Bowery. CBGB's. Punk was everywhere, and it was so incredible. So loud and irreverent. Free. It was unbelievable, especially after all those years in the Soviet Union. I have never been able to be anything other than what I was, and what I was very few people liked. My work doesn't make me many friends. In New York, though? People were being themselves, and to hell with what anyone else thought. I didn't want to leave. Everyone was so amazing. I wanted to be like that. Like them. I guess I still do," she admitted quietly.

"Well, I don't know why you'd want to be like anyone other than yourself," I said, "because the you I see is one-hundred percent cool."

Since I'd first hung out my shingle as a post-relationship personal effects repossession specialist, I'd had a lot of clients. Not once had one crossed the room to stand directly in front of me with chin tipped down, lips parted, and wide eyes searching mine. They certainly hadn't put a palm on my chest and the other on the back of my neck. And none of them had leaned in to press their lips against mine.

When the kiss ended, I opened my mouth to say some stupid something or other. Thankfully, she put a stop to that with another kiss. My hand reached around her waist, then my other hand joined it a moment later. The couch took our weight, and the floor took our clothes. Sometime later—and I was pretty impressed with myself at the amount of time—we lay intertwined. As we held one another, we spoke of little things. The weather, our favorite bands, how weird Minnesotans could be. I'd made some offhand remark about the one stoplight town she called home, and asked if there was a town drunk or if they all took turns. She laughed, and I screamed.

Since her head was nestled on my shoulder, I'd let my eyes shift their focus a bit and drift around the room. They'd landed on the living room window. What they saw was something just beyond the glass. Something that might've been called a face, if faces were made of burlap, noseless, had a gaping slit for a mouth, and two Xs where eyes might have been. I saw the Strach na wróble, and so, of course, I screamed.

Dagmara nimbly rolled over. The fluid movement continued with her standing and quickly striding to the window. I saw her naked backside and the reflection of her naked frontside in the glass, but that was all. There was nothing beyond the window's pane but a warm Minnesota night.

"There's nothing out there," she finally said. "Maybe there was, but not now."

I babbled about her ex and his face and it was right there and so on, sounding like an absolute loon. I couldn't help it. One glimpse of those X's over that gaping maw, and I was right back in the field being inundated with the full force of every terrifying thing the world had to offer.

"It's okay, August," Dagmara said. "You're okay. You're with me and you'll be okay. Just sleep."

"Sleep?" I asked, incredulous. "How in the hell am I supposed to..."

A weariness swept through me, from the bottom of my bare feet to the scalp that sprouted my unruly hair. A vast nothingness beckoned me, reached for me, wrapped around me, and I slept.

CHAPTER 9

"Farming is old magic. Before rabbits and hats, there was bounty and dirt."
- Jezelene the Astounding

"SHE'S GOTTA BE A PN, right? I mean, what she did to you and Blunder in the field. Knocking you out like that last night. Dating that, um. What's it called again?"

"Strachy-something. Strach na wróble, I think?"

"Right, that," Jay said. "Dating that. She has to be a PN. Has to be."

We were walking to Philo's to restock the beer cooler, and I'd been sharing my exploits from the previous few days. I'd woken up on Dagmara's couch. The sun streaming through the windows had let me know it was midmorning. The neatly folded clothes on the coffee table had let me know she'd been out to the fields. The note on top of my clothes had let me know she was gone.

There's coffee in the kitchen, it read. *When you go, stay on the road. Your motorcycle isn't far. I'm sorry about the Strach na wróble. I'm glad about last night. I don't have your money, but I will soon.*

That last bit had me borrow her raised eyebrow expression. I'd dressed, found the coffee pot ready to brew, and had fiddled around the kitchen while I waited for it to finish. I drank slowly, hoping she'd return. After finishing a second cup alone, I had decided it was time to leave.

"I guess," I agreed, answering Jay's question, "but I couldn't tell you what kind of paranormal she is."

"Why haven't you asked?"

Why haven't I? I wondered as well.

Part of it was propriety. Most circles considered it to be rude. PNs who could pass as human did, and they were perfectly happy with that. We weren't forced to live in the shadows like our fairy tale ancestors. It was commonplace to see all manner of creatures in all manner of places. That said, it was still by and large the humans' world. There were so damned many of them, I couldn't imagine things differently. If some paranormals wanted to go along to get along, who was I to complain? Hell, I did it. There was nothing to gain by saying, 'Hey! Look at me! I can change into some animals. Whoop-dee-doo!' I shifted when I had to, and that was pretty much it. I thought of the clients I'd had. Vampires and succubi. Werewolves, werecats, even a were-emu, the poor bastard. Nix, sprites and merfolk. Pretty much all of them lived as human of lives as they could manage. Yeah, PNs could usually tell when someone wasn't human despite their looks. That didn't mean we had to go prying into what they actually were. If someone wanted you to know, they'd tell you. If not, well, it was none of your damned business.

The other part was a little harder to 'pin' down, pun intended. Despite knowing beyond a doubt that Dagmara couldn't be human, I wanted her to be. Humans could be a pain, but at the end of the day, they were easy. They didn't eat a person's life force. They didn't have to avoid the sun, or make it back to water, or perform weird rituals, or sprout fur and fangs and who knew what else when the moon was full. I didn't know what Dagmara was, and I didn't want to. Why? I suppose it was because knowing would mean dealing with those strings. Those complications. I was many things, but not someone who wanted to deal with that.

"I guess I don't really want to know," I finally admitted.

"Well, whatever she is, she seems pretty cool. Way too cool for Vermillion. She should be here. Tell her to move up here. Maybe with you until she settles in."

"Whoa!" I said as I stopped in my tracks. Philo's Liquors was only a short distance away, but what Jay was suggesting wasn't your typical walk-and-talk kind of topic. It was a stop-and-look-completely-shocked kind of topic. "There is no way I'm asking her to move in. I mean, geezus. We haven't even really had a date, and anyway, you've seen my place."

Jay scrunched his face up in thought. "Yeah. Good point. Still, seems like she'd be a lot more at home in the city. Not some cornfield."

He wasn't wrong. Everything about her was diametrically opposed to life in farm country. My friend and I resumed our trek and talked about the immense gulf between urban and rural life in Minnesota, how a handful of miles could separate radically different worldviews, and how much we preferred living in the city. It felt good, shooting the breeze with my friend. I hadn't realized it, but our recent adventure had left a cloud hanging over me. Jay hadn't been Jay, and it had bothered me. Jay being Jay again was a relief.

"So that doll was a corn spirit?" he asked as we stepped into our favorite liquor store.

My shoulders lifted and fell. Dagmara had said something to that effect, but hell if I knew what it meant. I pushed the thought aside. It wasn't that I didn't feel like speculating. There just happened to be more important things to think about, like a sudden crisis. I'd passed the front counter and turned the corner to the beer coolers. I'd stopped at the door I always stopped at. I'd opened it like I always did, and I'd reached a hand down to grab what I always grabbed. This time, though, that brief sequence of perfectly normal actions resulted in a very abnormal situation.

"No Grain Belt?" I asked, stunned. There was always Grain Belt Pilsner. Always.

"August! Jay!" the store's proprietor cried out as he emerged from the storeroom. "My dear friends. How are you?"

I was fine and said as much. Jay echoed my sentiments. Philo, however, didn't look fine. In fact, the portly satyr looked terrible. His normally glossy hair was dull and unkempt, and his left eye had a shiner that would've landed at least a runner-up in the Guinness Book of World Records for Terrible Things You Can Do to an Eye. He was wearing pants, though, so at least he had that going for him.

"And how about you?" I asked guardedly. "You doing alright?"

Plump little fingers patted nervously at his chest pelt. "Oh, yes. Of course. Why would you ask?"

"You're wearing pants," Jay remarked.

"And your face looks like the other guy won with a knock-out in the fifth round. What?" I asked, as Jay cast me a dark look. "How was I not supposed to say something?"

Philo moved the nervous fingers of one hand to his cheek and gingerly brushed the edges of the bruise.

"Ah. This. Oh, dear. It's nothing."

I nodded sympathetically. "Yeah, I've had a 'nothing' now and then, too. Usually after a few too many Grain Belts. Speaking of, where'd you move them to?"

The satyr's eyes flicked to the empty shelf in the beer cooler. "Oh, those. Yes. Those. Oh, dear. You won't find any of those here."

With a world-weary sigh, I turned toward the door. "Sorry, Philo. Gonna have to hit up your competition. I'll be back when you're stocked up."

"August," the satyr said with tears in his voice. "You won't find any Grain Belt anywhere."

A coldness settled in my stomach.

"What happened? Did something happen at the brewery? Geezus, Philo. Tell me Grain Belt is okay. Please tell me the Grain Belt Brewery is okay."

A giggle burst from Philo's full lips like a flutter of sparrows, followed by a half-sob.

"You misunderstand, my friend. You won't find any Grain Belt anywhere. Even if it's in stock."

He'd emphasized the word 'you.' That coldness expanded, fueled by a realization that something much more sinister was at work.

"You were told not to sell me any beer," I said with a slow certainty.

Jay gasped in confusion. "But why? By who? August didn't do anything."

That was the point. I hadn't done anything. Yet. This was a certain someone's way of reminding me I had a job that needed doing.

"Because Blunder wants me to get that damned spoon back," I explained, "and this is his messed up way of reminding me to stay on task. Sorry you got mixed up in this, Philo."

I gave the satyr the really short version of my current situation and watched his short, curled horns and pointy goatee bob in understanding.

"Ah. Yes, that is a pickle. No, no. Don't worry. This wasn't your fault," he said when I apologized again for his shiner. "More importantly, we need to get you something to drink. With what you've endured, you've certainly earned it."

The satyr's hoofs clomped back and forth in indecision, then stopped.

"I heard you say corn spirits," Philo exclaimed, brightening. "Those nasty coblynau made no mention of spirits. Only that I couldn't sell you your favorite beer. Come. Come, come," he said as he tapped over the store's linoleum floor. "Here we are. Georgia Moon Peach. Mellow Corn Kentucky. Oh, and this one is local. Distilled right here in Minnesota," he proclaimed as he held out a bottle. "You'll not taste a better corn whiskey. It's on sale, too."

Jay took the offered bottle. "Uh, thanks? I'm not much for whiskey, but you are, aren't you August?"

I was still trying to catch up. The shock of seeing that empty shelf in the beer cooler followed by learning the reason why had my blood pressure up, making it hard to focus. And now Philo was shucking corn whiskey? I mean, sure. I drank whiskey, but I was more of a rye guy. The ones with corn mash were too sweet for my tastes.

"I appreciate it, Philo," I finally said as I took the bottle from Jay's hands and placed it back on the shelf. "That's not really my speed, though."

Those full lips pouted and quivered. "But you said corn spirits when you came in. Unless you meant vodka. You meant vodka. Ah, my friends. My brain was rattled by those nasty coblynau knuckles. Come. This way."

I grabbed the satyr's shoulders as he tried to pass me.

"Hold on a sec, Philo. We weren't looking for liquor. We were talking about a job, that's all. Just a job."

"Yeah," Jay chimed in. "August has a client down in Vermillion. She's cool, too. Way too punk for farmville. Anyway, she needed this little doll made from corn husks back from her scary ex. August got it back, then he got a little somethin' somethin' afterward," the artist finished with a waggle of his eyebrows.

A blush crept up my cheeks. "Ignore him. He might look grown up, but he's still in the fifth grade."

Philo looked up at me with his mismatched eyes. One was partially swollen shut, but the other sparkled with curiosity.

"A doll with a corn spirit? Ah. You mean a corn dolly. Oh, my. August, that's quite special. Quite special, indeed."

"Is it? If you say so," I muttered. Jay was still grinning at me and doing that weird thing with his eyebrows. It was annoying.

The satyr sighed. "Youth. So ignorant of the ways of the world and all its mysteries. Come, come," he said as he grabbed a bottle of red wine from a shelf and headed outside.

Jay and I followed. While Philo expertly uncorked his bottle by shoving a long thumbnail into it and giving a quick twist and pull, my friend and I dragged over a couple of patio chairs. The satyr took a long drink and smiled.

"The corn dolly," he started, "is a wondrous thing, indeed. He'd be quite cross to hear me say it, but old Dionysus had it easy. Winters back home can be chilly, to be sure. Greece does have its seasons," Philo advised sternly. When neither I nor Jay dared to suggest otherwise, he continued. "Nothing like what those poor sots in northern Europe have to deal with, though. For dear Dionysus, death and rebirth was an easy thing. The grape vines, dormant for the cooler months, would ripen with a wave of his hand, and the winepress would be busy as the flitting bees. In the harsher climes, though, coaxing life back from the frozen soil is not so easy."

"Entropy and negentropy," I blurted. When both Jay and the satyr frowned, I muttered, "Never mind. Just something Clarissa had talked about once."

Clarissa Steyer, my recent ex and ex-oracle, had given me a lesson about entropy and negentropy once. How the universe tilts toward chaos and decay—aka, entropy—and how forces work against that slide. It had seemed a bit academic at the time. Now, as Philo explained the circle of life, the full import of her words was starting to take root. It made my head hurt.

"Indeed," Philo resumed with a nod. "Your Clarissa was quite right. Death and rebirth is the constant cycle, the endless dance of all of creation."

"So what's that have to do with corn dolls?"

"Oh, August," he scolded. "Not corn dolls. Corn spirits. The corn spirit is the life of the field. Its very essence personified. She's a special, special spirit that must be kept safe and warm through the long, cold winter, else the next year's crop will struggle, even fail. And that doll you speak of so dismissively is where she harbors. Woven of husks from her field's corn, it is there the corn spirit will take shelter."

I considered what the satyr had shared, then shook my head.

"If the corn spirit is so important, why give it to a scarecrow?"

"The Strach na wróble," Jay corrected, then asked, "What?" when Philo's good eye widened.

"Really? The Polish Strach na wróble?" he breathed. "My, my, August. You have had an interesting time of late, haven't you?"

I shrugged. "Not the word I would have used, but sure. How do you know all this, anyway?" I asked the satyr.

Philo smiled. "I've lived a long life, August Shade, and not all of it here. I have drunk with many a friend. I have danced beneath the sun and moon with many a partner. I have spent long nights sharing whispers with many a lover. I'd be a sad satyr indeed if I'd traversed through all those years and long, long miles, and not learned a thing or two along the way."

The satyr lifted his wine to his lips. After a decadent sip, he seemed about to say more when he saw something over my shoulder. Philo's good eye narrowed, and his smile fell. I turned to see what he was looking at and saw a fancy sedan. It was a big ride for a coblyn, but they were endlessly resourceful. I imagined a booster seat and a variety of levers to work the gas, brake, and wipers. Whatever the contraption was, it was tall enough for Lefty to glare at us from the driver's seat. A darkly tinted rear window rolled down, and Blunder—also boosted high above the car's seat—added his own stink-eye to the mix.

"Oh, piss off!" I yelled. "He didn't sell me any beer, you jerk. Besides, I've still got a few days."

The coblyn's craggy eyebrows folded together and turned his eyes to dark pits.

"Best hurry, shifter," Blunder called out. "We wouldn't want anyone else getting hurt, now would we?"

The car drove off, leaving a confused artist, ruffled satyr, and very pissed shapeshifter in its wake.

"Let's get out of here," I said to Jay. "And sorry again about all this, Philo."

The satyr had pushed himself upright and kicked his short legs angrily as the car disappeared around the corner. "Ah, it is I who am sorry, August. To hell with those nasty coblynau. Come inside and get your beer."

I shook my head, not wanting to cause him any more trouble than I already had, but Jay stepped forward.

"Thanks, Philo," the artist said, "and don't worry about those guys. If they come round again, you call me. I'll take care of it."

I'm not sure which of us looked more shocked: me, or the satyr.

"You?" I asked. "No offense, Jay, but what in the hell are you going to do? Paint them to death?"

The artist looked at me with eyes gone unexpectedly hard. "Just get the beer, August."

Neither of us spoke for the entire walk back to the studio. It was only after we were back upstairs and the beer was in the fridge—minus a couple of cans—that I asked what he'd meant back at the liquor store.

"I mean, that was nice and all, you trying to make Philo feel better. Not smart, though. Blunder and his goons can do a lot worse than what they've already done," I advised. "We don't need to be adding gas to the fire."

"Thanks for the tip, August. Now, finish up your beer. We've got to go."

"Where?" I asked, perplexed.

"The Great Minnesota Get-Together," he replied. "They're judging the crop art to-day."

In my mind, there were only two reasons to like The Great Minnesota Get-Together. One of those reasons was in my right hand. The other was in my left. I took another bite of my footlong hotdog—which was like a hotdog, but so much better because there was so much more of it—and washed it down with a swig of beer. Jay sat across the picnic table from me. While I was enjoying my lunch, he'd taken his bandana off, shaken out his dreads, and retied them three times. Between each retying, he'd drummed a little drum solo on the metal tabletop, crossed and re-crossed his legs and arms, and sighed repeatedly.

"Come on," he finally complained. "How long does it take to eat a hotdog?"

"It's a foot long," I said around a half-chewed bite. "Takes a while."

"If we're late because of your lunch..." the artist threatened.

I knew we wouldn't be late. While I didn't know what time the judging would be done, or even what time it currently was, I knew Jay did. His nervous fidgets had also included checking his watch every twenty-seven seconds or so. There was no way we'd be late.

Wistfully, I considered the remaining bit of overly processed meat smooshed into an overly processed white bun and contemplated whether I should make it last or put my friend out of his misery. My mouth stretched wide, and I shoved the rest of my lunch in. I'm a jerk, not an asshole. After offering what I hoped was a convincing thumbs up, I followed the artist through the crowd and into the Agriculture and Horticulture Building.

It was a crowd, too. The textbook definition of a crowd. A mass of humanity that made my eyes twitch. Every animal living under my skin was clamoring to get as far from the place as possible, which made walking a bit of a production. I tried to affect a casual stroll, but instead felt like a puppet with mismatched strings. One knee kept bending too much, my arms refused to swing in time with my steps, and I couldn't stop my head from swiveling from side to side in an endless search for an exit from that particular hell.

"What was in your hotdog?" Jay asked. "Actually, don't tell me. I already know, and I know that none of it was good for you."

Before I could offer a rejoinder to his dig, a lady with a huge fanny pack bumped me into a guy eating a deep fried candy bar on a stick.

"Watch it!" the guy complained.

"Put another stick in it," I growled back.

Jay grabbed me by the jacket and yanked. The jacket had been a necessity. When you're forced to share a space with hundreds of thousands of people, you're inevitably going to bump into them and all their exposed sweaty skin. If I'd gone with a tee-shirt like Jay, I'd have had as much stranger sweat on my arms as my own. That would have been gross. Really gross. Ergo, jacket. The downsides were that I was really hot, and it offered Jay an easy lapel to grab and yank. Before the candy bar guy could try to put a stick in me, Jay had dragged me away and we'd lost ourselves in that damned crowd.

"Low profile, August," the artist reminded me sternly. "We're just two regular guys at the Fair, remember? Just two regular guys that happen to like seed art."

I shrugged off his hand. "Fanny pack lady started it."

"And I'm ending it. C'mon, August. Don't screw this up. I've worked too hard to have you blow it."

A deep breath and a nod of my head were enough to reassure Jay that I was—for the moment, at least—not going to derail his plan. We let the crowd push us along the circular building's wide hallway and pull us closer and closer to the main event. The long tables with their agricultural whatevers stretched along the walls, and soon those same walls were covered with all manner of crop art. I hadn't been able to take much of it in on my last visit, what with the clandestine operation and all. I wrestled my vexation into submission and let myself actually look at what Minnesota's more inspired types had created. The seed art caught my eye first. Jay had a knack for gluing seeds on to wood, but he wasn't the only one.

Many of the pictures were bucolic in theme. Fields of corn, wheat, and soy below rising or setting suns were prevalent, as were tractors and barns and grain silos. There was one of a mid-1950s pickup that reminded me of Dagmara's. Other pieces celebrated Minnesotan culture. A portrait of the musician, Prince, next to a portrait of Bob Dylan. Paul Bunyan and his blue ox, Babe. The Mall of America, the State Capital building in Saint Paul, and the skyline of downtown Minneapolis. There were comical pieces, too. I chucked at one that portrayed *Star Trek's* Captain Kirk arm wrestling with *Star Wars'* Han Solo. More than a few were flat-out surreal. If Salvador Dali had used seeds and grain as a medium, his works would have been right at home. I glanced at Jay and saw him admiring the more subversive pieces. Ones that skewed political or offered some tongue-in-cheek commentary on current events. There was a picture of the President with a corn dog—a hotdog rolled in cornmeal batter, deep fried, and served on a stick—going in one ear and coming out the other. Another showed a pack of werewolves waiting in the rain outside of a veterinarian's office, a clear rebuttal of a recent call for were-creatures to use vets instead of hospitals for their routine care.

The seed art was only part of the show. Spaced along the wall were all manner of things you could make from crops. Elaborate crop arrangements whose stalks of wheat and barley and garlands of nuts and berries were more impressive than the fanciest flower bouquets I'd ever seen. Some were as tall as I was and had obviously taken much time and care to create. Others were smaller, but no less ornate. My natural cynicism cooled a smidge as I realized how intricate and clever many of the creations were. Minnesotans were an odd bunch, to be sure, but at least we were creative.

What really got to me, though, were the scarecrows. Some were comical. Others were less so. There was one in particular that caught my attention like a glue trap. Its patched jacket hung limply from bent arms that ended in leathery glovelike hands. Its head was a gunny sack with two coarse X's sewn where eyes would be. A round and flat-brimmed hat sat on top.

It couldn't be, I thought as I held my breath and leaned in a bit closer. *No way.*

I stared, daring the thing to twitch, to bend, to do anything. The harder I stared, the more it did exactly nothing. Those Xs where eyes should have been didn't blink. Its gash of a mouth didn't stretch. I checked my innards for any hint of bowel-twisting fear. Nothing.

"These are so much better than the butter sculptures," Jay commented, pulling me out of my confused regard.

"The what now?" I asked.

"Butter sculptures. Princess Kay of the Milky Way?"

I shook my head, and Jay sighed at my ignorance.

"Princess Kay is like a beauty contest for farm girls."

"Okay…"

"The winner gets to represent Minnesota's dairy farmers to consumers," he explained, "and this butter sculptor lady carves her bust and the busts of all the contestants out of enormous blocks of butter."

"That's ridiculous."

His countenance darkened. "All part of the plan. Sucker people in with cute girls, then feed 'em the milk of animals that are pumped full of antibiotics and growth hormones and who knows what else."

"You."

"What?"

"You. You know what else, right?"

It was supposed to be funny, a typical jibe like the others we traded day in and day out. This one didn't land as expected, though. Jay ducked his head and glanced around.

"Geezus, August. Why don't you just paint a bullseye on my back?" he said with uncharacteristic agitation.

I had started to apologize when my friend shushed me, then pulled me away from the crop art and into the crowd. The judges were coming over to put ribbons on the winning pieces. The group of them were hilarious in the way that only a group of bona fide 'Sotans can be. One must've been a professor. That, or his cosplay skills were top-notch. Tweedy sport coat with patches on the elbows. Plaid bowtie. Tortoise-shell glasses. The woman beside him screamed suburban chic. Her highlighted blonde hair was puffed up in that way only strip mall stylists seem capable of, and a beige pantsuit made her look like a Lego person. Next was a farmer who looked like he'd just walked in from the field. Easily in his late sixties, his gut pushed his overalls out like they were hiding a beach ball. The missus had likely cut his hair with the help of a bowl, and his bristly beard was stained yellow around his mouth with tobacco smoke. The three of them walked a few steps at a time, regarded what was on the wall, nodded their heads and talked amongst themselves, then moved along. A few feet behind them, a teenager in a vibrant green 4-H smock followed. Occasionally, the tweedy professor would point, then hold up one, two, or three fingers. The three-fingered art got a white ribbon. Two fingers meant a red ribbon. The precious few that got a single finger were awarded a blue one. They stopped in front of the scarecrow I'd noticed a few moments before. Each gave it careful consideration. Farmer John said something. Suburban Barbie said something back. Professor McTweedy beamed and held up a finger. The 4-H kid's wide eyes shone as he pinned the blue ribbon to the scarecrow's lapel. I found myself agreeing with the decision. Whoever had made that particular entrant for the crop art contest had known what they were doing.

The judges continued their slow procession. Shuffling a few steps, stopping, conferring, and awarding ribbons. They drew closer to us, which also meant closer to Jay's seedy surprise.

"How are you going to make it fall?" I asked in what I thought was a quiet whisper, but Jay still shushed me.

"Just wait," he counseled. "Just wait…"

I did my best to impersonate someone who cared about being there and added my own *ooohs* and *aaahs* to the crowd's as the judges stuck their little ribbons on various displays. One had just awarded a red ribbon to the picture of the President with the corn dog through his ears when a shock of pink caught my eye. I squinted in disbelief as Dagmara pushed through the crowd and over to a gap between two display tables. Barely a half-breath later, a serious-looking guy in a dark suit stepped out of a door I hadn't noticed. In a way, he reminded me of her ex: Lanky and full of angles. The similarities stopped there, though. For example, this guy had a face, and that face had a nose that could have turned an ocean liner. They spoke. Dagmara looked pissed and shook her head. They spoke some more, and then I saw the corn dolly. She'd pulled it from a small, black backpack and was exchanging it for a thick manilla envelope.

"The hell?" I wondered out loud, and then there was a gust of wind, a heavy slam, and a gasp from the crowd.

I whipped my head around and saw Jay's massive tableau on full display. While the judges milled and barked questions, the crowd pressed in for a closer look.

"Ya don't say..." one voice said above the murmur of voices.

"Aliens? That tracks," another said. "My brother-in-law saw one once."

"I'm not pushing out no alien babies," a woman declared around bites of her funnel cake.

The crowd was getting agitated as more people added their cries of shocked surprise. I glimpsed Jay and saw him wink in my direction. Much as I wanted to celebrate his big moment with him, though, I had more pressing concerns. GMOs and alien babies would have to wait. I turned and pushed against the press of bodies in an effort to get through.

"Dagmara!" I yelled. "Dagmara!"

I saw her crook her head to the side, then look my direction.

"Dagmara! It's August!"

Our eyes locked, mine confused, hers stunned. A split second later, she turned and pushed off in the opposite direction.

"The hell?" I wondered out loud again, and then the suit guy was in front of me.

Suspicious eyes stared at me from either side of that gigantic and hooked schnozz. Then they flicked to where the judges were trying to obscure the view of Jay's art with their bodies. When they flicked back to mine, something like recognition flickered.

"Don't move," the gangly guy in the suit warned.

His voice made it very clear he wasn't going to be ignored. I didn't know who he was or what he wanted with me. What I did know was that the guy in the suit meant business, and at that moment, his business was me.

Chapter 10

"Save your catapults and trebuchets and battering rams. Wheat is the greatest weapon of all."
- General Odyr uth Naga

FUN FACT: WHEN SOMEONE tells me not to move, I can't not move. Maybe it's a survival instinct. Maybe I'm a natural contrarian. Either way, it's true. The giant nose with a guy in a suit attached to it told me not to move, so I moved. More specifically, I moved toward him, grabbed his bony shoulders, shoved him as hard as I could, and then chased after Dagmara. I tried to keep my eyes on her mohawk, but she was rounding the building's curve and I was about to lose her.

"Why the hell is she running?" I complained out loud, and then someone burst through the crowd and tackled me.

It wasn't the same suit guy. This one was bigger, burlier, and obviously had practiced tackling people. I hit the concrete hard and gasped as his weight came down on me, then I sent a knee straight for his groin. A moment later, I was back on my feet and moving as quickly as I could while the crowd pulled back from the kerfuffle. Three steps later, he hit me again.

"The hell is your problem?" I screamed. "I didn't do anything!"

"Liar," he shot back.

My legs kicked, and I heard a pained grunt. I twisted and brought a fist around in a clumsy haymaker. It connected and gave me the space I needed to scurry backward. Flipping over onto my hands and feet, I scrabbled a few yards and then pushed myself upright and looked around. I counted three guys all wearing the same dark suits and all moving menacingly toward me. I was outnumbered, but they were wearing dress shoes. When there's a foot race on a polished concrete floor, the guy in boots will always beat the dorks in dress shoes. I launched myself into a sprint and heard their feet skitter cartoon-style as they tried to catch up.

I careened through the hallway in search of an exit. Swear words, surprised cries of, 'What the heck?' and other yelps blended with my exclamations of 'Ope, sorry!' and 'Just gotta scoot by you!' Once outside, I could blend into the crowd, flit from building to building, and melt into a million faces. All I had to do was get through the crush of bodies inside and I'd be home free. While I frantically forged ahead, angry voices called out behind me.

"Stop him!"

"I'm trying!"

"Not you. You get that to Grey Cloud."

Who the hell is Grey Cloud? I wondered. Not that I really cared. It was more that the mind does funny things when you're being chased, like ask rhetorical questions when you should be thinking about more important stuff.

I needed to lose my pursuers, and fast. Who they were and why they were chasing me mattered, but not as much as getting away. There was light spilling through a garage door, so I knocked a guy hard enough to send his socks and sandals-clad feet up into the air and ran. I cut right, cut left, ran across the street, and crossed into another world.

Here's the thing about the Minnesota State Fair: it is one-hundred percent Minnesotan. There are chainsaw carving contests. A wavy slide you ride down on a gunny sack. The Agriculture and Horticulture Building I'd just come from. A fishery building full of fishing stuff with a stocked fish pond outside. Sportsman displays for all your hunting needs. Quilting, knitting, and macrame exhibits. Barns full of horses and cows and sheep and pigs. A coliseum with dressage events. The Grandstand concerts skewed country, which I hated, to classic rock, which I might have enjoyed had it been anywhere but the State Fair. Hell, you can buy a damned tractor there. The point is, the place was 'Sotan through and through, except for one little corner called The International Bazaar. My feet were pounding pavement in that direction, so I crossed under its archway and into an open plaza ringed with vendor stalls.

As a general rule, Fair food is deep fried, so to me, the Fair smelled like chicken. As I crossed over the International Bazaar's threshold, a wave of exotic smells hit me hard enough to make my head swim. Curries and spices colored the air, and a dazzling array of colors smacked my eyeballs like kids going after a piñata. Vendor stalls pressed against one another. Each was bursting with food and clothing and fabrics and gifts from places most Minnesotans could never find on a map. For a moment, I felt like old Dorothy crossing from her black-and-white Kansas into the Technicolor land of Oz. The crowd was especially dense, a fact I tried to use to my advantage. I bent my knees, hunched my back, and did my best to be well below-average height. As I passed a stall with the words 'Chile Winter' on a brightly painted sign, I spied a woolen poncho.

"How much?" I asked in a harsh whisper. "For that. How much?"

A wizened old woman smiled. "Ah, the chamanto? Good choice. So warm, so comfortable. The natural oils in the wool even repel water. Not much use in a thunderstorm, but you'll stay dry as a bone in a light rain."

"Uh huh. That's great. How much? And that," I added, pointing at a wide brimmed straw hat.

"And a chupalla? All you need is a horse, and you'll be a Chilean cowboy."

"Lady, tell me the price or I'm buying a kimono instead," I growled as I pointed to my left. The next stall had long silken robes embroidered with snaking dragons chasing bright koi. I didn't care what I wore, as long as it covered what I was wearing.

The creases of her face realigned from friendly and welcoming to irritated in a breath. "For both? Fifty."

"Fifty?" I repeated with a shocked gasp. "Fine. Fine. Here's..." I managed as I pulled my wallet free. "Sixty. Damn it." After cursing, I slapped three twenty-dollar bills—the entire contents of my wallet—onto the table. "Keep the change and just give me the chalupa or whatever."

I risked glancing nervously around. It only took a moment to spot the suits, so completely out of place did they look among the rest of the crowd. They'd spread out to cover more ground. One was moving along the wall of vendor stalls, and was only seven or eight away.

"No, no. I can give you a..." the woman dithered, "hmmm. For ten? A bolo tie. They aren't from Chile, you know, but most of you don't know where Chile is, so what's the harm?"

I'd already grabbed the poncho off its hangar and pulled it over my head. I'd been overdressed in my leather jacket. Adding a layer of thick wool on top was like adding steam to the sauna—especially after my foot race with the suits—but necessity trumped comfort. I slapped the straw hat on my head, grabbed the bolo—a perfectly worthless thing, in my opinion—from her hand, and turned my back on the encroaching suit. As long as no one saw my face, I'd hopefully just be another overly enthusiastic 'Sotan trying to look worldly.

I reversed course, tipped my chin down, and crept toward the bazaar's entrance. With my face pointing toward my toes, I couldn't see much in front of me, so I shifted my eyes from left to right. One suit passed by on my right with only a few people between us. Fortunately, he was too busy craning his neck to peer over everyone's heads to notice me. I'd just breathed a side of relief when I glanced left and locked eyes with the guy that had tackled me.

"Stop!" he yelled.

"You first!" I yelled back and then ran.

I passed under the bazaar's arches again and hung a left. Barely twenty steps later, I was outside of the Fair's haunted house. It was a big attraction, which meant there was a line. The people waiting had tickets, and I respected that. I really did. However, I'd blown all my cash on a disguise that hadn't helped in the least and didn't have time to get a ticket, anyway. I pushed past tweens and teens eager for the attraction's scares, and then I was at the entrance.

"Hey, you can't..." the pimply kid working the door blurted, and then I was inside.

The place had an old Victorian theme going on. Heavily patterned wallpaper. Wall sconces that created more shadows than light. Oil paintings of well-dressed skeletons in ornate frames. Hidden speakers piped in weird music underlaid with wolf howls, screams, rushing wind, and maniacal laughter. A single hallway wound through a series of live-action panoramas. There was a graveyard with crooked headstones and skeletal fingers reaching up from the ground. Another was a haunted bedroom with a canopy bed. The curtains drew back on their own, the mattress compressed, then a hidden fan blew a gust of cold air. The soft cries of a mourning woman accompanied it. One was a slaughterhouse with a chainsaw-wielding guy in a creepy mask and blood-spattered apron. I hurried past them all, then climbed a stairway to the second floor where more rooms waited. Each had a different theme, but all of them had one thing in common: jump-scares. As I pushed ahead, the haunted house cast hit me with all they had. I wasn't in the mood to play their games, so I hit back. When someone in a ghost sheet popped up and yelled, "Boo!" I slapped my wide-brimmed hat on their ghosty head. When a woman in a high-necked, long-sleeved dress appeared to wail at me, my discarded poncho hit her in the face. I ducked under a giant spider that dropped from the ceiling, shoved a couple of tweenagers over the hallway's bannister and into a zombie apocalypse, then ran down a flight of stairs to the main floor. That final length of hallway had a scary clown, a maniac in a straightjacket, and a witch lit by a glowing cauldron. Every few steps, I looked back to see if my pursuers were gaining on me, but all I saw were the strobe-lit faces of annoyed people. I was in the home stretch when a jump scare finally got me. A doctor in surgical scrubs leaned out with a ridiculously long scalpel in his hand. The room he was in had an operating table. Something under a blood-soaked sheet kicked and writhed while a nurse with an eye patch and yellow claws instead of fingernails danced around the table. A broken fluorescent light flickered madly, and the sound of a buzz saw filled the surrounding space.

"Not funny!" I screamed as I jumped back and slammed against the opposite wall. "Scary hospitals are not funny!"

"August?" a raspy voice called out.

The sheet flipped to the side, and a familiar revenant sat up. While everyone else working the haunted house had fake stitches and scars, I knew this guy's were one-hundred percent genuine.

"Leonard!" I exclaimed in surprise. "Wow. Small world."

The breathing cadaver walked over while ignoring the angry complaints of his cast-mates. He extended a hand, and I gave it a quick shake.

"Enjoying the haunted house?" he asked.

I glanced at the wake of annoyed people behind me.

"Uh, sure. I didn't know you were working here."

The undead dead guy nodded sheepishly. "Deacon's castle is neat and all, but the property taxes are through the roof. Me and Mona needed a little extra money, so I'm here. She's working security for the Grandstand concerts."

One of the many unexpected outcomes of that summer's debacle at Nicollet Island had been the death of an old and rich vampire named Deacon Saint James. On top of being a spray-tanned douchebag, the guy had been a bona fide necromancer. Leonard had been one of his projects. Another had been Mona, a woman who had died of cancer. Deacon brought her back to be his personal henchwoman. After the end of the world had been averted, Leonard and Mona had become a thing. A gory thing, sure—because two reanimated corpses in love was nothing if not gory—but a thing, nonetheless. They'd taken possession of the dead vampire's lakeside castle in a very rich suburb. The thought had never occurred to me before, but when people say there are only two sure things in life—death and taxes—they were only half right. You might not stay dead, but you always have to pay your taxes.

"Yikes," I sympathized. "Well, I'll keep an ear to the ground for gigs. If anything pops up, I'll let you know."

The talking corpse smiled a bashful smile and said he'd appreciate that.

"Anything for a friend," I replied, then gave another nervous glance down the hall. The people I'd shoved past were shoving their way forward again. I didn't see any suits in the mix, but it was dark.

"You're in trouble again, aren't you?" Leonard said with a hint of recrimination.

"Is it a day ending in Y?" I asked.

He chuckled, then gave a small wave when I said I had to get going.

"It was nice seeing you," he replied as he got himself back on the hospital table and pulled up his bloody sheet.

My feet were already moving, but I called over my shoulder, "You too! Say hi to Mona."

I jogged the remaining distance to the exit, hoping that my detour had given my pursuers the slip. When I burst out of the door, though, my folly slapped me full in the face: the entrance and exit doors were side by side. The suits hadn't needed to bother chasing me through the haunted house. They were simply waiting outside.

"Get him!" Schnozz yelled.

I grabbed what was likely a parent waiting for their kid and shoved hard. The lady let out an angry, "What in the heck?" and then she was tangling with the suits while I sprinted away.

The building next door was the architectural antithesis to the faux-Victorian mansion I'd emerged from. Concrete blocks were stacked into a single-story box with a garage door-style entrance. The Dairy Building's complete lack of aesthetic made a certain amount of sense. No need to be fancy when you're catering to people who are passionate about lactose. I ducked and wove through a fresh press of bodies, then plunged into the mouth of madness.

Don't get me wrong. I like cheese. I love butter. There will always be milk on my cereal, and I can crush a chocolate shake in under a minute without getting brain freeze. Jay will never approve, but I remain convinced that he's secretly jealous. It's hard not to like dairy products, and I fully expect to like them 'til the day I die.

But love them? Worship them? Yeah, that's a bit much.

My feet slid to a stop, and I looked with disbelieving eyes at the insanity. The Dairy Building was a shrine to all the things you can do after squeezing an udder. Its blandness was a testament to its god. The walls were butter-yellow. Fluorescent light filled the room like skim milk. People shuffled along to look at the various displays about curd and culture and calcium, their faces as bland as the products. Most folks, though, congregated around the center of the building. A big, multi-pane glass room filled the center. Caught up in the moment, I forgot about my pursuers and moved closer. Inside the room, small tables were set up around the circumference. Each held a bust of a different girl carved from a block of butter. Yellow hair framed yellow faces with yellow eyeballs above yellow noses above wide and smiling yellow mouths full of yellow teeth. A woman sat at a larger table in the middle, hard at work on another butter block. The artist was more fortunate than her subject. She at least had a heavy sweatshirt, thick pants, and a bulky knit cap. The other girl was sitting in a glass-walled refrigerator in nothing more than a sparkly pageant gown and a tiara. A thousand-watt smile was literally frozen on her face.

"He wasn't kidding," I breathed, realizing Jay had been serious when he said there was a butter sculpture exhibit.

"Right?" a guy said as he pushed his way up alongside me.

I was sick of being jostled. Sick of being chased. One-hundred percent done with people. Too bad the guy didn't know those things. If he had, he might've stopped talking to me.

"Aren't they great?" he continued, thinking I cared about what he had to say. "She's been carving all them Princess Kay contestants for almost fifty years."

"Ya don't say," I replied, adding a healthy scoop of sarcasm to my hokey 'Sotan accent. "You sure could butter a lot of biscuits with them there princesses."

I watched the guy try to process my comment, then he pointed at one of the busts. His shoulder bumped mine as he did, and damn if it didn't seem intentional.

"That one there? She's my niece," he said, a challenge in his tone.

Don't say it. Don't say it, I cautioned myself. So of course, I said it.

"She's got a nice figure. Butter face..."

I was about to add, "I'd spread that one there, that's for darned sure," just to be a Grade-A salted jerk, when a cry of, "He's in here!" reminded me why I was there in the first place. Three suits were converging on me from three sides. I backed toward the butter room and feinted in one direction, then another. The suits didn't bite. We all knew the chase was at its end. Whoever they were, whatever they wanted with me, they were going to get it if I didn't think of something quick.

Gotta give 'em the slip, I thought, then smiled.

As luck would have it, I was on the side of the butter room with a door. My hand grabbed the handle, and I leaped inside. The princess being immortalized—assuming her sculpted likeness stayed below thirty-five degrees or so—screamed, and the sculptor yelled something like I shouldn't be in there. I was used to hearing stuff like that, and ignored it like I always did. Besides, the suits were hot on my tail, and I didn't have the luxury of trading snark with a butter sculptor and her dairy queen. I thrust my hand into the half-carved creamy face on the table and then rubbed my arms. The impromptu move was accomplished in the nick of time. One suit had already followed me inside. He grabbed my wrist, and I literally slipped his grasp. My delighted laugh came to an abrupt end when I stepped on a yellow glob and went down hard.

While I dragged myself to my feet, two more suits entered. It would've been a serious mismatch had it not been for all the butter. I darted back and forth while knocking princesses from their pedestals. After slapping each bust with both hands, I smeared myself with the good, old-fashioned results of churning milk for a living. I also hurled handfuls at my pursuers. I think it was the sheer randomness that kept them at bay more than anything else. The sight of me must've been something else. A middle-aged guy in jeans and a leather jacket throwing a butter-slathered tantrum? In their eyes, I was bona fide crackpot. Hey, don't judge. Desperate times called for desperate measures. If acting all Looney Tunes meant I'd have an edge, it was an edge I'd happily grab. Unfortunately, my antics only gave them pause. After a moment of incredulous regard, they attacked.

What followed was classic comedy. Laurel and Hardy, Buster Keaton, and the Marx Brothers would've been proud. Hands that tried to grab me slid off with nothing to show but globs of yellow goo. Punches that should've knocked a tooth or two free glanced off my jaw. Hard to get a lot of force behind a fist when your feet are sliding on a greased floor. One suit tried to wield a pedestal like a club. I thought my brains were going to be splattered across a glass wall, and then the guy was flat on his back. At one point, all three of them hog piled me, but I slithered out with ease. I won't go so far as to say things were going according to plan—there definitely hadn't been a plan—but they weren't going badly. It helped that my attackers were slowing down. Not stopping. Just slowing down. It was weird, the way their steps became more sluggish, their grabs and punches more lethargic. It also wasn't something I needed to contemplate. I only needed to stay out of their slow-moving hands.

The folks that had gathered to watch the butter sculpting were shocked, then appalled, then raucously approving of the mayhem. Each slip, slap, folly, and fall brought out a roar and a round of applause. I tried to use the bolo tie to lash an assailant. Seeing me defend myself with little more than a string sent the crowd into fits. After dodging a wide swing by falling on my butt, I got hoots and hollers. When I kicked my legs out and sent that suit skidding backward, the cheers got louder. I'd never wanted to be on stage, but suddenly understood the appeal of applause. I found my feet again, took a theatrical bow, and was body-checked hockey style into the glass wall. The crowd loved it.

My cheek and one palm pressed against the pane, and I saw Jay. Barely a foot from my face was the reason I was in this mess.

"Asshole," I managed, which was pretty impressive with half my face smooshed against the glass.

I knew that wasn't fair. Jay hadn't planned for strange guys in suits to chase me. He hadn't made me run from them, and he definitely wasn't the one that started a butter-brawl. Still, it felt good to have a target for my annoyance.

He couldn't have heard me curse, but he was saying something back. His lips moved, and he did some weird stuff with his hands. A moment later, a gust of wind buffeted my hair and pulled at my jacket. The wind picked up speed, spiraling through the room with growing force. The guy who'd been smooshing me against the glass slid away. I pushed away from the wall and was instantly caught in the wind's grasp. A pedestal that had remained upright tipped over, and chunks of fallen butter began a counterclockwise slide around the room. Soon, we were doing our best impressions of laundry in a washing machine. After I'd made four or maybe five revolutions, the door opened. I shot out like a rock from a slingshot and bowled over an unfortunate family in the front row.

"Come on!" Jay yelled.

I wobbled and lurched, then bent at the waist and gave back that footlong hotdog I'd packed away earlier.

"There's no time for that," Jay scolded. "Run, August. Run!"

I straightened and moved toward where he'd been a second before, but the artist had vanished. Questions were swirling through my mind like I'd been swirling around the butter room, but they'd have to wait. The wind had stopped, and the suits were pulling themselves together. To make matters worse, someone had called Fair security, and guards were pushing their way through the crowd. Jay—if it had been Jay that had done what I was pretty sure he'd somehow done—had given me a narrow window, and I had to use it. Getting through the crowd was easier with a jacket coated in butter. Once outside, I ran down the street toward the barns. I'd tried hiding among the humans. It was time for more drastic measures.

The cow beside me lowed. I rolled my eyes at her, willing her to shut up. I wasn't in a chatty mood. Unfortunately, no one ever cared what I wanted. No sooner had she offered her commentary on whatever it was cows enjoyed commenting on, than the cow on the other side of me answered. I lowered my head, deliberately trying to stay out of the conversation. That, and I wanted to hide my horns. In my haste to find a place to hide, I'd stupidly jumped into the lady's room.

The State Fair's Cattle Barn was an immense structure full of long rows of partitioned pens. Each held a few head of cattle, dragged there to endure ogling fair-goers and maybe win their farmer a prize. It had seemed like the perfect hiding spot. The mysterious suits were looking for August Shade, the human. August Shade, the bull? He wasn't on anyone's most-wanted list. All I needed to do was keep my head down. The prospect of staying in a shift until the barn closed was frightening. The longer I wasn't human, the harder it was to shift back. I didn't have many options, though. To keep my human mind occupied, and to ensure it remained intact, I chewed on the events of the past week while my big bull mouth chewed on hay.

The most recent events were naturally front and center. What had Dagmara been doing at the Fair? Why had she given the corn dolly to that guy in the suit? Who were the suits? Their attire didn't fit with the Great Minnesota Get Together at all. It was a place of cargo shorts and tee-shirts, Zubaz and sports jerseys, socks and sandals. The suits looked like car salesmen. Accountants.

G-Men, a traitorous corner of my brain added.

Get out of my head, Jay, the rest of my brain snapped back.

Government agents in dark suits were the stuff of cheap thrillers and bad movies. I knew because I'd indulged in my fair share of fiction. I also knew that none of those books or films were set in Midwestern farm festivals. They were always in the big cities and always had the serious acronyms: FBI, CIA, NSA. The thought of those agencies at The Great Minnesota Get-Together was absurd.

But Dagmara and the suit guy and that envelope, I thought.

I'm no expert in envelopes, but I know when one looks like it's full of cash. The manilla package Dagmara had received fit the bill, pun intended, so it was likely she'd sold the little doll of woven corn husks to the guy in the suit. But why? I considered my glimpse of that envelope. It had been thick. Really thick.

Bills are pretty skinny, I reminded myself, *and if they were Benjamins...*

The bull's nostrils flared in surprise. That envelope could've had a few hundred grand inside. For a little doll. Damn. Suddenly, clandestine hand-offs with secretive agent-types didn't seem so far-fetched. Another detail surfaced as that note she'd left me came to mind. The bit about not having the money, but having it soon.

So, if she hit pay dirt, why did she run? I wondered.

I replayed the moment in my mind. Me seeing her pink mohawk and calling her name. Her turning and seeing me, then hightailing it in the opposite direction. What happened in that second or two? What had she thought? What had she felt?

A few more thoughts flitted through my brain, then I mooed a bull's equivalent of a curse. I wouldn't get any answers by standing around and chewing my cud. Only Dagmara could tell me what I needed to know. My next trip to Vermillion would not be a fun one. I had to rip off one client and then shake down another for answers. Most of the time, my jobs were just jobs. I helped someone get their special whatever back, and that was it. I didn't want to get caught up in people's problems, yet there I was, wondering incessantly. About Dagmara, strange people in suits, hag sisters, and architectural blueprints. About a baby spoon and the nasty coblyn that wanted it so badly. My mind whirled, caught up in a vortex, and that gave me another thing to wonder about. Something I really didn't want to wonder about. Something I wished hadn't happened at all.

I tried and tried to convince myself that my experience in the butter room had nothing to do with Jay. Nothing. It simply wasn't possible. Jay was an odd duck, but artists were like that. So were conspiracy theorists. The combination made Jay exceptionally weird, but that didn't mean he was warlock weird. Elemental magic weird. Someone else had to have been there.

Another Tony?

I pawed with irritation at the stall's straw-covered floor. Tony the Douchebag Warlock had almost killed me earlier that summer, and had damned near destroyed the entire world in the process. He had loved to toss things around with his magical wind. Dropping a tornado in a butter carving room had Tony written all over it, but he was dead. Electrocuted by a giant beer sign and carried off by a troll for a crispy late-night snack dead. You just can't get any deader.

So, Jay.

My insides went cold. Jay had known Tony as the Vortex Virtuoso. Had listened to the guy's podcast. Had gone to see him at the local cuckoo convention. If he'd picked up where Tony had left off...

Oh, Jay, I thought with a growing sense of dread. *What have you done? What in the actual fuck have you done?*

I let out an angry bellow and tossed my head. The cows caught the mood and added their own dismayed moos. Soon, the stalls on either side were fussing as well. It was getting harder to exert my will over the bull's inclinations, but I did my best. The last thing I needed was to spark a bovine uprising in the Fair's cattle barn. I took a few deep breaths and gave myself a good shake, then opened my mouth wide and filled it with hay. My jaw's circular chewing was a meditative mantra meant to still my swirling thoughts. I willed my forced Zen to spread as effectively as my earlier agitation. Unfortunately, it wasn't working. Worse, we were drawing attention.

The barn had emptied considerably. Judging from the light slanting through the windows, the Fair was likely to close down soon. The number of curious monkeys had diminished, which meant the minor commotion in my pen was easier for the barn's staff to notice.

"What in the holy heck is wrong with you three?" a fellow wondered out loud as he hooked his thumbs through his overalls and ambled my way. "Nothing to get so worked up over, I'm sure. You just settle down there. Just settle down. There we go."

His soothing words were having the desired effect, even on me. I felt my eyelids droop. All that worry I'd worked up evaporated like the cow fart that slipped out of my derriere. It was loud enough—and apparently pungent enough—to catch the guy's attention. He gave me a long once-over, then unclipped a walkie talkie from his belt and clicked the switch.

"Callie, this is George. Any idea why there's an untagged bull in with a couple of cows in stall forty-eight? Over."

There was a burst of static. "What's that, now? A bull in forty-eight? One sec, hon."

George regarded me while he waited. "You sure as heck aren't from around here," he mused.

He wasn't wrong. How was I to know that good old George would have such a keen eye for cattle?

He's working in the cattle bar, I pointed out.

Yeah, but that doesn't mean someone's an expert, I replied churlishly.

It isn't that hard to tell a boy cow from a girl cow, I reminded myself.

I'm a bull, not a boy cow, I replied.

My internal bickering might have continued 'til those cows came home, but a fresh burst of static got my attention.

"You stay put, George. Help with a capital H is on the way. Over."

"Help? You mean…" he said with a press of the walkie's button, "them? Over."

Callie's voice was as flat as the barn's floor. "Yes. Them."

I shuddered to think of what that meant. All I needed was a little luck—just a smidge—and I'd be home free. A few minutes later, that luck I was hoping for gave me a big, fat middle finger. Two of the suits came walking down my row. Schnozz had a split lip and swollen cheek. His hand snapped sharply at the wrist, and old George took off at a run. The other suit, the one that was built like a tractor, had a rifle. Before I could think of a way out of the manure pile I'd landed in, he'd unslung it from his shoulder, worked its bolt, and sent a tranquilizer dart into my shoulder. I wobbled on my hooves, gave a sad little moo, and dropped to the straw as my knees buckled. The bull's wide field of vision narrowed, and then all was dark.

Chapter 11

"I would rather be on my farm than be emperor of the world."
- George Washington

F OR THE RECORD, TRANQUILIZERS are flippin' awesome. When something akin to awareness returned, I let myself float for a good, long while. I'd never felt as good as I did under that industrial strength cocktail. I knew I had dreamed, although I don't know what I'd dreamed about. Maybe grazing verdant fields. Maybe having an entire herd of four-legged hotties show up in my pasture with a few bales of hay and a hankering for a good time. I'll never know. I did know that I was more relaxed than I had been in years. Sadly, that euphoria was short-lived. As my wits returned, I realized I was still shifted. Still a bull. I didn't know how much time had passed, but I knew it had been too much. I tried to nudge the bull. Reassert myself in its consciousness. Convince my bully self that I was still me. I wasn't getting through, though. Most of my brain was thinking woozy bull thoughts. With a growing sense of panic, I tried to shake the damned thing out of its tranq stupor.

C'mon, you stupid boy cow. You fucking hamburger waiting to happen! Gimme the wheel.

My eyes fluttered, and a few labored breaths steamed out from my wide nose. I offered a groggy snort and raised my head from its bed of straw. It wasn't directly my doing, but it was a start. I needed to assess my situation. Mismatched memories of a guy with a rifle mixed with the remnants of the bull's dreams. While my head swayed back and forth, I took stock of my surroundings. They were the same. I was still in Fair's cattle barn. The only change was that instead of two cows to keep me company, there were two guys in dark suits perched on milking stools.

"Wakey, wakey. Eggs and bakey," the big one, the one who had tranquilized me, said.

"Finally," the other remarked while scratching that long and hooked nose. "I thought we'd be here all night."

His comment opened the door to more observations. The windows showed a darkness outside, broken only by the glow of quaint streetlamps. Most of the lights inside were off. The rest left the immense space in a textured gloom. The barn echoed with the contented snores of a thousand head of cattle. If it weren't for the annoying chatter of the two humans in the room, it would have been serene.

"How do we get it to shift?" Tranq asked. "No point in asking it questions if it can't answer."

"Shifter," Schnozz said authoritatively. "Paw once if you can understand me, and twice if you can't."

I concentrated, focused, harnessed my humanness, and pressed my will onto the dumb bull's brain. For a moment, nothing happened. Then my foreleg pawed at the straw twice.

Guffaws erupted from the two men. When they subsided, the one that had tranquilized me reached inside his coat and withdrew a huge gun. The damn pistol looked as long as one of my horns. With a psychopathic calm, he leaned forward and pressed the barrel between my eyes.

"You will shift into your human form now," he instructed. "If I see even the slightest hint of any other animal, I'll blow your freak brains out the back of your freak head."

"Hey," Schnozz said, "Easy. There's no need to get mean."

"I can't stand PNs."

"My neighbor's wife is a werecat."

"Oh," Tranq replied after a moment's hesitation. "I didn't know."

Schnozz nodded. "Yes, she is, and she works for the DNR. So you just take that nasty crap about the paranormals and stow it. They aren't the problem. Not yet, anyway."

Tranq held up his free hand. "Sorry, alright? Sorry." Returning his attention to me, he pressed the gun more firmly against my skull. "If I see even the slightest hint of any another animal, I'll blow your different but perfectly acceptable and in no way deserving of disparaging remarks brains out the back of your different but perfectly acceptable and in no way deserving of disparaging remarks head."

"Now you're being obnoxious," Schnozz whined.

While the two bickered, I considered whether I could shift faster than he could pull the trigger. On a good day, maybe. Not likely... but maybe. It didn't matter. Today wasn't a good day. I was exhausted. I'd been drugged. I'd been the bull so long it was getting harder and harder to think of myself in any other terms. After a long pause, during which Tranq tapped me on the skull a couple of times and said, "Hey! Shifter. Get to shifting. Hey! You in there?" I started the old mantra that had saved me time and again as a kid.

Me, me, on the count of three. Me, me, on the count of three.

Usually, shifting is like standing up too quickly. My head swims a bit, and then I'm good. The longer I stay shifted, though, the more it sucks when I change back. Instead of a brief head rush, it's more like standing up too quickly and having a head rush, brain freeze, vertigo, stubbed toe, stomach cramp, and tinnitus. And that's if I'm lucky and actually can shift back to my human form. I'd never been not lucky, but I'd been close. The doctors at that damned hospital were always pushing and pushing and pushing. If I hadn't gotten free when I did, who knows what I'd be today? An irritable gorilla, forever scratching its butt? A coyote endlessly pacing its cage? I'd always been careful not to stay shifted too long. Then along came these assholes and their top-shelf cocktail in a red-tailed dart, and I'd been the bull for hours and hours. For all I knew, I'd jumped over that invisible line. For all I knew, this was it. Maybe I'd passed from being full of metaphorical bullshit to being literally full of the stuff. Maybe I'd spend the rest of my days as the Hereford formerly known as August Shade.

That thought whammed my panic button. With a gut-wrenching push, I concentrated all of my awareness. I was a human. Not a bull. A human. A middle-aged, irritable human of average height with a fondness for beer, hotdogs, and 90s grunge and an aversion to pretty much everything else.

Me, me, on the count of three. Me, me, on the count of three. Three, two...

"Moo," I complained, then followed it with a much more human, "Argh."

My hands and knees pressed into the damp straw covering the floor. I dropped to my elbows and caught my head in my hands. For a moment, I thought Blunder had shoved his punchy contraption inside my skull. The whamming was all that existed. Tears streamed down my cheeks as I pressed my palms hard against by eye sockets.

"Aw, the little vandal is crying," I heard someone say. With a little effort, I figured out it was Tranq. Made sense. He was obviously the big softy of the two.

"I'm in touch with my feelings," I muttered, "and right now, I feel awful."

Schnozz squatted down in front of me. "You should. What you did was awful. Getting folks worked up like that. It was a rotten thing to do."

"How'd you know?" Tranq demanded, the gun inching closer to my head. "Who told you?"

"There's nothing to know," Schnozz said hastily. "Now, put that thing away. He's naked. He's obviously a wreck. He isn't going to do anything. Are you, August Shade?"

I pried a palm off of one socket and rolled an eye at the good cop, bad cop routine.

"No. Maybe. I might throw up," I admitted. "Besides that, though? No, I'm not going to do anything."

Schnozz nodded, pressed his hands to his knees, and stood. The unfolding of his lanky frame reminded me of that damned Strach na wróble. To be honest, I wasn't sure who was scarier. There was something about Schnozz that gave me the creeps.

"That's good. The cameras are off," he said with a wave of his hand, "so we can do whatever we want."

The suit let his comment sink in, then he smiled an almost pleasant smile. Almost.

"Let's get you into some clothes, then we'll chat about your little stunt," he said. A moment later, my boots, jeans, shirt and jacket were laying on the straw beside me. After dropping them, Schnozz looked disgustedly at his palm, then scraped his hand across the stall's railing. Clumps of yellow slid down the rough wood and fell to the ground. "We can't turn our backs to give you privacy, unfortunately. I'm sure you understand."

"Sure, everything about this is completely understandable," I growled, then set myself to dressing.

After lacing the second boot—all the more challenging because of the damned butter—I picked loose bits of straw from my jacket and turned my attention to Tranq and Schnozz.

"Okay. Let's get this cleared up," I growled through an epic headache. "I have no idea why you were chasing me, but you were. Since you're the aggressors in this situation, everything that happened is your fault. Don't bother trying to sue."

Tranq chortled. "Oh, why's that? You some fancy, big shot lawyer?"

"No. I'm broke."

"We aren't going to sue," Schnozz assured me. "We just have questions. Answer them to our satisfaction, and we can all go home. You'd like that, wouldn't you, August? You'd like to go home?"

My face scrunched. "How do you know who I am?"

"You're trending," Schnozz replied. "Honestly, if I were planning to do what you did, I'd have opted to stay a bit more anonymous."

"He could've auditioned for that *World's Dumbest Criminals* show. He'd have been a shoo-in."

"I'm about to put a shoe in your ass," I warned, but we both knew I didn't mean it. "And what do you mean, I'm trending?"

Schnozz reached into his suit coat's inner pocket and pulled out a smartphone. A moment after that, he pulled a pair of cheaters from another pocket, hooked their temples behind his ears and perched them on his boat rudder of a nose. After a few taps of his finger, he turned the phone's screen to face me.

The video was a bit jarring, which made sense. I'd been trying to squirm away while the guy was filming it. Not the best of conditions for a smooth recording. His voice was perfectly clear, though.

"Wazzup, peeps? I'm here with August Shade. That's right! The shady shifter that trashed Nicollet Island and kicked some serious ass. Me and Auggie are just kickin' it in the hood. Peace out, bitches!"

"See? Hashtag 'Shady Shifter.' We already had you on camera," he explained as he pulled the phone back and fiddled some more with its screen.

When he showed its display to me again, it was a still image. The quality wasn't great. Despite the pixilation, the face was one I knew all too well. A face that could have been hidden behind the bandana Jay had offered me. I logged yet another entry in my register of bad decisions and sighed.

"This was captured moments before the power went out. Fair security and the police weren't able to turn anything up, but they didn't have our resources. Our facial recognition scans matched you with that little video, and we've been keeping an eye out ever since. We knew that, whoever you were, you must've been up to something."

"You just had to be a big, dumb showboater," Tranq tacked on. "Dummy. You're a terrible criminal. Or a narcissist. Lots of criminals are narcissists."

Schnozz waved off Tranq's criticism. "Never mind him. The important thing is that we get to the bottom of why you sabotaged the crop art competition. Who are you working for? Why did you decide to show those particular images? What was your end game? Enlighten us."

My mind was a rockhopper full of disjointed thoughts, but a few fell into place. They thought I was Jay. Me. It was such an absurd thought that a laugh slipped through my lips.

"Wrong guy," I chuckled. "It definitely wasn't me."

Fun fact: Getting pistol whipped sucks. Funner fact: Getting pistol whipped after being chased, tranquilized, and stuck as a bull for hours before finally being able to shift back really sucks.

"Why?" I cried out.

"We don't like liars," Tranq replied tartly. "We don't like them at all."

"Okay. Okay," I managed as I wiped at a trickle of blood on my forehead. "I'll tell you what you want to hear. Just give me a sec. I think I'm going to throw up."

They leaned back on their milking stools while a couple of dry heaves bent my back. After the third, I coughed up a bit of masticated hay and burped.

"That was unpleasant," Schnozz remarked.

I looked up with bleary eyes. "Imagine being me."

The back of my hand slid across my mouth, and I coughed another time or two. When I felt like I could speak without risking another hay-filled burp, I held up a hand to beg for a moment.

"I hate you, Jay," I muttered, then saw my tormentor's eyes light up. "...Kowski. I hate you, Shannon Jakowski. So much. I wish I'd never met you, you terrible white lady with your blond hair and gigantic ass and terrible ideas."

Tranq cast a look at Schnozz, and Schnozz leaned in. His giant nose almost touched my much more reasonably sized one, and he asked who Shannon Jakowski was.

"Uh, real piece of work from... Bemidji," I winged. "Yeah. She came down from Bemidji. She forced me to help her do that really terrible thing. I didn't want to, but she made me. I'm so glad you're going to catch her and hit her with the gun. She totally has it coming."

Schnozz had put his phone and glasses back into their respective pockets. When his hand reached back into his suit coat's inner pocket, it came out with a small notepad. He flipped to a blank page and then pulled a ballpoint pen from his shirt pocket.

"You've got a lot of pockets," I observed.

"Shannon..." Schnozz prompted.

"Jakowski," I agreed, then spelled it. "From Bemidji. You know. Little town way up north. She's up there. Making her weird seed art things and causing all sorts of trouble."

Schnozz made a few notes in his pad, then flipped it shut and returned it to his project.

"Thank you, August Shade. You have been most helpful. Now, if you could scoot back a little bit to where the straw is piled up? It will help soak up the blood."

Time slowed down in that weird way it does when you're pretty sure your ticket to the Fair is about to get punched. Tranq raised his gun. My mouth stretched around a wide, "No!" I leaned back like that might somehow help me dodge a literal bullet, and then I looked over Tranq's shoulder.

I saw two things. Neither made sense, and neither made me feel better, but that happens. We don't get to choose what we see.

First, I saw myself—clear as fucking day—standing across the wide row between the cattle stalls. I was wearing my Schott Perfecto jacket, tee-shirt, and blue jeans. I looked at myself, and myself looked back. That me shook his head and shrugged. At what, I had no clue, and I wasn't likely to find out. After giving that little shake of his—my—head, that other me disappeared. Where it had been a moment before, a collection of sticks unfurled into a tall and tattered simulacrum of a person. It had a flat-brimmed hat, like what preachers in the Old West might've worn. A threadbare canvas jacket sporting a jaunty blue ribbon on one lapel hung from the sharp points of its shoulders and stretched along thin arms. A ragged slit of a mouth in a burlap sack face widened, and a sound like rotting meat, like blistering flesh, like festering wounds, erupted.

Tranq turned first. The gun drifted sideways, then fell to the straw as the big guy screamed. Schnozz turned a second later. He didn't have a gun to drop, but drop something, he did. The smell of poo hit my nostrils hard, and then Schnozz was falling backward off his milking stool. I had the slightest moment of sympathy. The Strach na wróble had scared the crap out of me, too. I hadn't been wearing pants at the time, though. That had to suck.

Oddly, the fear that was twisting up the suits wasn't affecting me. Or it was, but in a distant sort of way. Like watching a serial killer in a B horror flick as opposed to being confronted by an ax wielding psychopath in real life. Yeah, I was scared, but not shit-myself scared. Not fall-off-my-milk-stool scared. Not scrabble-backward-in-abject-terror scared. I was just, you know, scared. When the walking nightmare factory screamed, I realized why. I wasn't the source of its ire.

"The corn dolly!" it wailed in its barbed, abrasive, and rotting voice. "Where is the corn dolly?"

The scarecrow's arms rattled. Its long fingers twitched. Its weird face wrinkled and stretched. Arms splayed impossibly wide, its threadbare canvas jacket spread out like the topsail of a ghost ship. The few lights above flickered and dimmed, and the thousand-head of cattle lowed.

"Where?" the Strach na wróble demanded.

In response, Tranq and Schnozz ran. The two suits tripped as they launched themselves over the stall's railing, then grabbed and shoved at each other as they raced for the exit. Their screams echoed for a moment, and then quiet reclaimed the cavernous space. The meager light showed me the Strach na wróble folding back in on itself. What had been an immense nightmare became nothing more than a tall, skinny scarecrow. A collection of second-hand clothes tossed over a lanky frame with oddly jointed limbs. A burlap face that wasn't all that scary. Rather, it looked sad.

"Are you... Are you crying?" I asked when a soft, hitching rasp reached my ears.

"No," it replied, then drew the back of a leather-glove hand across its Xs.

How many times had I been in that exact moment? Well, not exactly. I mean, it was my first time consoling someone in the cattle barn at the Minnesota State Fair. And it was my first time consoling a terrifying Strach na wróble. Those details aside, though, I was in my element. Was I the best shoulder to cry on? No, and I never would be, but any port in a storm, right? I hopped over the stall's railing and rested a hand on the strachy-thing's quivering back. It tensed, then long arms wrapped around me and a burlapy face pressed into my shoulder. For a long moment, I awkwardly patted its dusty coat and listened to the sandpaper-on-rough-wood sound of its cries.

"You really liked that corn doll, huh?" I finally said.

"Dolly," the strachy-thing replied, "And yes. I have to save her."

"From those guys?" I asked, tilting my head in the direction the suits had run. "Why? Who are they?"

The Strach na wróble released me from its embrace, and a shaky sigh of relief crept through my quivering jaw. I don't care who you are. Hugging a scarecrow is creepy.

"The Department of Agriculture," it whispered ominously.

I laughed. When the strachy-thing didn't, I stopped. For a moment, I tried to take it seriously. I couldn't, though, so I laughed again.

"C'mon," I finally said. "Seriously? Since when does the Minnesota Department of Agriculture have heat-packing G-Men?"

In response, the talking scarecrow raised its Xs to look up at me.

"Decades," it replied seriously. "Perhaps longer. They are horrible. Horrible."

I scratched my chin in thought. A door in my brain cracked open. It led to a world where people like Jay were actually onto something, so I slammed it shut again.

"Whatever. Sure. Welp, I'm sorry they got your doll."

"Dolly."

"Right. But it wasn't yours to begin with. It was Dagmara's, and she can do whatever she wants with it. If that means selling it to those douchebags, so be it."

The strachy-thing rattled its collection of limbs in agitation. "The wraith doesn't know what she's doing," it whispered.

Wraith? I thought.

"Wraith?" I asked.

I'm not sure how two stitched Xs in a burlap sack could look disbelieving, but they did.

"Of course. The Cornflower Wraith. The noon demon."

Demon? I thought.

"Demon?" I asked, my voice hitching a bit higher. "Dagmara is not a demon. Look, buddy. Getting dumped sucks. I get it. Doesn't mean you can just start calling your ex a demon. That's. You know. Rude. Calling a human a demon. A really attractive human. That you, you know. Did stuff with."

"Foolish shifter," the Strach na wróble replied.

An uncomfortable silence settled like a wet fog between us, and then the strachy-thing straightened its hat.

"I must go," it proclaimed. "I must find the corn dolly."

"Uh, sure," I replied distractedly. I was still trying to process the whole demon thing. "Um. Thanks and all. I mean, I know you weren't trying to help me, but sometimes things work out. Maybe things will work out for you, too. Clouds and silver linings, right?"

The Strach na wróble shrugged and turned to go, but stopped when I blurted out two words.

"Grey Clouds," I said. When those weird X-eyes looked confused, I added, "One of those suits told another one to bring the doll to Grey Cloud. No clue who that is, but maybe it'll help."

Its sigh was an icy wind through a frozen field.

"Not who. Where," the Strach na wróble said. It tipped forward in a half-bow, then said, "Thank you, shifter. Tell Dagmara... I understand why she did what she did. Tell her it is alright. If I don't return, tell her I forgive her."

"Okay," I replied, but the thing's long legs had already carried it well beyond the range of my quiet voice. I didn't have a chance to explain that I'd likely never see her again. That the last time I had, she'd run away. Not really an auspicious sign from someone you're dating.

My brain chugged on that last bit. Dagmara and I hadn't been dating. We hadn't even had a real date. I mean, sure, there was that night, and that night was something. Dating, though?

I rolled the thought around and considered it from a few angles. Dating a demon. A Cornflower Wraith, whatever that was. Didn't seem like a great idea. The more I considered it, the more it seemed like a terrible idea. What future could a shapeshifter and a demon have?

A naked one, a very persuasive part of my brain replied.

Maybe, I conceded, assuming her reason for running was something we could work through.

First things first, though. I had an artist-turned-warlock to deal with and a spoon to re-repo. Neither was a chore I wanted to do, but when a thing needs doing, you do it.

CHAPTER 12

"**Y**OU'VE GOT SOME EXPLAINING to do, Mister."

Rolling out of bed at the crack of dawn was definitely not on my list of favorite things. I'd made the painful sacrifice to ensure I'd be at the art studio when Jay rolled in. As my usual luck would have it, Jay had decided not to start his day until almost noon. I'd tried to pass the time by being productive, but my job didn't exactly have administrative overhead. Mine was strictly a cash operation. No bank statements to balance. No reports to compile. No employees to manage or timesheets to approve. It was just me, a phone, and a few safes to keep stuff in until its rightful owner stopped by. Needless to say, there wasn't much to fill the time. When Jay did arrive, he didn't walk in to me shoving a finger into his chest. He passed my office, did his own whatever for a bit, realized I was there when he'd passed my office again to take a bathroom break, and woke me up with a chipper rapping on the open door and a bright, "Hey, August!" I'd startled awake and fallen off my chair. It was only after I'd let a few choice swear words out, righted myself in the chair, and shook the cobwebs out of my head that I finally got to shove my finger into his chest.

"The Great Minnesota Get-Together turned into the Great Minnesota Get August Shade."

"I'm sorry, August," he sputtered in shock. "I didn't. I mean, I don't. You weren't supposed to..."

"Get chased through half the fairgrounds? Get into a butter-brawl?"

"... Yeah. That wasn't supposed to happen."

"Well, it did. But let's set that—and the fun that happened after all that—aside for a minute. What I really want to talk about is the freak tornado in the butter room. That happened," I seethed. When he proceeded to look at everything except me, I prompted him with, "Now's the part where you explain exactly how."

"That was so weird. Must've been, you know. The air conditioner. The fan, probably. Must've been a glitch in the fan."

"Damn it, Jay!" I swore. "It wasn't the fan, and you know it."

"It wasn't?" he asked, all innocence. "I mean, no. You're right. Whatever that was, it was way too intense to just be a fan," he agreed with a nervous laugh. "You don't think. I mean, there must've been someone there who... You know. Like maybe a warlock or something?"

"Like maybe a warlock, or something," I repeated coldly.

Jay's head nodded vigorously. "What are the odds, right? After all that stuff this summer with the Vortex Virtuoso... I mean, Tony the Douchebag."

"It was definitely a douchebag," I agreed. "Come on. Cut the crap, Jay. Talk to me. What was that? What did you do?"

A twinge of hurt thrummed somewhere inside of me as I watched the wheels of my friend's mind work like a loom spinning threads of bullshit. Finally, thankfully, those wheels slowed.

"Have you eaten? You want lunch? Uncle Sid's?" he asked.

The vegetarian offering to go to my favorite hotdog spot was a hell of an olive branch. I nodded and slung my jacket over my shoulder. Despite my best efforts to clean off the butter, the leather was still slick, and it slipped from my hand. With a curse, I picked it up from the floor, shoved my arms into its sleeves, and glowered to cover the gaffe.

"Fine, but I'm driving. I'm not letting you out of my sight until you tell me what the hell is going on."

After killing the bike's engine, Jay quietly climbed out of the sidecar. He politely held the door for me, then followed me into Sid's.

"Two dogs, Chicago style, Coke, and these," I said as I held up a small bag of chips.

The guy behind the counter would normally punch a few keys on the cash register, take my money, and give me back my change. That's how these things worked. When he didn't do those things, when instead he just stood there looking at me, I repeated my order.

"Hello? Did whoever give you that split lip break your ears, too?" I asked, finally looking, really looking, at the guy.

He was always there. Twenty-something human. A little scruffy. No clue what his name was, but why would I know that? I gave him money. He gave me hotdogs. No need to complicate things with names. I thought we had a perfectly normal customer-cashier relationship going on. When he continued to not do his half of the transaction, I started to get annoyed.

Jay's messing with the dark arts, and now my hotdog guy is broken, I thought.

"I can't serve you," he finally said. "Uh, sorry. But no hotdogs for you."

"What in the...?" I asked, stunned. "No hotdogs? Why? Wait, no. Shit. Oh, shit. Mother fucker."

"Um, if you're going to use that kind of language," the guy said in a shaky voice, "I'll have to ask you to leave. Actually, you might as well leave, anyway. I can't, uh, serve you anything."

I shook my head angrily. I wasn't mad at him. Honestly, I felt terrible for him. I was mad at someone a lot shorter than him.

"Sorry, bud. This is my fault," I muttered while sliding a few crumpled bills across the countertop. "You didn't need to be mixed up in this."

Jay and I had to try two more spots—a burrito joint I was fond of, and a gyro place that I loved almost as much as Sid's—before we finally found a corporate chain diner where they didn't know who I was. I made a mental calculation of how far I was from my regular hood and whistled. We'd had to travel over two miles away from the studio to find a place that would serve me.

"Blunder's really got it in for you, huh?" Jay remarked worriedly after I mentioned the sphere of his influence.

"Looks like," I said.

It infuriated me that the thug was roughing up innocents, and it scared me that he knew all of my regular spots. Betty popped into my head, and my stomach did a somersault. Then I remembered that Betty was everyone's favorite bartender. If Blunder and his pals had plans to rough her up, they'd have to get through every single person—PN and otherwise—in the place first. Even if she had been in danger, there wasn't anything I could do. Well, besides getting the damned spoon back.

"Don't worry. I'll get the spoon tonight and put an end to all this."

The artist looked down at the salad he'd ordered but hadn't touched.

"I could help," he said quietly.

"Sure, Jay. Maybe you could paint over that black eye Philo got, or glue some seeds on that split lip the poor guy at Sid's has. I mean, that's what you could do to help, right? Right?"

"Okay. Yes. It was me," he shot back. "I made the wind in the butter room. Is that what you wanted to hear?"

The sun was shining through the diner's window, but it felt darker inside.

"No, Jay. That isn't what I wanted to hear," I said sadly.

He straightened his spine and crossed his arms. "Well, too bad. You're not the only special one anymore. I'm special, too."

My jaw landed in my half-finished burger. "Special? What the hell are you talking about?"

"Oh, come on," he almost yelled. "You can shift. Leonard can lift a BMW off the ground. Betty can get any guy or girl she wants. Clarissa could see the goddamned future. Even Blunder. He might be a jerk, but coblynau can build all the crazy stuff they build. Well, now I can do something that none of you can."

"Jay," I tried, "you already do something we can't. You're an artist. You think Leonard could do what you do? Or me?"

That last bit should've gotten a laugh. It didn't.

"Don't mock me, August. Not you. I know what you think about my art. You don't have to lie to my face, though."

"Lie? When did I lie? Do I get art? No, but I know enough to know you're talented. More than talented, and I've told you that. The only one here that's been lying is you. Why didn't you tell me you were doing magic stuff?"

"Sorry, mom. Must've slipped my mind."

The waitress chose that moment to check on us. When she asked if we were doing alright, I said, "Whatever," and Jay said, "No." The poor lady took a surprised step back then hurried over to her next table, leaving me and my friend to glare at each other. It didn't last, though. That's the funny thing about friendship. Even when people are being total asshats, it's hard to stay angry for long.

"You're grounded," I muttered while trying to suppress a grin. When the corner of my mouth crooked up, Jay's face let the sun back into the diner.

"But it was great, right?" he said with wide eyes and a wider smile. "I mean, those guys—whoever they were—totally got their asses kicked, and you got away. I mean, you did, right? You got away."

That moment of light faded.

"Oh, no, Jay," I said after a bite of my burger and a swig of pop. "I did not get away. Not until much, much later."

For the next few minutes, I unfurled how I'd spent the rest of my night. Getting chased through the bazaar and the haunted house. Almost getting stuck as a bull for the rest of my life. Having a gun shoved against my forehead. Being saved by the Strach na wróble's serendipitous appearance. I almost mentioned seeing myself, too, but decided against it. I was still trying to process that bit.

While I spoke, Jay's head sank further into his shoulders, and his mouth stretched in shock. When I finished my tale of woe by talking about how much the walk home sucked, since the buses weren't running that early in the morning, he actually cried. We got a few sideways looks from another couple a few tables down, but I didn't care. I had wanted to rattle Jay. Impress on him that whatever he'd been up to, he needed to stop. I didn't mean to make the poor guy cry, though.

Still, a little corner of my brain observed, *he deserves it.*

"August, this is serious. I had no idea those guys were Department of Agriculture. I mean, sure, I knew my project was going to churn the butter, so to speak, but I did not know they'd send operatives. I swear!"

"Operatives?" I scoffed? "It's the Department of Agriculture, for cripe's sake."

"Oh, August," he sighed. "There is so much you don't know."

I shoved the last of my lunch into my mouth and chewed it angrily. Jay watched with his usual reserved disgust, but this time, the lecture that followed wasn't about my sodium intake or cruelty to animals.

"Do you ever think about the bun that burger was on? Where it comes from?"

"No."

Jay rubbed his cheeks and exhaled slowly. "Of course not. Okay. Let's do a little math. How many people are in America?"

I shrugged. "A lot?"

"Yes, August. A lot. Over three-hundred and thirty million people. And Canada?"

"More?"

"Less. A lot less. Still, thirty-eight million people. A hundred and thirty-odd million people in Mexico. All things told, there are almost six-hundred million people in North America. Sadly, a lot of them—the vast majority, if we're being honest—like hotdogs and brats and hamburgers and chicken sandwiches and chips and English muffins and tortillas and on and on and on. They like wheat and corn and meat. People like to eat, August, and American farms produce a lot of food. A lot. For us, and to export to other countries."

"So?" I asked. "You eat."

"Organic, small-farm, non-GMO as much as humanly possible," he replied tartly, while poking the diner's salad with a fork. "But yes, I eat. We all eat. Food is the single most important thing on the planet. Which means..." he prompted.

"... that everyone likes food?" I answered.

"That the Department of Agriculture is really, really powerful."

"That, too," I agreed, trying not to sound dumb. I hated it when I sounded dumb.

The artist's fingers drummed on the tabletop in agitation.

"That's why what they're doing is so insidious. Messing with our food. Chemicals. GMOs. We can't not be a part of their experiments. We're all unknowing guinea pigs. That's why my tableau was so important. Why people needed to see it."

He frowned and scratched at the dark stubble on his chin. I was worried he was going to take off a few layers of skin.

"But why you?" he wondered, with an edge to his voice. "Why would they think it was you?"

"Oh, that," I said, more curse than comment. "Whatever you thought you did to the cameras and stuff the other night didn't work. At least, not enough. They had a picture of me."

Fresh tears welled up in the artist's eyes. Jay knew how desperate I was to keep a low profile.

"That's not possible," he gasped. "I burned the circuits."

"We'll come back to exactly how you did that," I promised menacingly, "but apparently you missed one. They had a picture of me, and they matched it to some stupid video of me online."

"I saw that!" he exclaimed. "Holy crap. I completely forgot to tell you. How did I forget about that? You're trending. Hashtag 'Shady Shifter.' Kinda catchy," he remarked, then backpedaled. "But totally not cool. Not cool at all."

It was my turn to sink further into my chair. The knowledge that a video of me was running laps around the internets was giving me heartburn. Well, that and the burger.

"I still don't get why you're so scared of the internet," he remarked. "I mean, I get it from my perspective. I just don't get it from your perspective."

Jay knew I had an unpleasant past, but I'd never shared all the details.

"I don't want to be found. I don't want to be findable," I said. "You think the Department of Agriculture is bad? There are worse people in the world, Jay. Much worse."

"Worse than people in cahoots with aliens that are trying to alter our DNA and breed us out of existence?"

I'd just taken a sip of pop. When I snorted, most of it came out of my nose. After squeezing my nostrils into a napkin, I waved off his comments.

"Cahoots," I said with a roll of my eyes. "Sure, Jay. Aliens are totally real."

"You're a shapeshifter. You've done jobs for werewolves and huldras. You've hooked up with a succubus. Well, you tried, anyway. You've had beers with a reanimated corpse. You dated an oracle. But aliens are unbelievable," he said, his words rolled in sarcasm and sprinkled with scorn.

"All those things you mentioned didn't come from the Planet Xenon or whatever. They came from here," I protested as I jabbed a finger at the table.

"Denny's?" he asked with a laugh.

I couldn't stop the grin that twisted my lips.

"Shut up, you big dummy."

"You first, you big oaf."

Our usual routine—him trying to illuminate me on the dark machinations of nefarious no-gooders, and me being my usual cynical self—was a thin veneer over the tension between us. Even so, it felt good. I finished my pop while enjoying the more companionable silence that had settled between us. I wanted to make the most of it, because I knew it wouldn't last.

"So, you're a warlock now," I said.

Jay squirmed.

"Oh, I don't know about that," he finally protested. "I just. I mean. Tony had his podcast, and I took his Masterclass, and... What? I didn't know he was a psycho douchebag until later."

I took a deep breath and didn't say any of the things I wanted to say. When Jay saw I was biting my tongue, he pressed on.

"I'm good at it, August. Most people that try get nowhere. I think it's because I'm an artist. I'm in this chat group. Don't worry. It's on a private server. Super encrypted. The lady who runs it is a cybersecurity expert. First rate."

He'd obviously misinterpreted my raised eyebrow. I didn't know the first thing about servers or cybersecurity. Hell, I didn't know about most of what happened on the internets. Old ladies that ate life force, reanimated corpses, people changing into animals and back, that I could understand. The internets? Forget about it. But even I knew that a private chat group for aspiring warlocks was approaching peak dorkiness.

"Creatives apparently pick up magic more easily. Weird, right? Maybe Merlin painted in his spare time," Jay added with a laugh. "Anyway, I'm good, August, and getting better."

It was hard to stay mad when he was obviously so excited. There weren't any laws against practicing magic or casting spells. Consequences, sure, but like anything else, it was a matter of degrees. If no one was seriously hurt, the wrong spell at the wrong time might get you a slap on the wrist and a fine. If something bad did happen, though…

I pushed those worries aside. Whatever Jay was doing, he wasn't one to cross that line.

And he saved your ass in the butter room, I admitted to myself.

"Geezus, Jay. Just be careful, okay? Promise me you'll be careful?"

The artist nodded enthusiastically. "Oh, yeah. No more stunts like the Fair for a while. I swear. So, um. Are we, you know. Are we okay?"

Reluctantly, I dipped my chin.

"Good. Then let's get out of here before I open up a pit in the ground to swallow this place whole."

"You wouldn't!" I gasped.

"No," Jay agreed with a good-natured laugh as he dropped some cash on the table and walked to the door. "Not yet, anyway. Tony had mastered air magic. I'm pretty good with air, and now I'm learning fire. It's how I killed the power at the Fair. Heated up the wires until all the breakers popped. I want to work on earth magic next."

I tried to keep the surprise off my face. I didn't know a lot about elemental magic. Honestly, most of what I knew I'd learned that summer at a dinner party while Tony the Douchebag Warlock and a mean old vampire traded barbs. What I knew was that mastering a single element was apparently pretty tough. Learning Jay had already tackled two and was delving into a third was stunning.

"Just stop talking," I grumbled while shoving him through the door.

"PNs could have been aliens," he said after climbing into my Guzzi's sidecar. "Ancient aliens. They came down here and mixed with the locals, and now we have weres and vampires and coblynau and stuff. And you. People like you. Maybe you're part alien."

"Stop talking," I begged again with a twist of the key.

He didn't. He kept unfurling conspiracy theory after conspiracy theory the entire way back to the studio. Thankfully, I was pretty terrible about maintaining my bike, and the engine's whine made him impossible to hear.

CHAPTER 13

*"In undertaking farming we undertake a responsibility covering the whole
life cycle. We can break it or keep it whole."*
- Lord Northbourne

LUNCH WITH JAY HAD eaten up the afternoon like I'd eaten that greasy diner burger,
one big bite at a time. I dropped Jay off at the studio, adjusted the strap on my
helmet for the long drive ahead, and pointed the bike south. As soon as I hit the highway,
I wound the poor bike's engine up to an unsafe speed. Dropping by Fannie's would not
be a pleasant experience, but I'd decided to confront her directly. That meant getting to
her hovel before she snuck out to feed after dark.

It was always weird heading out of the metro. You went from city to suburbs to exurbs,
and then—boom—there was a whole lot of nothing. The countryside undulated to either
side of the road. Just a few days prior, I'd been appreciating the view. My conversation with
Jay put the kibosh on that. Those swaying cornstalks? Alien arms reaching up from the
ground. Those tassels? Their grasping alien fingers. Those giant irrigation rigs stretching
over the fields? Stainless steel strands of enormous alien DNA. I shook my head to clear
out the crazy thoughts and caused the bike to fishtail a bit. Visceral reactions while doing
seventy on an old motorcycle were not allowed, so I switched off my brain and kept
heading toward Vermillion.

A state trooper passed me going the other direction, and I glanced down and swore.
Not at my speed. I was going fast by the bike's standards, but still within a comfortable
range of the speed limit. What elicited my curse was my gas gauge. It was feeling neglected.
If I didn't find a gas station soon, I'd have a long walk ahead of me.

Fortunately, an exit appeared over the next rise, along with signs for gas. I guided the
Guzzi off the main highway and wound my way to an open pump. Tank full, I decided

to pop inside for a bathroom break and a quick snack. Roadside gas stations had some of the best food in America. I'd be a fool not to take advantage. After putting the pump's nozzle back in its cradle, I headed inside and went straight for what I'd known would be there: a hotbox of steel rollers endlessly turning a collection of glistening hotdogs.

"You'd honestly eat one of those?" a voice asked in disbelief.

I turned to see who had decided I needed their opinion, but didn't spot them until I looked down. Looking up at me from his three-footish height was an old man with young eyes and a bright red beard. I immediately cursed my luck, which was funny in its way. Leprechauns were supposed to be lucky.

"I honestly would," I replied, "and I honestly will."

"You must be feeling brave," the leprechaun said with a wink.

"Better that than loquacious," I snarled, hoping to shut him up before things got worse.

Leprechauns were fine and all. I'd helped one or two in my day. They just got on my nerves. Always running their mouths. Always deedleydee'ing. Always kicking their little feet around like not doing a jig could be fatal. After a break-up, they were the worst. Imagine someone whining about losing the love of their life using only limericks.

There once was a lass from Dublin
Whose wayward ways were troublin'

Yeah, annoying.

"Loquacious. Ah, that's a big word, there, isn't it?" he remarked with a lopsided grin.

I nodded as I used some tongs to nab a dog and set it in a bun. "Almost as big as some of the mouths around here."

That got a good-natured laugh from the little man. He ambled off—thank Saint Patrick or whoever—and I immediately forgot about him. That is, I forgot about him until I went to pay. The cashier punched in the cost of a hotdog and pop, then told me the guy ahead of me had already paid.

"But not really," the woman added as she snapped on her chewing gum. "Because he only gave me this."

A golden coin appeared in her hand.

"We don't take gold," she explained, "so you still owe four eighty-seven."

I slid a five across the counter, and she slid the gold coin toward me. I gave her as suspicious a look as I could muster.

"Lady, that's a gold coin."

"No, it ain't," she replied with an emphysemic laugh.

I picked it up, and my fingers confirmed what she'd said. It was plastic. Cheap, painted plastic.

"Them leprechauns," she continued with another wheezy laugh. "Always with their tricks. Ain't they just adorable?"

"No," I replied, then headed for my bike while slipping my change and a worthless plastic coin into my pocket. "No, they are not."

Too soon, I was maneuvering down the narrow stretch of road that would first pass Dagmara's farmhouse, then branch onto a dirt road that led to Elouise' and Fannie's place, and, finally, the goblin's hovel. That brief stretch of old country road had caused me a lot of hassle. With a grimace, I resolved to never leave the cities again. Old country roads—no matter how scenic—were nothing but trouble. After making the turn to Elouise's and Fannie's, I slowed down to manage its bumps and ruts, and finally let the bike roll to a stop. The mid-evening's low sun silhouetted Fannie's shed. It looked exactly as foreboding as a vacant old building occupied by a life-force sucking hag should. My boots crunched over the mostly dead weeds that served as a front yard, and then I was at her door.

"What are you doing here?" the hag asked suspiciously through the narrow crack she'd opened after I'd knocked. Her eyes flicked over my shoulder. "You're lucky my sister is away. If she'd seen you walking up, pretty as you please, she would'a sucked you dry."

"Probably," I agreed with a nod.

"Is that why you're wearing that stupid helmet?"

I tapped the side of my half-shell and offered what I hoped was a charming, lopsided smile.

"No, this is for you. Because you aren't going to like what I have to say, and your sister might not be the only one with a frying pan."

The hag ushered me in with an unsure chuckle. I looked around the shed and felt a twinge of sympathy. Gaps showed between the boards, and light filtered down from holes in the roof. It was a dank and drafty place.

This is where she lives, I realized. *No wonder Fannie isn't in charge of interior decorating.*

The hag tottered to a three-legged stool and settled onto it like a fussy hen. Her foot shot out and kicked an overturned apple cart. Invitation clear, I set it on its side and sat across from her.

"Well," she snapped. "What are you here for, you stupid shifter?"

I took a deep breath, then said as calmly as I could, "I need the spoon."

"Why?" the hag asked without emotion.

A mental image of Blunder's punchy chair popped into my mind.

"It's complicated. Well, it's actually not. Your sister's partnered up with a nasty piece of work named Blunder. He's a coblyn, and a loan shark, and a bully. I guess he's been fronting her the cash for the B&B."

I studied Fannie's face as she took in what I'd told her. When she didn't react, I realized that she'd known all along.

"Huh. Okay, then," I muttered. "Well, this next part makes no sense. None at all, but it is what it is. Blunder wants that spoon for the B&B. I've got no clue why, and I honestly don't care. Either I get it for him, or I'm dead. I know you like your spoon and all, but I don't want to be dead."

She twisted in her chair, and I leapt out of mine.

"Wussy," she spat, then waddled back to the doors. After pushing one open, she looked across the unkempt lawn at the house she'd shared with her sister.

"Blunder," I heard her whisper. "Oh, yes. Yes, indeed. There's been a blunder. There's been a great many blunders."

The hag waddled back to me, arthritic hands patting and pulling at her housecoat's many pockets along the way. When she reached her stool, she found what she'd been looking for and held it up.

"Here she is," Fannie said softly. "Sorry, dear. Didn't want you to be easily found."

"You're talking to a spoon," I said carefully.

"And now I'm talking to a damned idiot," came the hag's tart reply as she glared at me. "Does that contraption you ride fit two?"

I blinked. "Yes... Why? Where are we going?"

"To Grey Cloud. We're putting an end to all of this."

The honks and friendly waves we elicited as we motored up Northfield Avenue toward Highway Sixty-One were perplexing. I couldn't help but think of Fannie as what she was: a scary old hag. To the outside observer, though, seeing a guy taking his grandma for a toodle in his motorcycle's sidecar must've been quite the spectacle. With each honk and wave, I grit my teeth a little tighter. Fannie, though, was delighted. I guess it was nice that one of us was having a good time.

Our route took us up through Hastings, a small town north and east of Vermillion that teetered on the edge of Minnesota's border with Wisconsin. After crossing the Mississippi, Fannie waved me on to Highway Ten and kept us heading north. A short while later, I hung a U-turn and headed south, parallel to the wide river to our right. A glimpse of a sign informed me we'd turned on to Third Street. Not long after, Third turned into Grey Cloud Island Drive, and I finally realized what the suits and the Strach na wróble had been talking about. Grey Cloud was a place. A muddy arm of the river had carved out a small island connected to the mainland by a short bridge on its northern tip. As I slowed my bike, I turned my head and took in the surroundings.

The first thing that hit me was the smell. Having come through farm country and the residential streets of small-town Minnesota, the smell of soot, diesel smoke, and rotten eggs caught me by surprise.

"What is that?" I complained over the bike engine's rumble.

"Gravel quarry," Fannie yelled back. "Used to be they mined limestone here. They used half the island for mining. When the wind is right, it mingles with the oil refineries a few miles off. Lovely, isn't it?"

I risked a sideways glance to see if she had been kidding. She hadn't. The hag had her head back and mouth open wide to savor each breath. Yeah, hags are pretty gross.

"So, where now?" I asked.

"Just keep driving, shifter. Cemetery's not far."

"Cemetery?"

"Cemetery. Now, shut up and hurry. My poor knees. This damned bucket on wheels has ruined them."

Our destination only took a few more minutes to reach. Tucked off the main road and hidden by wide trees, the little cemetery looked almost as old as Fannie. When I said as much, I expected a typical response of 'stupid shifter' or something to that effect. Her silence was equal parts unexpected and disturbing.

"So, we're going in there?" I asked, head tilting toward the plots, markers, and headstones.

"We are. Now, c'mon, shifter. If I can make it on these old knees, I'll not be hearing any complaints from you."

Dusk had stretched the trees' shadows and blended them into an unrelenting gray. I followed the old hag toward as she moved with purpose through the grave markers and then stopped.

"Here," she said with a downward jab of a bent finger. "Here."

"Here, what?" I asked.

She didn't reply, so I leaned down to see what she'd been pointing at. It was a grave marker. A roughly square slab of stone lying flat on the earth. I pushed a few stray leaves aside and read its engraving out loud.

"Baby Boy O'Brien. Born January Nine, 1873. Died January Nine, 1873. Parents: Henri and Guinevere Blanchet O'Brien. First known burial in cemetery."

I looked up at the hag and caught a single tear finding its way through the many creases on her cheek.

"What is this, Fannie?" I asked.

"Stupid shifter. I've had bowel movements with more sense than you. It's a baby's grave. A baby taken so soon, he didn't even have a name."

I squinted in the fading sunlight. "Okay. Sad story. Which has what, exactly, to do with anything?"

The hag pushed the back of a hand across her dampened cheek, then plunged that hand into a pocket of her voluminous housecoat. It emerged with the spoon.

"Here," she commanded, and thrust it in front of my face.

Confused, I took the spoon. For a moment, I held it in front of my eyes and studied its details. Its tarnished bowl. Its decorative handle. As things went, it was just a thing. Nothing special. Old, sure, and likely handmade. Beyond that, I couldn't fathom why such a trivial thing had driven such a wedge between two sisters. Unless...

"Fannie. Was that your baby?" I asked, shocked.

"Stupid shifter. Shut up. Open your ears. Open your eyes. And if you got one in that wussy chest of yours, open your heart."

I bit back an impulsive retort and humored the old lady. I looked again at the spoon. Really looked and, at the same time, listened.

"I don't..." I started, and then I did.

At first, I thought Fannie had let out a soft sob. It hadn't come from her, though. It had come from further away. I turned my head first left, then right. No sooner had I looked to the right than something caught the corner of my eye off to my left. I whipped my head back to see it, but whatever it had been, it was gone. Another sob sounded from behind me. I pivoted and again glimpsed something.

"Who's there?" I called out.

A woman's voice that wasn't Fannie's answered. Younger, much younger, but somehow so much older and infinitely sadder. Her words were a mystery, so laden with sorrow as to be incomprehensible.

"Who is that?" I asked in a whisper.

The hag sniffed. "Guinevere Blanchet O'Brien."

I looked again at the gravestone by my feet.

"The mother?"

"The mother," she confirmed. "Poor, poor woman."

I held the spoon a moment longer, but couldn't bear its sudden weight. Haunted objects are like that. Not that I'd been around many, but it only takes one or two before you learn to appreciate the difference. From that moment forward, I knew I'd never be able to touch that spoon and not hear the mournful wails, be split in two by the ache as raw a century and a half later as it had been in 1873. I grabbed the hag's hand and shoved the spoon against her lax palm, then squeezed her fingers around it.

"I don't want to see that thing again," I said, my voice quavering almost as much as the hag's shaking hand.

"Of course ya don't, ya wussy," she replied distractedly. "Who would? I told Elouise it wasn't right, using poor old Guinevere that way."

A puzzle piece slid into place. A dot connected to another dot. A domino tipped another domino. Fannie's words and my very recent experience made it all make sense.

"A haunted bed-and-breakfast. She wants to run a haunted B&B. People come from all over to see the ghost, spend the night, and you two get to eat to your heart's content. And the key to the whole thing is that spoon."

The hag nodded sadly. "She's most active when she's close to her boy. Her poor, poor child."

My mind was spinning. "Sure, and that makes it legit. The whispering. The moans and wails. A glimpse of the wandering woman. Textbook ghost story, but it's real. Word of mouth advertising explodes. The place is legit. Genuinely haunted. Reservations go through the roof. You're booked out for years." I rubbed my chin. "I gotta give it to Elouise. She's a work-smarter kinda lady, that's for sure."

It was easy to forget how damned fast the hag could be, to underestimate the unnatural strength hidden under her saggy flaps of skin. That said, I shouldn't have forgotten. She'd thrown me to the ground before. Small wonder she could do it again.

"Hey!" I cried after I got my breath back. "What the hell was that for?"

Fannie was seething. I'd never seen a truly pissed-off hag, and decided I never needed to see one again. She was terrifying in her fury.

"Don't you say that. Don't you ever say a single kind word about what she's doing. She's monstrous. She's cruel."

"She's a hag," I said, perplexed. "Sorry, lady, but that's kind of in the job description."

I added 'makes old ladies cry' to my list of less than desirable attributes. It was plenty long already, but there was always room for more.

"Geez," I offered as the hag's sniffles graduated to full-on sobs. "I didn't mean it like that. I mean, I guess I did, but not in a make-you-cry sort of way."

"Stupid shifter," she huffed, then succumbed to a fresh round of chest-heaving sobs.

I left her alone for a few minutes, unsure of what to say and—for once—wisely opting to say nothing. Eventually, the sobs diminished to sad little mewls and the waterfalls springing from each eye became trickles. She fished a cloth kerchief from a pocket and roughly blew her nose as the sun dipped below the trees. There were no lights in the graveyard, so the two of us stood in darkness. When a blurry luminescence appeared, it was so faint I thought it was a trick of my eyes. The amorphous glow took on first a shape, then a moment later features. She was across the graveyard from us, which meant her eyes were little more than shadows and her mouth was little more than a dark line. Even so, I could see the sadness.

"Guinevere?" I asked haltingly. "Guinevere O'Brien?"

"It's her," Fannie breathed. When she spoke again, her words weren't for me.

"I was different then. Different. Worse. Terrible. I shouldn't have done what I did, and it haunts me. Sure as you haunt your little boy's spoon."

I put a gentle hand on the hag's shoulder and guided her out of the cemetery. When we reached my old Moto Guzzi, I made a bench of its seat and crossed my ankles and arms.

"Spill it," I commanded. "You brought me out here. You made me see... that. What the hell is going on, Fannie?"

The words fell haltingly from her purple lips at first. Having been locked inside for so long, it was a wonder they could be set free at all. Once the first few had come out, though, the rest followed more easily. I kept my mouth shut and let her talk. Not that I could have said anything, anyway. By the time she reached the end of her tale, I was on the verge of sobs. I kept my jaw locked and my arms wrapped tightly around my chest, trying in vain to hold my broken heart together.

"The Civil War had ended," she began. "Me and Elouise had spent a good part of it in the Virginias, and it had been a fine time indeed. There's no sweeter nightmares than ones dreamt by exhausted soldiers. We was fed and full and fat as cows. Soon, though, those tent cities, those encampments, they came down. Those soldiers went home, some of their own volition, others in rough pine boxes. Too soon, it was getting harder and harder to feed. The cities were bustling, but too many folks were learning the wardings. The war had stirred things up, you see. Forced many a night dweller into the light. As our kin and kind grew bolder, the humans got wise. More and more, hag stones and horseshoes hung over their doors and beds. Pitchforks and torches were clutched in their hands. Feeding was hard and getting harder. Once fat and full, we got slight and slender. More nights than not, we supped on only our memories of better times and better meals. 'Twas time to move on, so we did.

Folks was heading west. Some to stick their toes in that far-off ocean. Many, though, went in search of nothing more than good, black dirt. Farming settlements were sprouting up from that dirt like the green shoots of their fresh-planted fields. The thing those farm towns all had in common was that life was hard. So darned hard. The farmer, he'd work the fields from dawn to dusk, then collapse into a fitful sleep. Worried dreams would plague him. Would there be rain? Would there be pestilence? Would there be blight? Would the sheep get the pox, or the cows get that Texas fever? The farmer's missus would bounce a babe on her knee, herd up the little 'uns running 'round and making a fuss. Her nights would fill her sleeping head with worries of cholera and scarlet fever.

Worries, they had, and with them those delicious nightmares. Common sense, though. That was lacking. You might have thought those folks working their way across the country to the Midwest would've brought at least a sprinkle of their elders' wisdom. Lucky for me and my sister, a good many did not. 'Twasn't a hag stone or horseshoe or other such nonsense on a one of 'em. We laughed and fed, fed and laughed. Stupid farmers had it coming."

The hag paused and looked up at the waking stars.

"After a time, we found our way to this here island. Grey Cloud, the humans called it, named after some European fella's Native mother-in-law. It was nice here. There was the limestone quarry and kiln up at the top to sweeten the air, and farm folk down below. The first families to truly put down roots were the Courteriors and the O'Briens, the Bourciers and the Blanchets."

Her voice hitched on that last name. I shifted quietly on my bike's saddle and waited.

"For me and Elouise, it was perfect. 'Tween the woods and river caves, there was plenty of places for two hags to hide. Them's that was mining the lime and working the kiln dreamt terrible dreams of explosions and cave-ins. And them's that was farming could dream of nothing but the inevitable end of their farms. The feeding was sweet and easy, as it should be."

"As it should be," I agreed sarcastically.

"You eat to live. Would you begrudge the likes of me and mine that very thing?"

She had a point. My conversation with Betty came to mind. Hags fed on nightmares. It was how they survived. Who was I to judge?

"So, what happened next?" I asked.

"That Guinevere Blanchet. Ginny, they called her," she said, suddenly remembering. "She married Henri O'Brien. They lived not far from here, where the first folk had built their bark huts and the newcomers had built their log homes. They were a happy pair, those two. So happy. Their nights were easy. Their slumbers, peaceful. No dark dreams for those two. Drove me half mad with hunger, it did. Time and again, I tried to feed. Time and again, I was left unslaked. Then she had the babe, and I was hungry. So hungry..."

According to Fannie, the night terrors of a newborn were too hard to resist. She'd tried to take but a taste, the smallest taste.

"And you sucked him dry," I finished through jaws locked with sadness and rigid with fury. "A newborn baby."

My heart kicked in my chest at the injustice. My fingers squeezed my arms, and my elbows pressed my sides so hard I was sure I was going to crack a rib.

"And the spoon?" I finally managed.

"The spoon," Fannie whispered. "'Twas a gift, as was customary then more so than now. A gift for the mother. That poor child's first bites of corn mash should'a been with that spoon. Fed to him by a loving mother's hand. Instead..."

The hag sighed a deep, anguished sigh.

"The poor woman was driven half-mad with grief. Oh, that Elouise, she was delighted. 'Come eat, sister,' she'd say. 'The nightmares are sweet as a newborn's tears. Eat!' But I could not. I would not. Not Ginny O'Brien, and no others for a long time. I near died of starvation. 'Twas a long winter, that winter of '73. Longer years followed. Was twenty-two more years before Guinevere herself died. That spoon, that little spoon, was with her every minute of 'em. Many was the night I looked on as Elouise fed. Many was the times I was tempted, but always that spoon was there. Always."

I shuddered at the imagined cold of winter in 1873. At the imagined grief a mother must have suffered. As I looked at Fannie with sudden insight, I realized she hadn't needed to imagine. She'd witnessed it firsthand and had carried that with her ever since.

"Guinevere died. Her possessions, including that spoon, was passed on," Fannie continued. "Eventually, folks stopped farming the island, so me and Elouise moved on. Farming town to farming town, but never too far. Something was keeping me here. All them years, something wouldn't let me leave these parts behind. Then there I was, just this spring past, antiquing."

That last word came out with a spit and a mirthless laugh.

"Oh, Elouise and her antiquing. As if the likes of us had any need of such things. But there we were, in a little shop in Hastings, passing as we can for human and looking at things that once were fine. There, among the riffraff sifted down through the years, was this spoon."

"And that's it? You did... what you did, and now that woman is trapped? Like, forever?"

Fannie's head was a shadow among shadows, but I saw it nod.

"I did what I did, and yes, shifter. For all I can tell, for all that I've tried, Guinevere O'Brien's spirit is bound to this spoon."

"And Elouise wants to use it as a prop in her haunted bed-and-breakfast," I spat.

"It's just past them trees, ya know," Fannie said with the half-hearted wave of an arm. "Nice and close to the cemetery, so Ginny's torment can be on display for all to see, every night."

I grabbed my helmet and strapped it to my head, then kicked the bike harder than needed. The engine gave a surprised bark before settling into its customary ill-content rumble. The headlamp cast its light across the cemetery, but to my eyes it was still draped in darkness.

"I don't know how, but we'll fix this," I promised as I pointed at the sidecar and Fannie clambered in. "I return things to their proper owner, and that baby boy needs his mother. But first, you're going to give me that damned spoon."

CHAPTER 14

"If the farmer is poor then so is the whole country."
- Polish Proverb

A MIX OF EMOTIONS too confusing to explain churned in my stomach and made me belch. I'd been standing on the edge of Dagmara's yard for ten, maybe fifteen minutes. After dropping Fannie off, I'd backtracked up the dirt road to the wraith's house. It hadn't given me nearly enough time to process all that I had I'd learned. I should've headed home, knocked back what was left in my current whiskey bottle, chased that with a good two or three beers, and passed the hell out. Maybe after a day or two, I'd find myself able to cope with the knowledge that there was a tormented spirit perpetually caught between two feuding hags. Maybe I'd know how to set things right. Hell, maybe I'd even know what to say to the woman that had snagged my unsuspecting heart, then run in the opposite direction when she'd last seen me. Tonight, though...

Nope, I thought. *I got nothing.*

Moving with a resolve I didn't feel, I crossed the uncut grass and climbed the porch steps.

"Hey, Dagmara," I practiced. "I was just in the neighborhood."

"Oh, hey. You're home. I was just passing by."

"Hi. Please don't run away again. We need to talk."

"Hey, Dags. What's up? We should probably talk, but want to get naked first? Ugh. I suck at this stuff."

I gave myself a good shake, paced back and forth across the porch, and stopped again in front of the door. My hand lifted to knock, and it opened.

"August."

"... Hi."

She had obviously settled in for the night. Gone were the short shorts and punky top, the fishnets and Doc Martens. In their place were those sweats and the oversized sweatshirt she'd let me wear the other night. On me, they'd looked silly. On her, they looked fantastic. I hadn't heard the music when the door had been closed. When it opened, the sound of drums and electric guitar filtered through from a far-off stereo. I recognized a ubiquitous 80s punk band and nodded approvingly.

"I liked those guys," I remarked.

"They were great live. Why are you here?"

My mind went blank. All the questions I wanted to ask, the things I wanted to say, were gone. Just gone. All I could come up with was—of course—something stupid.

"You never paid me."

She went very still. Every line of her radiated tension. I took a half step back to make sure the door wouldn't hit me in the face when she slammed it. My reaction was unnecessary, though. Rather than kick me to the proverbial curb, her shoulders slumped, and she opened the door wider. I stepped inside—no mean feat considering I was kicking myself at the same time—and followed her. This time, we didn't head to her living room, and we didn't follow my fantasies up to her bedroom. Instead, she took me to the kitchen.

"Tea?" she asked, lifting a kettle to the sink.

"Uh," I replied.

"Tea, it is."

The faucet ran. Then she twisted a knob on an old stove and set the kettle.

"I only have black tea. No honey."

"Okay."

Dagmara leaned against the counter, crossed her arms, and stared at something on the floor. I slid a chair back from the kitchen table and moved a few envelopes aside to make room for my elbows. I hadn't meant to look, but my eye caught the words 'past due' stamped on more than a few. While the kettle heated, she stared at nothing, and I tried to do the same. When the kettle's whistle did its thing, I was instantly envious. At least it could blow off some steam. Whatever was going on between me and Dagmara was still coming to a boil.

She dropped a couple of tea bags into mismatched mugs, poured the water, and set one in front of me. Hot water sloshed over the mug's lip and soaked the corner of one of the many unpaid bills.

"Christ," I swore as a few hot drops hit my hand. The burn touched off my temper, and I snapped, "I got your stupid doll back, and you throw boiling water at me."

"She's not a stupid doll!" Dagmara screamed as she slammed a fist on the table.

Thankfully, I'd thrown my hands up in surrender. It saved me from another scalding when more of my tea jumped out of its mug.

"Okay, okay. Geez. You're awfully touchy about something you turned around and sold the second you got it back," I said, then added petulantly, "and stiffed me in the process."

Her eyes flashed, and her lips pressed so tightly together that they disappeared. Had I thought the visit would go this way? No, but to be fair, I hadn't really thought about how the visit would go at all. I mean, I'd thought about it, but somehow all those thoughts had skipped all the messy stuff and gone straight to me and her and the naked stuff.

"I don't have the money," she practically screamed. "I don't have any money. Damn it. You're as bad as they are."

"Who? The bank?" I asked. "Or the Department of Agriculture?"

Something about those four words changed everything. Dagmara stumbled back and would've fallen had she not caught herself on the counter. I lept to my feet and ran to put an arm around her. The woman was trembling.

"You know?" she whispered. "How did you find out?"

"That the suit guy was a Department of Agriculture operative? Long story."

I gave her shoulder a light squeeze, and she pressed into me. Arms went around my waist, and her face pressed into my chest. Her back hitched a few times, but no sound came out. Whatever was inside of her, she seemed intent on keeping it locked in.

"It's an exciting story, too," I said gently. "You should definitely hear it sometime. I wore a funny hat and ran through a haunted house. The fake one at the Fair, not a real one. That's another story. Then I got into a fight in the Princess Kay of the Milky Way butter-sculpting room and got tranquilized."

"You really are bad at your job," she said, but at least I heard the hint of a smile behind it.

"Well, obviously. To go through all that and not get paid? Definitely not a sustainable business model."

I'd meant it as a joke, but no one ever liked my jokes. Her back stiffened, and she pushed herself away.

"I'm sorry, August. I didn't mean to get you involved. I had no idea you'd be at the Fair. Why were you there? You shouldn't have been there."

While I collected my thoughts, I went back to the table and my cooling tea. Absently, I collected her chaotic pile of past-due notices and unpaid bills, stacked them, and set them aside.

"You aren't wrong," I said with a resigned sigh. "But, them's the breaks. Why were you there, though? Why did you sell the corn dolly? These?" I asked with a wave at the stack of bills.

Dagmara took a sip of her tea and grimaced. Instead of answering me, she said, "Sorry. It's better with honey." Then, "Did you know that the word farmer used to mean 'to rent?'"

"Sure," I lied. "Everyone knows that."

"Uh huh," she replied while doing her eyebrow lifty thing. "It comes from the Anglo-French word 'fermer.' Long ago—like the Middle Ages long ago—people had to rent good land for a fixed amount. Nowadays, it's more common to pay a percentage of the crop. Anyway, that lump sum to use the land was called 'ferme.' Farm. The farmer wasn't the person tilling the soil, the one doing the actual work. The farmer was the person collecting the rent. Over the centuries, the meaning of the word farmer changed. Now, it means the person working the land, harvesting its bounty. Doesn't change the fact that it is hardly ever their land. The land always belongs to some rich asshole that couldn't tell the difference between a corn cob and his... you know."

My eyes crinkled as I smiled, and Dagmara softened a bit. Her lips crooked up at the corner, but that almost-smile didn't last.

"The fields have never belonged to the one with his hands in the dirt," she said. "The real farmer—that rent collector—has always held all the cards. That," she said with a disgusted wave at the pile of bills, "is just another day on the farm. Doing everything you can to have a good harvest, and knowing it won't be enough to pay all the bills because the bank, the agriculture conglomerates, just keep squeezing and squeezing and squeezing. And the Department of Agriculture," she added, practically spitting the words, "aren't just letting it happen. They're making it worse."

That anger gave way to a new emotion, and the lines of her face changed. The tension in her jaw became a nervous chewing of her lower lip. Eyes that had bored into mine a moment before looked away.

"I can't pay, August. I'm sorry. I really am, but there's no blood left in this turnip. How did you say it? 'Them's the breaks?' Well, there you go. Thanks for stopping by."

I muttered a curse and tried to salvage the wreck I'd made.

"I didn't come here for money. I don't care about that, and I don't know why I said it. I'm an asshole. Just, you know. Ignore me, I guess."

"So, why did you come here?"

"You," I said honestly. "And me. And, I don't know. Us."

"Us," she said quietly.

That one syllable spoke volumes, but the tale those volumes told was actually pretty short. There wasn't an 'us.'

"If you knew me. Really knew me," she said apologetically.

Yeah, yeah, I thought. *It's not you. It's me. Heard that one before.*

My mind drifted back to my conversation with Ted. He'd talked about yesterday and tomorrow and today. When it came to relationships, all my yesterdays were the same. Every time I met someone and started to think about tomorrow, those tomorrows became todays. And days like today sucked. Maybe it was her. More likely, it was me. Whatever it was, it sucked.

"Um. Since we're on the subject. What are you, anyway?" I asked. If I was getting dumped before even getting a real date, I figured asking couldn't make things any worse.

Her eyes widened. "You know what I am."

I shrugged and shook my head. "No. Maybe. I might've heard something, but I don't. I didn't. Uh..."

"Seriously?" she asked. "Then this is definitely not going to work. I thought maybe. I mean, I thought you knew and still wanted to be with me. Which was crazy, but it's been so long. Oh, shit..." she trailed off. "You really don't know?"

I hunched my shoulders and ducked my head.

"Are you a demon?" I asked, then flinched.

When nothing hit me, I cracked open one eye, then the other. I didn't appear to be in imminent danger, but Dagmara's face had gone very still.

"The strachy-thing. Your ex. He told me," I explained. "Said you were a Cornflower Wraith. A noon demon."

"You spoke with the Strach na wróble?"

I shrugged. "Yeah, a little. He sort of saved me from those Department of Agriculture douche-nozzles, and we talked a bit after. He was trying to get that corn doll back."

"Oh, for the love of... It's a dolly, August. A dolly."

"Right. So the strachy-thing,"

"Strach na wróble."

"Right. He was trying to get it back, I guess. He knows you sold it, you know. Said it's okay. That he understands. I guess he knew about this?" I finished with a tap on the bills.

Dagmara nodded, and her gaze turned inward.

"The Strach na wróble knows," she finally said. "He and I are not that different. We've both lived in the fields for a long time. A very long time. I told you I was from Poland. Before I came to this country, I was working for a farmer there. He came here in search of a better life. The Strach na wróble and I followed. Our farmer passed not so long ago, and his children had no interest in the fields. I have tried to keep his dream alive. It hasn't been easy. The world our farmer lived in is gone. He and others like him worked the fields because they loved the green and growing things and the life those things provided. The banks could care less about that. They want maximum yield. They want the profit. I understand that. I don't like it, but I understand it. The Strach na wróble, though, is stuck in the past. Stupid old fool."

"Yeah. Okay, but back to the other stuff," I asked, switching gears to the more pressing question in my mind. "The part about you being a demon..."

"A noon demon."

"The time of day matters?"

She laughed bitterly. "Maybe not. Honestly, none of it matters. Not anymore. We can't change who we are, though, and this is who I am," she said as she placed a palm on her breast and tapped at where her tattoo's blue flowers peeked over her collar. "A Cornflower Wraith. When field hands are careless or lazy, I punish them. Set them straight. Make sure they respect the field and its crops. At least, I used to. It's mostly just one guy with a combine now, and he doesn't take much watching. I'm the product of an earlier time. The Strach na wróble, too. There was a time when every farmer wished the Strach na wróble would visit their field. A scarecrow on a stick was an invitation, an entreaty, practically a prayer. Now, they use lasers and sonic emitters. Scarecrows are nothing more than arts and crafts projects for bored farm kids." A long sigh escaped her lips. "We were unliked, unloved, but at least we were relevant. Vital to the farmer's success. No longer, though. Now, we're unliked, unloved, and unnecessary. Just relics."

"And when you say 'relic,' exactly how relicy are we talking about, here?"

Dagmara gave me that look. The one I tended to get every time I talked to a member of the opposite sex.

"Rude much?" she said. "But if you must know... Oh, wow. I'm not sure I know. Hang on."

Her eyes rolled up, her lips worked silently, and she folded the fingers of first one hand, then the other down. She shook her head a couple of times and restarted her count, then finally said, "Fifteen."

"Wait, what?" I asked with a rising panic. "You're only fifteen years old?"

"Hundred. Fifteen hundred years old, give or take. When I said I was from Poland, I probably should have been more specific. I was old long before the Kingdom of Poland was founded early in the 11th century. I came over here from Poland in the late 1970s."

That panic that had jumped into my throat did a U-turn and plummeted into my gut.

"See?" she said. "You'd be better off with someone closer to your own age. Like Fannie."

"Oh, you had to go there, huh?" I griped. "Couldn't just let it be. You had to go there."

A quiet settled between us. I tried to rearrange my thoughts and feelings, but wasn't having much luck. I kept getting stuck on the whole fifteen-hundred years old thing.

"Cougar doesn't even come close to covering that," I muttered.

And there goes that eyebrow of hers again, I thought.

"So, what now?" I finally asked when she stopped glowering at me.

Dagmara sighed. "You go your way. I go mine and use the money from the corn dolly to pay as many of these bills as I can."

Her words awoke an itch I'd forgotten about.

"Why did the suits want the corn dolly, anyway? Why pay so much for one?"

Dagmara looked off to the side.

"I don't know. They never told me."

There wasn't much to say after that. I made my farewells. She apologized again for not being able to pay me. I told her to forget about it. She said she wouldn't, that she'd always appreciate how I'd helped. We fell into an awkward silence. Finally, I turned and left.

The drive back to Minneapolis was a lonely one, and not because I was the only one on the highway. First Jay had lied to me, and then Dagmara. And she'd lied to me after not paying me and dumping me. So, yeah. I was feeling a bit lonely.

And if we're being honest, a bit pissed.

But mostly, just lonely.

CHAPTER 15

"The farmer is the only man in our economy who buys everything at retail, sells everything at wholesale, and pays the freight both ways."
- John F. Kennedy

"WHAT?" I SNAPPED INTO my phone's receiver.

"Soon, August Shade. Soon."

"Fucking knock it off!"

I slammed the phone down hard and caught my finger between the receiver and its cradle. After another barrage of the worst words I knew, I grabbed the phone, yanked its cord from the wall, and threw the whole damned thing through my office door.

"Whoah," Jay blurted. "Careful. They definitely don't make that model anymore."

I glared at where the telephone hovered above the floor. It turned slowly, like it was sitting on an invisible record player, and an errant breeze ruffled papers on my desk.

"Not helping," I complained.

The artist's head poked through my door.

"Sorry. Here," he said as he lifted the phone free of its little pillar of air. "You caught me off guard, is all. Scared me. That was just a reflex. Won't happen again."

Jay's tee-shirt added to my angst. Unlike others in his wardrobe, it didn't have a pithy conspiracy quip. Instead, it had a picture of a Tarot card. Specifically the card for The Magician. I took a deep breath and pinched the bridge of my nose. After holding it for a few seconds, I exhaled and tried to shed a few blood pressure points.

"I'm sorry, too. It's that damned prank caller. That was the third call today."

It didn't help that I was rocking one hell of a hangover. After getting home from Dagmara's the prior night, I'd intended to have a shot of whiskey and a couple of beers. That was it. Unfortunately, that one shot had become many, and those couple of beers had become six, maybe seven. I'd woken up with my head in one of the kitchen cupboards, nestled between a dented saucepan and an old—and thankfully, empty—mousetrap.

"And I'm not exactly in top form," I admitted.

Jay leaned a shoulder against the door frame. "You don't say..." he quipped. "Would some hair of the dog help?"

A half can of pilsner later, I felt better. Not much, but I took what I could get and called it a win.

"So," my friend asked. "You plan on telling me why you have a nine on the hangover scale?"

"Only if you swear that nothing else will float around your studio on magic air while I'm here."

We shook on it, and I caught him up on the prior day. At the end of Fannie's tale, he was visibly shaken. At the end of Dagmara's tale, the big softy was teary-eyed. He'd untied the handkerchief that had held up his dreads and was using it to blow his nose.

"Please don't put that back in your hair," I implored. "So, yeah. Rough couple of days. Not likely to get better, either," I complained. "I need to get that spoon to Blunder today."

Jay gasped.

"To Blunder? You said you told Fannie you were going to fix things. Free that poor woman. Why would you give the spoon to Blunder?"

"Because I have to. Look, I want to help, and I will, but later. Not today. Today, I make sure that damned coblyn bastard gets off my back. That's enough for one day, thank you very much."

I lifted my jacket off the chair's back and followed Jay into his studio.

"What about you? Busy day ahead?" I asked.

"I guess," he shrugged. "Might paint a little. Remember the old Cream of Wheat tin signs from the 1930s? I was thinking of doing some variations with little squid babies sucking down the oatmeal instead of little human kids. What do you think? August? August?"

I'd meant to listen. I really had. Then I'd glanced at a stack of newspaper Jay kept on hand for catching drips and wiping brushes. The top of the pile was the week's *Metro Pages*, the local free paper. I looked at its front page, and my face looked back.

"Oh, shit. Yeah. I was going to tell you that," Jay apologized. "You're more than trending now. You're on the front page of the newspaper."

"I see that."

"But they don't actually accuse you of anything. Not really. The story should be about my seed art. About the aliens. But you can't trust the media. If they aren't changing the story for the own ends, they're getting censored by the shadow government. Happens all the time."

I'd lifted the paper from the pile's top and was reading the article. Jay had been right. It wasn't about me per se, nor was it about aliens. It was an article about the declining state of mental health in the Twin Cities Metro, and the rise of paranoid and delusional disorders. I was simply the face of the problem, loosely and clumsily associated with the sabotaging of the State Fair's crop art contest. People like me, the article explained, might look perfectly normal but could be afflicted with deep-rooted mental trauma. I growled at that part, but grudgingly approved of the next bit. The general advice the article offered was to give people like me a wide berth.

Works for me, I thought.

I finished skimming the article, then frowned.

"There's nothing about the butter fight."

"Yeah, I noticed that, too," Jay said. "There are videos online, but none have many likes or shares. See? You ruined a Fair tradition that's been going on for half a century, and there's no mention of it. Squashed like a genetically modified squash. At least a few butter fight videos should have gone viral, but did they? Nope. I dropped the truth-bomb of the century, and I didn't even get a mention. It said the authorities are looking for a Shannon Jakowski, whoever that is."

"I hate to say it, but she's proof you and your conspiracies might be onto something. If she's mentioned, then those goons that tranquilized me in the cattle barn are definitely behind this article. I fed them that bogus name."

The artist's eyes widened in surprise, then crinkled in appreciation.

"Nice. Jakowski. I like it. I'll bet there isn't a Jakowski in the world with this complexion," he said with a tap on his cheek. "And yeah. You've got to be right. The Ag Ops are definitely behind this."

"I don't get it," I admitted. "Not that I want to be in the know—I don't—but c'mon. Someone broke into the Fair. Sabotaged the crop art contest. A bunch of perfectly good butter that had already been wasted was completely ruined. There isn't any of that here. Only a fluffy, 'Watch out! This guy's crazy!' story."

The artist rolled his eyes. "Classic misdirection. Now it's a mental health story. Just another crazy doing crazy things. Sorry. No offense. But if the story is about some crazy guy, then it's not about strange guys in suits making deals with Midwestern farmers or aliens changing our DNA. Like I said, it's classic misdirection," he finished with a dismissive wave of a hand. "Oh, and I think we both know those guys in the suits weren't actually guys. Or humans. Or anything from this planet."

"Do we?" I asked, all innocence.

"Don't get me started."

Unfortunately, I already had. I let Jay go on about ancient aliens, and modern aliens, and alien plots, and alien schemes. I won't lie. He was convincing. How the guy found time to do his research, I don't know. Research he had, though. As he talked, he referenced this group and that site. This person and that blog. Government reports and corporate press releases and countless clues. To quote his favorite show, the truth was out there. According to Jay, that truth was often right in front of our noses. You just had to know what to look for.

"Okay, sure," I agreed. "I'll be better about that, I promise. I'll definitely pay more attention. Right now, though? I really need to get that spoon back to Blunder, and it's a quarter past time-to-go-and-do-that o'clock."

Jay rolled his eyes. "I still can't believe you're going to give it to him, but yeah. I get it. One problem at a time, right? I can't take down the illuminati and the Bilderbergs and the rest of the cryptocracy all at once. Gotta choose my battles."

"Uh, sure. Yeah. Like that. You going to be okay while I'm gone?" I asked. "No elemental stuff, no dark arts, right? Just you and some paint fumes to huff?"

Jay assured me I had nothing to worry about and waved me toward the door. It didn't take much prompting to send me on my way. I wasn't looking forward to seeing Blunder, but was more than ready to get the whole damned spoon ordeal over with.

Until you figure out how to fix it, I reminded myself.

Right, I agreed in what I hoped was a convincing way. *Totally.*

The coblyn had told me to bring the spoon to the railyard warehouse. The bike's engine had barely enough time to warm up before its tires were crunching across a gravel lot, bumping over railroad ties, and maneuvering its way to my destination. After parking out front, I pushed inside the warehouse, squeamishly avoided looking at the chair and its swinging arms, and headed for where a phone hung on the wall. It was from the same era as my office phone, which is a long way of saying it was old.

As I lifted the receiver and twirled its spiral cord on a finger, it occurred to me that Blunder hadn't given me a number.

"Well, shitski," I muttered.

A tinny voice said something back, so I pressed the receiver to my ear.

"What? Who's this?" I asked.

"Will Schichtsky isn't available," a crunchy voice replied. "Would you like to leave a message?"

I laughed a surprised laugh and asked if there really was a Will Schichtsky working there.

"I don't understand what's so funny, sir," the voice replied. "You asked for Mr. Schichtsky. He isn't in. Would you like to leave a message?"

Why that made me laugh even harder, I couldn't say, but I did. Only when the operator threatened to hang up did I ask if I could talk to Blunder instead.

"Full name?" the voice asked.

Crap.

"Hang on a sec. I need to find all of my Scrabble letters."

I thought that was funny. Again, I was alone in my assessment.

"Tordundanragnorfolsteck. Mastiwallerick. Blundergibalfronalbesk," I recited with a mental back pat. Remembering all of that was tough.

"Thank you. Please take a seat. He will be there soon."

"But there's only one..." I tried, but the line had disconnected. "Seat."

The last time I'd used that chair, I'd left with a split lip and a bruised kidney. Small wonder I was standing when Blunder arrived with one of his henchies. I think it was Lefty.

"August!" the coblyn said with a wide smile. "So good to see you again."

There was no reason to return the pleasantry. I wanted to keep the visit as short as the reason I was there. My hand grasped the spoon's handle, held it out above Blunder's waiting palm, and let it drop.

"Excellent," the cob replied. "Now we can finally get on with the testing."

"Testing?" I asked, then I yelped at a sudden and sharp jab in my butt cheek.

The world doubled and spun. My mouth filled with cotton, and my fingers went numb. As I fell to my knees and then slumped over on my side, I saw Righty grinning vindictively.

"You're a pain in the ass," I managed.

Three bearded and gloating little faces peered down at mine. Lefty gave Righty a high-five, Blunder offered me a wink, and then all was dark.

I came to on a wooden floor. My head hurt a lot. My ass cheek hurt worse. I found myself missing the tranquilizer the suits had used. Theirs had been a fuzzy, floaty dream. Whatever the cobs had used was more akin to a hangover in a syringe. Added to the hangover I already had, it made for a rude awakening.

"Where...?" I managed.

"You are right where you need to be, shifter," Elouise said in what she probably thought was a bright and cheery tone. "You are going to be our first guest. Well, my first guest, anyway. That Fannie, she'll come around, though. Just you wait."

I looked at her stupidly.

"Guest?" I asked.

"Of course," the hag cackled. "Everything has to be in order before we commence with reservations. Oh, this house is a wonder. That it is. Mr. Blunder and his crew have done a fine job."

Blunder built a house? I wondered idly.

That didn't track. Coblynau were miners first, contraptionists second. But carpenters? As my brain drifted on the drug's fading currents, I tried to imagine what a house built by coblynau would look like. All I could come up with is something that didn't look anything like a house.

"And I'm expecting a substantial return on my investment," the cob's voice proclaimed a moment before he stepped into the room.

Blunder dragged an ottoman over, set it in front of me, and hopped up. Once perched, he pulled his little pipe from one pocket, a box of matches from another, and put the two to good use. Elouise protested, saying the property was non-smoking, and that smoke was simply impossible to get out of the throw pillows. Her concerns met one look from the cob and became petulant mumbles, then nothing more than a sour pursing of her lips. Satisfied she didn't have anything more to say on the matter of his pipe or her throw pillows, he turned back to me.

"Enjoy your stay, Mr. Shade," he said brightly after a few puffs. "Explore. No room is off limits. You can go anywhere you want, so long as you stay inside the house. Try to leave—as a human or anything else—and, well..."

He let the warning hang unspoken between us like the clouds of pipe smoke. Whatever they'd drugged me with was making it hard to concentrate. I felt like I got the important part, though. I wasn't supposed to leave.

"You bet, little fella," I said groggily, then gave a hearty thumbs up. At least, I wanted it to be hearty. As my blurry eyes watched my arm make lazy figure eights in the air, I decided it didn't quite meet the definition of hearty. Woozy, though. It was definitely woozy.

A small hand struck my cheek with surprising force. "Snap out of it, shifter."

"Whaaa?" I cried. "How are you so small and so strong at the same time?"

Blunder laughed and headed for the door. On the way, he waggled his glowing pipe at the old hag.

"We've done our part. You make sure that the spoon lady does hers. You hear?"

Elouise wrung her hands. "Oh, absolutely, Mr. Blunder. You have nothing to worry about. Not a thing," she groveled.

Seeing the terrifying hag behaving like a boot-licking sycophant to a coblyn that was a third her size seemed like it should've been funny, so I laughed.

"Go on and lick those itty bitty boots," I said with a giggle, but stopped when that giggle turned into a disoriented, "Whoaaah boy."

I placed a palm on the floor to steady myself and took a slow breath. When the competing urges to pass out and throw up had both resolved to take a number and wait a bit, I looked up at Elouise.

"What?" I asked in response to her glare. "You sucking on Blunder's little toes is funny."

The hag raised a hand threateningly, then let it drop.

"Eh. What's the point of knocking you around again? It obviously won't do a thing to knock some common sense loose. You just have a nice evening, August Shade. A fine evening, indeed. One that is full of sweet, sweet dreams."

With that proclamation, the hag smiled a horrible smile, then turned her back and left.

After taking a slow assessment of my body, I decided it could probably stand. I was wrong. I did manage to get up onto a divan that sat below a large window, though, and congratulated myself on that accomplishment. While the fog between my ears dissipated, I surveyed my surroundings.

With a start, I realized exactly where I was: Elouise's bed-and-breakfast. There was the small concierge desk from the illustrations, complete with an open guest book, the old-fashioned key cubbies, and the corresponding keys. Just past it was the wide staircase leading up to the second story. Memory of the pages I'd flipped through on the hag's kitchen table filled in the rest of the floor plan. The hallway past the desk would lead to the main floor bedrooms. The archway near the stairs opened to a modest but tasteful dining room, where the guests would get the second 'B' of their stay. Up the stairs, there'd be a hallway that led to three bedrooms: a suite overlooking the house's front yard, and two overlooking its back. I pivoted to look out the living room window and confirmed what Fannie had told me. The house faced the cemetery. There were a few trees marring the view, but they were decorative and spaced enough to show a glimpse of the headstones. The hag had been right. If the ghost of Guinevere O'Brien was riled up enough, she'd be plenty easy to see from any of the windows on that side of the house. Hell, night was fast approaching. If I waited, I'd be able to see the ghost myself.

"Ooooh," I said with dawning understanding.

Blunder had talked about tests, and Elouise called me her first guest. I was testing the house, whatever that meant.

And after that? a highly suspicious part of my brain asked.

You'll go home, an obliviously idiotic part of my brain replied.

I liked the idiot part of my brain's optimism. I was tired, so tired. Would it be so bad to grab a room key, find a bed, and call it a night? Come morning, I'd tell Elouise that her house had worked like a house.

Sure. In the morning.

I considered the hag's parting smile. I'd thought of it as horrible, but that wasn't quite right. It was hungry. This wasn't just a haunted house. It was a haunted dinner platter, and I was the main course. Sleep was out of the question. Unfortunately, Blunder's warning meant that so was escaping.

"Welp, guess I'm exploring," I decided.

With nothing better to do, it made for a fine decision. If nothing else, it would keep the terror of my situation at bay.

The kitchen was first. My stomach was letting me know I'd neglected it, and that I was a right bastard for doing so. Unfortunately, Fannie hadn't been being facetious when she'd said Elouise planned to serve dry toast. The pantry was empty. Aside from a few plates and coffee mugs, the cupboards were bare. She hadn't even plugged in the fridge. There was a large bread box. Inside, there was a loaf of cheap bread. I snorted a laugh.

"Nice place. Comfy divan in the living room. Saw a real ghost. Had some of my life force sucked out, and got white bread for breakfast. Two stars."

I grabbed a slice of bread and took slow bites as I drifted from the kitchen to the dining room, the dining room back to the front sitting room, and from there to the hallway. The rooms were unlocked, so it was easy enough to crack their doors and give each a quick look-see. My wealth of interior design experience informed me they each looked like a bedroom, and that both were much nicer than my own.

After leaning through the second room's door and craning my neck a bit, I stepped back into the hallway and pulled the room's door shut. A few steps later, I heard the click of a door latch and the soft creak of hinges. With a quick backtrack, I grabbed the door's knob again, pulled it firmly shut, and continued down the hallway until a click-creak brought me to a stop again. When I turned back, that damned bedroom door had opened again. In addition, there was a soft light spilling into the hallway.

"The hell?" I wondered.

The room had been empty. I was sure of it. At that point, my curiosity was dialed up a lot higher than my common sense, so I headed back up the hallway and poked my head past the open jamb. I hadn't noticed it on my first quick inspection, but the bedside table had a decorative oil lamp, and someone—or something—had lit it. The small flame illuminated the frosted glass shade and chimney from within and bathed the room in a faint, flickering light. I let my wide eyes roam the space, noticing more of the details. Sharing a workspace with an artist might not have imbued me with any creativity of my own, but it gave me the vocabulary to describe someone else's. And though it pained me to say it, Elouise was an artful decorator.

The wallpaper was mossy green with a pattern of yellow birds on slender branches. The bedspread was rust-colored velvet with ochre pillows. Two arm chairs, one a subdued brown leather, the other covered in a fabric floral print, framed a decorative table preset with hard-covered books on bird watching and—I had to step further in the room to see—topiary. There was a low, wide wooden dresser. A large, ornate mirror and framed needlepoints adorned its top. The room was charming. It was cozy.

It was decorated by a hag, I reminded myself.

Yeah, sure, but the lady's got taste, I pushed back.

A taste for human nightmares, I pointed out.

It was a study in contradictions, to be sure. Elouise had all the charm of a heat rash and the culinary chops of a gulag jailer. When it came to interior decorating, though, the old hag was a natural. So surprised was I by this realization that I didn't notice the reflection in the room's mirror. Well, not at first. When I did, though...

I'd just finished a slow circuit of the room. I'd pinched the bedspread fabric between my fingers and fluffed the decorative pillows. The armchairs had beckoned, so I tried them out. Both were decadently comfortable, but I preferred the leather one over its fabric companion. I'd opened a few dresser drawers and found additional blankets neatly folded inside one and an extra pillow in another. Everything felt like it was quality. Genuine quality, too. Not mass-produced. Handmade. High end. Even the needlepoints displayed on the dresser looked expensive. The frames were real wood and clearly hand-carved. No cheap plastic imitations, here. Nothing but the real deal for every detail.

"What did all this cost?" I wondered. "How much did Blunder have to put up?"

It was a mystery. Not a very interesting one, granted. Certainly not as interesting as the mirror on the dresser. That was interesting because I wasn't the only one in its reflection. There was someone else standing behind me.

"The fuck?" I swore as I spun around.

Despite what my eyes had clearly seen in the glass, there was no one else in the room. I shared that news with my pounding heart and suggested that it calm down a bit before it killed us both. It had just agreed when the room's door decided it was finally time to close.

It didn't slam shut, nothing that dramatic. Instead, it swung slowly on creaky hinges until it was good and firmly closed.

"Okay, weird," I decided.

Here's the thing about me and ghosts: I know next to nothing about them, aside from what I've seen in movies and read in books. If we're being honest, the night before in the Grey Cloud Cemetery had been my first and only experience with the beyond. That meant I couldn't say one way or the other if ghosts were a health hazard or not. When I'd seen Guinevere O'Brien wandering the cemetery the night before, it had been eerie and sad, but not frightening. Nothing about the woman had made me think I was in danger. No vengeful spirit shenanigans. No poltergeist tantrums. Just a heartbroken woman in a dress. That said, she might've been the exception that proves the rule. Maybe ghosts were something to worry about. The more I thought about it, the more it made sense. You died, but your spirit didn't move on? I'd be pissed if that were my fate. Maybe pissed enough to take out my angsty rage on complete strangers. Like irritable shapeshifters.

"Knock it off, August," I complained. "There's one ghost. Just one, and she's out there somewhere. She's not in here messing with the doors and lamps."

And that wasn't Guinevere in the mirror.

Did ghosts congregate? Were they suckers for peer pressure, like pigeons on a power line? I didn't know and cursed my lack of knowledge. If I survived the night, I planned to study up a bit on the beyond. If I didn't survive the night...

I guess I'll know firsthand, I decided. If I died, I fully intended to haunt the living shit out of Elouise for the rest of her haggy days.

"You hear that, Elouise?" I called out, embarrassed at the quaver in my voice. "If I die here, I'm gonna haunt the shit out of you."

I paused for a minute to see if the hag was still hanging around and in a mood to respond. Either she wasn't or she wasn't, because nothing answered me but a chilling quiet. Well, that and a soft moan. So soft that I might've imagined it. It had come from upstairs, and whoever had made the sound had not been Genevieve McCoy, unless she had sung baritone in the old church choir.

"Okay. Fuck this," I decided, Blunder's warning be damned.

Deliberate steps carried me up the hallway and to the front of the house. The door had a cut glass knob. I wrapped my fingers around it, turned, and pulled. It opened a foot, then two, then the knob was ripped from my hand as it slammed shut.

"The fuck?" I swore again as I jumped back.

I glared at the door, then glared around the door, too. For good measure, I glared behind me at the empty front desk, glared around the living room, glared at the stairs going up, and glared down the hallway going back. I glared into the dining room. I glared at all the parts of the house I couldn't see.

"That's enough!" I declared with one more glare. "No more. No self-lighting lamps. No spooky reflections. And enough with the doors that don't do what doors should do."

I gave a satisfied nod, opened the door, and swore once again as an invisible force slammed it shut a second time. I took a careful step backward. Elouise and Blunder had wanted me to test out their haunted house. So far, the house was acing it.

The front door was obviously not an option, so I returned to the living room's divan. For a little while, I looked out the front window and regretted all of my life choices. While self pity sloshed around my insides, my eyes wandered. Up the deep folds of drawn velvet curtains to the ceiling's elaborate crown molding. Along the intricate and repeating pattern of the quatrefoil wallpaper that stretched beneath its length. Down the wall beyond the window's far edge. I paused to study a still life painting of posies in a vase. My mood made them appear wilted. Listlessly, my eyes retraced their journey to the window's other side and the expanse of wall that held the front door. Centered between that door and the window was a small, simple display case. In the room's dim light and set against the dark patterns of the wallpaper, it was easy to overlook. Roughly the size of a shoebox, its sides were deeply stained wood and its front was a single pane of glass. Inside hung a single item: the spoon.

Something flickered in the corner of my eye, and I looked at the world beyond the window. There was poor Guinevere, pacing the cemetery's plots. Like me, she seemed trapped, and like me, she was restless. I moaned a long and frustrated moan, imagined the ghostly woman in the distance echoing my sentiments, then jumped when that damned thing upstairs added its own lament.

"Geezus," I complained over my pounding heart. "Screw you. I'm not going up there."

My arms crossed, and I fixed a defiant scowl on my face. Whoever or whatever was upstairs had nothing to do with me. I wasn't going to investigate. Ghost hunters investigated ghosts, and good for them. I wasn't a ghost hunter. As of that moment, I decided I was a ghost avoider. It was a much better fit. I avoided a lot of things. Paying taxes. Cleaning my apartment. Country music. Adding ghosts to the list was easy.

Yup, I decided with a satisfied nod. *Ghost avoider. That's me. So I'm avoiding the hell out of Guinevere, and I'm not going upstairs. Just gonna sit right here and avoid all of you.*

It was a good plan, at least for the interim. I knew that eventually I'd have to find a way out of the house, or risk Elouise sucking out my nightmares like marrow from a bone. For the moment, though, I'd just stay put and not go anywhere.

Except I had to go. Like, go go.

With a muttered curse, I launched off the divan in search of a bathroom. Groany McGroanster upstairs gave voice to his wordless complaints again, followed by the sound of something heavy sliding above my head. It was a sudden, harsh dragging that likely left deep gouges in the floor above, and definitely left gouges in my nerves.

"Nope. Nope, nope, nope," I said as I passed the stairs leading up and instead headed back down the hallway.

The bedrooms had bathrooms. I knew because I'd seen the drawings. I entered the first room, headed for its commode, and almost had my nose broken when the bathroom door slammed in my face. I spun around, stomped down the hallway, flipped on the ceiling light of the next bedroom, and again watched a bathroom door firmly shut itself.

"Oh, come on!" I yelled as I jumped back.

As if in answer, the ceiling light flickered, and a breeze ruffled the window's curtains. I yanked one aside. There was nothing behind it. I shivered at a sudden chill and glowered at the night. There was no sign of Guinevere or anything else. Just a grassy lawn and shadowy trees I couldn't get to. If I could, I'd happily pee on a tree. It certainly wouldn't be the first time. That wasn't an option, though. The bedroom corner, perhaps? Seemed fair. I'd been drugged, abducted, and forced to spend the night haunted by whatever and hunted by a hag. The urgency of my situation was escalating. After extending a middle finger to the room and its unseen inhabitants, I unzipped. There was a decorative chair in the corner that I lightly kicked with a toe to make room for my impending puddle.

And the damned thing kicked me back.

My yelp sounded like a twelve-year-old ghost had possessed my throat. I fled the room and didn't re-zip my zipper until I'd made it back to the relative safety of the living room. Fists clenched at my sides and knees pressed together, I cursed every ghost that had ever been, but especially the ones that wouldn't let people pee. If someone took the time to rank rotten ghosts, those would definitely be at the top.

The moan from upstairs wound its way down to my ears again, but this time, it sounded apologetic.

"Fine. Fine. If you promise to let me pee, I'll go up there. Well?" I asked. "Do you promise?"

Another moan, and I decided it sounded agreeable.

I took the stairs two at a time. When I reached the top, I made a slow pivot. Behind me was a door to what had to be the home's main suite. As big as the downstairs living room and dining room combined, it would have the best view of the cemetery. The other direction led to two additional doors, one on the left-hand side and one on the right. Picking one at random, I twisted its knob and pushed, then something pushed back. I tried twice more with the same effect. I spun around and tried the other door. Same outcome. Whatever was in that damned house with me did not want me going in those rooms. That left only one option.

I stomped up to the main suite's door—no easy task when you really have to pee—and tried to incinerate the door with my angry glare.

"Open up, you son of a bitch," I growled.

I heard the soft moan from the other side, and the door swung open.

"Thanks, pal. You're just swell."

As expected, the main suite was an exercise in tasteful decor. This room was large enough to have its own sitting area, complete with an old gramophone. Like everything else in the house, it looked like the real deal, not some cheap knock-off. It sounded like the real deal, too. I knew because it had started to play by itself.

"Nice," I commented. "The spooky factor, not the music. Honestly, the music sucks."

As if offended, it stopped. On the upside, it meant no more of the sucky music. On the downside, it meant I could hear the moaning again. I penguin-waddled toward the bathroom and gave a small sob of relief when its door didn't slam in my face. I made it to the toilet, flipped up its lid, and sighed a heavy sigh of relief. A sigh that turned into a, "What the fuck?" when I heard a shower curtain being drawn behind me.

I spun, forgetting that I'd been right in the middle of doing something else, and finished my business on the bathroom's wall and floor. I didn't care, though. I was too busy being terrified.

The bathroom had a cast iron clawfoot tub. A shower ring held a decorative curtain in an oval around it. It was slowing drawing back, which was creepy as hell, but this time there was something doing it. The bathroom had wall sconces for lights, and two were on the wall behind the tub. The others flickered and extinguished, but not those two. They stayed on, and damned if they didn't get brighter. Bright enough to back-light the thing that was in the tub. As the curtain hooks slowly scraped along their ring, the large and oddly shaped shadow behind it came closer and closer to being revealed. That moan sounded again, but louder, so much louder.

And then it coughed. A lot.

"What the?" I asked aloud.

My hand shot out on impulse, and I yanked the curtain aside. The tub was empty, and the coughing was coming up from its drain. I pulled the back half of the curtain to reveal those sconces on the wall. In front of one, a tiny version of the shadow's shape was affixed to a small, jointed lever that held it in front of the light. My hand moved a bit to catch the light's edge, and I saw my fingers enlarged on the shower curtain. I was looking at a shadow puppet. A stupid kid's trick. Something in my brain flickered like the bathroom's lights had a moment before. I zipped up my jeans and returned to the bedroom. Like the room downstairs, a simple wooden chair sat in a corner. While I watched, it turned on its axis then slid a few inches forward. Unperturbed, I tipped it over and dropped to my hands and knees. The bottom of its legs were shiny disks of metal. I rapped my knuckled on the floor experimentally, then righted the chair and balanced it on two legs. Moving as slowly as I could, I let the other legs inch closer to the floor. When there was maybe a finger's width between those metal discs and the wooden boards, I felt the pull. An almost imperceptible force drew on those legs. When I relaxed my grip, they dropped firmly down. A second later, the chair slid back as if affronted.

"Magnets?" I guessed. "Moving magnets under the floor?"

The gramophone was next. It took a minute to find what I was looking for. The wires were so thin they were almost impossible to see. The end of one was affixed to the switch that would set its record spinning. The other would pull the needle down to the record's groove. I bit back a laugh as I straightened my spine. The whole thing was a farce, a lie, but every good lie had a kernel of truth.

Yeah, there was a ghost. I strode from the bathroom to the main suite's enormous windows and peered out across the house's front yard. Sure enough, there was Guinevere among the gravestones. She was real, but she was also the only actual ghost in the place. The pieces of Elouise and Blunder's schemes finally clicked into place. I understood what the hag had meant when she'd praised Blunder and his crew. Everything inside the house was smoke and mirrors. Coblynau contraptions. It also explained why the spoon had been so important to the whole mad venture. Guinevere O'Brien was the lynchpin, sure. The coup de grâce. If a guest found the source of the other scares, they still wouldn't be able to explain away her. I could see the online reviews for the place stacking up. Most would be from people who had been completely fooled. A few would discover 'the truth,' and try to debunk the whole thing. No one, though, would be able to explain the sad woman pacing slowly beyond the trees. Not being able to debunk her would mean those other revelations of hidden gears and levers would be suspect, and you'd be right back to thinking maybe the place actually was haunted. It was brilliant.

The coughing from the tub's drain sounded again, followed by a soft, "Crap." Then the moan wailed again, as loud as it had ever been. The laugh I'd been holding in burst out, and I ran from the room. Furniture rattled and lights flickered behind me, and the old gramophone blurted out a few bars of its eerie tune. I was moving too quickly to be ensnared by its mystery, though. Like Dorothy in The Wizard of Oz, my hand was already reaching for that curtain.

I took the stairs two at a time again, wrapped a hand around the wooden ball at the end of the banister, and swung myself behind the front desk. I was good at finding stuff that didn't want to be found, and intuition set me looking for what I knew had to be there. When I found it, I cackled in delight. A seam was cleverly concealed in the groove between two of the beadboards. My fingers searched for some button or catch. When they came up empty, I turned my attention to the small desk and guest registry. Nothing. I poked at a wall sconce behind the desk and pressed my feet on various floorboards. Nothing. It wasn't until I examined the key rack on the wall behind the desk that I got lucky. There was one more key than rooms in the boarding house. When I pulled on it, that section of wall with the seam opened. A moment later, I was inside a crawlspace so narrow I had to turn sideways to slide between its walls. When the crawlspace opened up, it was into a space about the size of a walk-in closet. And there, I found the source of the moans and whispers.

"Snarchurraga?" I exclaimed.

I'd expected a coblyn. Not Blunder. He was too important to spend his nights pulling the levers, turning the wheels, flipping the switches, and pumping the bellows that cluttered the small room. Lefty, though, or maybe Righty. When I saw the goblin instead, I was taken aback. Only when I actually considered the control room did I understand. Coblynau were inventive and clever, sure, but also small. Their diminutive frames and small hands could never work the devices they'd built into that room. They needed someone bigger and stronger, but dull enough to not mind spending hours in a tiny room doing drudgery. They needed a goblin.

"August?" the goblin exclaimed right back. "What are you doing here?"

"Bit of a story behind that one," I admitted in answer to Snarchurraga's question. "Honestly, it started with that hafada ring you wanted back..."

"Hush," the goblin snapped, as she covered a brass horn shaped like a trombone's bell. "I'm working."

I watched in amusement as she made a few more moans into the horn thing and flipped a couple of switches up and down.

"Okay," she rasped. "I got a few minutes. No one said they hired a new guy. Am I training you?" she asked, then more worriedly, followed with, "Unless you're the boss?"

It took a few tries—goblins weren't always the quickest on the uptake—but I finally convinced her I was neither. I was, in fact, the one she'd been trying to scare. When that finally got through to her, she was crestfallen.

"I screwed up," she lamented. "Uncle Blunder will be so mad."

"Uncle Blunder?" I asked.

"Momma's side, thrice-removed," she affirmed.

My face scrunched up with confusion. "I don't think it's possible to have an uncle thrice-removed."

The goblin's shrug effectively ended my inquiry. I'd known cobs and gobs shared a family tree. I'd figured it was a weird tree. It'd have to be. Even so, discovering that Snarchurraga was a relative—even a distant one—of my little nemesis was a surprise.

"Well, your uncle thrice-removed is trying to kill me," I complained. "I'm trapped in here. I guess the plan was to scare me into exhaustion, then Elouise would stop by and suck me dry."

"The hag," Snarchurraga agreed. "A hag will do that."

"Uh huh. Which is why I have to get out of here."

The goblin rubbed her chin. "I scared you, though, yeah? Really scared you. I did a good job, and you were scared?"

"Terrified," I confirmed. "I almost peed myself, I was so scared."

That brought a wide smile to her face. On the upside, I was glad to put her worries about her job performance at ease. On the downside, I had to look at her jagged and yellow teeth.

"You got so scared, you ran away," she decided. "Right out the door. I'll let it open. You ran because you were so scared, and Uncle Blunder will know I did a good job."

Defeat settled on my shoulders and pressed them down into a sad sag. "I can't leave. Blunder's watching, or one of his goons. If I try to go outside, I'm pretty sure I'll get shot, or worse."

Snarchurraga scratched her chin again, then something like resolve steeled her black eyes and pressed her black lips tightly together. She shoved past me and clambered toward the exit, then looked back. I tilted my head to the side, unsure of what her plan was. In response, she hooked her fingers and beckoned me to follow.

Perplexed, I followed the goblin through the narrow crawlway, down an iron rung ladder I hadn't noticed when I'd crawled in, and into the home's cellar. A large boiler squatted like an iron leviathan in one corner. The goblin scurried around the side, warned me where not to touch for fear of burns, and disappeared.

"Hey. What the hell? Where'd you go?"

"Here, shifter. Here," her voice said.

I leaned in and spotted the gap a second before her gray-green hand poked out and waggled its bony fingers and blackened nails. A few seconds after that, I was hunched over in total darkness. There was a scratch, a whiff of sulfur, and a flickering light. Snarchurraga held a wooden match to a small lantern. When the wick caught, I inspected where I was.

"Limestone," I said as I ran my hand across the tunnel's rough surface. "A limestone tunnel. Did you make this?"

"Nah," she remarked. "Here for a long time, I'd bet."

"How did you know it was here? How do you know where it goes?"

She wrinkled her brow and tapped her breastbone proudly. "Goblins got a nose for tunnels. Easy to find. Go that way, shifter. Pass four branches on the left, take the fifth. Pass one on the left, then take the second one on the right. Look up after thirty paces. Hmmm. Long legs. Maybe twenty-five. Go up and out."

"Wait. You aren't coming?"

"Job," she replied as she hooked a thumb over her shoulder. "Scared you good. So good you disappeared. Maybe I'll get a raise."

"Thanks, Snarchurraga," I said with genuine warmth.

In reply, she snorked and grunted and finally hawked a big glob onto the tunnel's floor. I nodded my understanding and added my own phlegm to hers to seal the bargain. A favor for a favor. A trinket for a tunnel. Our business transaction had come to a satisfactory end. She passed the small oil lantern to my hand, then turned and scrabbled out through the hidden gap in the wall.

"Another satisfied customer," I said with a bemused smile, then turned toward the unknown.

Chapter 16

"WAIT. DID SHE SAY pass four branches, then take the fifth? Or pass the fifth?"

The tunnel was obviously not a made thing. Its height and width varied. Its floor barely fit that description. I'd hunched and squeezed and crouched and crawled my way through with only the lantern's weak light to guide me. There was one spot where I was certain I'd have to go back until I remembered I was a shifter. The goblin would've had no issue squeezing through, but human me definitely wouldn't have fit. I set my lantern aside and stripped. After the coyote had easily hopped through the narrow gap, I reluctantly shifted back, pulled on my clothes, and retrieved the lantern. Unfortunately, while I'd been a coyote, I'd forgotten half of what Snarchurraga had told me.

"Damn it," I complained. "Think. Think think think."

If there'd been more room—a lot more room—I might've tried the elephant trick. Elephants have incredible memories, but they gather and retain information a little differently from humans. There was no guarantee that I'd harken back to the conversation I'd had barely thirty minutes ago and remember Snarchurraga's exact words. Ambient sounds, colors, details, sure. Specific words? Maybe. It was a moot point, anyway. There was no way an elephant would fit in the limestone seam. Instead, I was stuck with my human brain, a brain I really wished was better at remembering things.

"Pretty sure she said pass four, take the fifth," I decided.

I rolled that around in my brain for a moment and liked the certainty it had. Confident I'd remembered her words correctly, I held the lantern up to the branch.

"So, is this the fourth or the fifth?" I asked, and that moment of confidence fell like the floor of the branching tunnel before me.

"Crap. This can't be right," I muttered.

I held the lantern back the way I'd come, but its flame only revealed a few feet and then all was dark. I swung it in front of me to similar effect. There was no way of knowing how far back the prior branch had been, or how far ahead the next one was.

"Figures," I complained as I dropped to my seat, stuck my legs out in front of me, and hoped like hell that I was choosing the right tunnel.

The grade of the descent wasn't too bad for the first twenty feet or so, and then I was falling. It felt like forever, but was only a second or so. It was a damn scary second, though. Without knowing when I'd land, I inevitably landed awkwardly. Thankfully, the lantern hadn't gone out. If it had, I would've likely gone insane. The chute I'd come down would've been a bitch to climb back up, especially in complete darkness. I let the lantern paint the worn limestone with oranges and yellows as I tried like hell to recall my journey so far.

"I know I passed four branches. There was the one that I would've had to belly-crawl through. The one with the opening a couple of feet up the wall. The one that smelled like something had died. And, um. Hmmm. Shit."

Had there been another one? Hell if I knew, so I decided to soldier on. The goblin had said to pass an opening on the left, then take the second one on the right, then look up. I was sure of that bit. Mostly sure. Pretty sure.

"Damn it!" I yelled. The tunnel threw my words back at me, then resumed its usual silence.

I held the lantern up and pivoted. The new shaft I was in was big enough to travel through in one direction, and too small for anything bigger than a rat to go in the other direction. That meant there was only one way forward. I liked it when decisions were made for me. Saved me the trouble of weighing pros and cons and whatnots. I pointed myself in the only direction I could fit and kept moving.

Time passed, but it was meaningless to consider how much. Pitch black tunnels are funny that way. All I could do was put one foot in front of the other. Eventually, I knew I would pass an opening on the left, then one on the right.

Any minute now, I thought. *The island isn't that big and I'm not that deep underground. I'll be home free any minute now.*

More time passed. My back ached from being hunched. My shoulder shook from holding the lantern in front of me. My tongue was dry. My eyes wouldn't stop watering. I was misery in motion, but what could I do? Trudge, trudge, and trudge some more.

Any minute now.

Finally, I stopped. There was no way I was in the right tunnel. I couldn't have been. Unless Snarchurraga had been messing with me. Unless this was part of the hag's plan. Send the stupid shifter underground and let him die of stupidity. It didn't seem likely, but rational thought and being lost underground didn't exactly go hand in hand. I tried to concentrate, to focus, but I couldn't think over the heavy sound of my panting breaths.

But I'm not breathing that hard, I realized. *Someone is, but not me...*

I stood very still and strained my ears. There was definitely someone—or something—breathing. A long inhale. A firm exhale. Inhale. Exhale.

I'd been holding my own breath long enough for spots to swim in front of my eyes when it hit me. That wasn't someone breathing.

"That sounds like bellows."

Whatever I'd expected when I'd followed the goblin into the B&B's basement, this was nowhere in the ballpark. Hell, it wasn't in the same league. Not even the same sport. Weird bellows in a tunnel under a river island? Definitely on the unexpected end of things that could exist. Curiosity pulled me onward until I finally saw something truly glorious: light. I took a few more steps to confirm what I hoped to be true, then gave the lantern's wick a turn and extinguished the small flame. I won't lie. There was a moment of panic when I thought the light ahead might've been nothing more than a trick of my eyes. Thankfully, it wasn't, but neither was it something I would have ever expected.

The tunnel narrowed as I drew closer. Soon, I was on my hands and knees. The limestone scraped my palms, but I was too eager to be out of the dark tunnel to care. The steady sound of the bellows grew louder as I crawled. When I finally got to the source of light, I discovered it was a rough opening about the size of a car tire. I brought my fingers to its lip, leaned forward, and simply stared at the unexpected scene my vantage point revealed.

I was looking into a limestone cave. It must've been over thirty feet high in the middle, and easily twice as long across. The walls curved up, giving the impression of being inside half a giant football. I could make out all those details because large, gymnasium-style sodium lights hung down in a circle from that high ceiling and bathed the space in an anemic glow. The natural hole in the porous limestone that was serving as my window was roughly at the same height as those big lights. I spotted what had to be the source of the bellows. A big HVAC unit emitted a rhythmic whoosh as it circulated air through the underground space. Below my crude window in the cave's wall, a smooth floor held what looked like—I rubbed my eyes—big stainless steel tanks.

"Beer?" I gasped.

A smile split my face from ear to ear. Beer did that. It didn't matter that I'd been abducted by a criminal coblyn, turned into a haunted house test case by a mean old hag, saved by a goblin, and had crawled like the state's namesake gopher through deep, dark tunnels. All that mattered was that I'd discovered a wonderful secret: an underground brewery.

"Jay is going to be so jealous," I said.

"Do you think so?" a voice behind me said.

I jumped. Well, I would have jumped, had I been standing in a place with enough headroom to jump. I wasn't, though. I was lying on my belly in a small tunnel. I guess whatever I did was more like a spasm. My body bucked, the back of my head smacked the limestone above, and I used every curse word I knew, plus a few I made up on the spot.

"Yeah, that looked like it hurt."

I hadn't turned to see who was talking to me. All I knew was that one, they were behind me, and two, I recognized the voice.

"Prank caller?" I gasped.

"Yup," the familiar voice replied.

"What in the hell? How in the hell?" I stammered as I tried to twist and jackknife enough to look back toward my feet. I bent my chin toward my chest, pressed my back against the tunnel to let as much light pass as possible, and peered back down the tunnel behind me. Maybe a foot or two past my boots, I saw a face. An unexpected face. One I'd seen plenty of times before, but never quite like this. Usually, I only saw it in the mirror.

"Enjoying the view?" the guy said in that familiar voice.

Looking at the guy, it made sense why his voice had been so familiar and so hard to place at the same time. I mean, how often do you call yourself on the phone? My brain broke a little. Seeing yourself—your actual self—will do that. Words bubbled up from some mad place in the far reaches of my brain and tumbled from my lips.

"You're me. How are you me? Why am I looking at me?"

"Just doing my job," I replied matter-of-factly.

"Your job?" I asked.

"Yup. I'm your Fetch, and you… Well, you're going to die soon."

His words, my words, reached my ears. They tapped on my eardrums and passed into my brain. They sort of stopped there, though. Usually, when words make it that far, you can make some sort of sense out of them. The words I'd just heard, though, made no sense at all.

"You're going to kill me?" I asked, struggling to understand.

"What?" that me exclaimed. "No! Hell, no. That's not how it works. I'm here to herald your death. Your death's portent, so to speak."

Fetch, I thought. *My Fetch.*

Again, my brain's gears caught. Something about the words, 'You're going to die soon,' had thrown a spanner in my mental works.

"Fetches are Irish," I pointed out. It seemed like an important detail.

"We are," I agreed.

"I'm Irish?" I asked. Why that seemed important, I couldn't say.

"Irish enough," I replied. "Okay. I think we're good here. Oh, I should probably do the spiel. You know. The whole, 'Soon, August Shade. Soon!' thing. Kinda in the job description."

My eyes narrowed. "Were you behind me in the mirror, back at the hag's house?"

I nodded in response. "Cool, right? Spooky as hell."

"And the Fair. At the barn. That was you. Me. You."

Another nod.

"Plus all those annoying phone calls."

"Yeah, those too. Ringing you up wasn't exactly in the manual, but I thought it'd be fun to experiment. Try something new. I mean, why just show up right before you're going to die? Why not stretch things out a bit?"

"You're an asshole," I muttered.

"Hey, I'm you, remember? What'd you expect?"

And with that, my twin was gone. Not in a left-by-crawling-back-up-the-tunnel sort of way. Just gone. There one second, not the next.

Those sticky gears in my brain turned again. I understood what had just happened. I knew what a Fetch was. That didn't make it any easier to accept my impending death. Impending heartburn after too many hotdogs? Sure. Impending hangover after too many beers? Of course. But death? Nope. Especially when there didn't seem to be anything all that deadly in the immediate future. I took a slow breath and looked back out through the limestone tunnel's opening. What could possibly happen down there? Unless I was going to slip and fall while exiting the tunnel. Possible, maybe even probable, but it wasn't too far of a drop. It certainly didn't seem like it could be fatal. And once I was down there, what danger would I be in? Sure, I'd stumbled across an underground brewery. If the brewmaster wanted to keep things a secret, I'd likely get a stern warning for having trespassed. But killed? Not likely. The real danger was far behind me, but even that wasn't too serious, was it? I mean, Elouise and Blunder obviously had it in for me, but would they actually kill me? I reflected on my recent past. Yes, Elouise was a hungry old hag, and yes, Blunder and his buddies were fond of punching things with their punchy little contraptions. That said, neither of them seemed so far gone as to completely disregard the Northern Quorum. It was like Betty had said: crossing the Quorum meant there'd be hell to pay. If a PN killed another PN in what clearly wasn't a case of self-defense, and the Quorum got wind of it, the punishment was severe. No. Elouise might want a taste, but she'd never suck me dry. And Blunder? Same. The little monster would threaten and bruise and even maim, but kill?

"Must have been a mistake," I decided. "The Fetch made a mistake. That happens. Everyone makes mistakes."

The cold certainty that there had not, in fact, been a mistake stayed lodged in my gut.

"Dead? Today? Here? What are the flippin' odds?" I complained quietly. "After everything. After that damned hospital. After Tony and Dieter Saint James and Canute. All the shit I've been through, and I'm going to die in a cave?"

At least it's a beer cave, a chipper corner of my brain added.

Yeah, at least it's that, the rest of my brain agreed.

A stillness settled over me as I took stock of my life. It didn't take long.

"Fuck it. If my number is up, maybe I can at least get a pint of whatever they're brewing down there before I go."

Chapter 17

"The end of the growing season can only be death, but from that death, life."
- Felloshna Grimfaerie

I**T TOOK A MINUTE** to get turned around. I wasn't flexible by any stretch, and the narrow tunnel didn't give me much room. The effort seemed worthwhile, though. Climbing through a small hole in a cave wall that was maybe twenty, maybe thirty feet above the floor head-first would've been tossing my damned Fetch a softball.

Hell with that, I decided. *If I have any say in this matter, I'm not dying like an idiot.*

After I got my head pointing back the way I'd come and my feet pointing toward the opening, I used my shoulders and butt to inchworm my way closer to freedom. My ankles cleared the opening's lip, then my calves. When I had scooted far enough for my knees to bend, I was able to crunch a bit, flop onto my stomach, stretch my arms, and press my palms against the opening's sides. I scooched a bit further through the hole, then kicked my feet around in hope of finding a ledge. When they didn't, I muttered a curse squeezed my eyes shut, and dangled for a long moment.

"It wasn't that far of a drop, right?" I asked myself.

"Not far, no," I replied.

I opened my eyes. There I was.

"Hey!" I exclaimed. "I thought you were... shit!"

I'm no physics expert, but here's what I think happened. Pressing my palms against the tunnel walls and squeezing with my fingers had created just enough friction to resist the pull of gravity on my lower half. However, when I looked up in surprise at my Fetch, that motion was enough to shift the equation in gravity's favor. Gravity eagerly took hold, I slid backward on my belly, and I fell. Science is like that, I guess, and I decided mid-fall that I hated science.

There were a number of painful stages in my landing. My heels struck the cave's floor first, which damn near shoved my legs up through my lungs. My tailbone was next, followed by my back, and lastly, the back of my skull. It felt about as good as it sounds. A miserable wheeze slipped out, which in its way was a comfort. Dead people don't bother with miserable wheezing.

"See? Not far," my Fetch said from above.

"Asshole," I replied.

He shrugged exactly like I would've and vanished again. I continued to watch the dark hole in case the guy had any other cameos planned for my final act. After a few moments, I gave up, flopped onto my belly, and gingerly made my way to my feet. For a guy that had crawled through a tunnel, discovered he was going to die soon, and then fallen from a hole in the wall, I felt pretty good. Granted, it was a low bar.

I was behind one of the big stainless steel tanks and took a minute to bask in its glory. I'd never tried to brew beer before. It took patience and no small measure of skill, two things I had in very short supply. Knowing that I'd never be able to do it myself made me appreciate those that could all the more. To me, brewmasters were the real magicians of the world. What they did with barley and hops and yeast... Yeah. Definitely magic.

Minneapolis and Saint Paul had no shortage of breweries, and I'd taken a few of the free tours. Words came back as I worked my way past a tank to its neighbor, and from there to a third. I hadn't thought to count the number of tanks from my earlier vantage point, but there were a lot. The ones I was creeping around were Brite Tanks, more commonly called serving tanks. In a nutshell, they were the last stop of the brewing process. They kept the beer pressurized until it was ready to be transferred to kegs, cans, and bottles. I could tell them apart from the fermentors, mainly because Brite Tank bottoms were flat, whereas the fermentors were cone-shaped. They were also where the cool stuff happened. Brewing yeast and oxygen were pumped in, and then little microbes basically breathed a lot. The resulting carbon dioxide was vented out and created the smell filling my nose. Depending on the beer, that smell could be anything from fruity and sweet to bready and yeasty, or—as in this particular case— something more like bad eggs. Once the fermentation was done, the used up microbes settled in the fermentor's conical bottom. The resulting elixir was pumped out the side to a Brite Tank. If memory served—and there was no way I'd forget what I'd learned about my favorite drink—there would be kettles for malt mashing nearby, probably up a level so gravity could move the evolving product through its stages. I let my eyes follow a couple of pipes over, around, and up, and then chuckled when my assumption proved out. Scaffolding held those kettles high above the cave's floor. They were where it all started. Malted barley and other grains got mixed with hot water into a slurry with big mechanical paddles. That warm slurry would activate the malt's enzymes and turn the starches into fermentable sugars. The liquid wort flowed down to the fermentors, and wet mashed grains were scooped out later.

"And I'll bet it gets collected there to ship back to some farmers for feed," I said, completely geeked out by the whole thing.

The entire process from start to finish was strangely cool. Easily explained by science, sure, but I preferred to believe it was magic. How could it not be? As I marveled at it all, thoughts of hags and coblynau and Fetches and impending death floated away like the off-gassed carbon dioxide from the fermentors. I was a kid in a candy store. An underground candy store. A candy store no one knew about. A completely empty, underground, secret candy story. It was awesome. Super cool. It was also—I had to admit to myself—very weird.

"Must be a private brewery," I decided, "and it's the middle of the night. That's why no one knows about it, and why there's no one here."

My rationalization made me feel a little better. Unfortunately, the next detail I saw brought my elevating spirits right back down. I knew a little about the brewing process, but I wasn't an expert. The extent of my knowledge was the same as any Joe Schmo that went on the free half-hour tour and drank the finished product at the end. Even so, I was pretty sure the tours I'd taken hadn't had biohazard signage plastered all over. Or yellow rubber smocks hung on the wall next to plastic face shields. Or an emergency eyewash station and a dousing shower. Also, beer went into a limited number of containers: kegs, growlers, crowlers, bottles, cans. I'd never once seen it distributed in bright orange fifty-five gallon drums, and definitely not drums marked 'DANGER.'

"Okay, fine," I complained, irate at my deflating mood. "Maybe this isn't a brewery."

The sound of a rising garage door split the silence and sent me ducking back behind one of the Brite Tanks. The squeaking of wheels and a couple of voices pressed me deeper into my hiding spot.

"Last batch for tonight," a voice I knew said. "Good crop, too."

It was Tranq, a.k.a. the suit guy that had tranquilized me.

"It had better be. We're behind schedule and under quota."

Hooray, I thought. *Schnozz, too.*

I inched my nose past the edge of the tank. The two suits were wheeling what looked like an industrial laundry bin down a ramp and through the garage door. They pushed it up alongside the scaffolding, and a plate on the floor rose on a hydraulic piston. Tranq climbed a steel ladder on the scaffolding's side and rolled the cart onto the platform.

"They can't blame us," he grumbled. "We've been busting our asses. These spirits don't grow on trees, you know."

"Of course they don't," Schnozz agreed as he craned his neck to look up. "They grow in corn."

The two laughed at what felt like an old joke. While I watched, the bigger man turned to one of the large kettles, gripped a steel wheel on its top, twisted, and opened a pressure-sealed hatch. He rolled the laundry bin closer, then plunged his hands down and pulled up an armful of what looked like dried husks. With a quick twist of his torso, he dropped them into the malt masher. I heard a mechanical thrum and knew those automated paddles inside had started their work. Another armful went into the kettle, then another. While Tranq worked, Schnozz walked to a small office on the far side of the cave and occupied himself with filling out papers on a clipboard. It hung from a length of string tacked to a tall metal locker. Black letters proclaiming 'CAUTION!' and 'WARNING!' leaped from bright yellow signs affixed to its gunmetal gray door.

"What lot was this again?" he asked.

His burly partner paused his efforts to respond. "Four-oh-seven, sub-B. Vermillion. South, southwest."

"Ah, that's right. Expensive lot."

Tranq snorted in agreement. "Don't know why you paid for it in the first place. That girl is getting a little too big for her sparkly britches."

Schnozz clicked his tongue in a quiet reprimand. "You know as well as I do she is definitely not some little girl, no matter how sparkly her britches. This way is better."

"Dagmara?" I gasped. "They can't be talking about Dagmara."

It wasn't the first time I'd made a mess of things by failing to keep my inside voice inside, and I knew it wouldn't be the last. That said, I really wished the previous time had been the last. If it had been, I wouldn't have said what I said out loud, Schnozz wouldn't have whipped his head around and pointed that gigantic nose directly at my shitty hiding place, and Tranq wouldn't have pulled out that hand cannon he was so fond of.

"Who's there?" Schnozz asked loudly.

I'd pressed my back hard against the steel tank, and clenched every muscle I had, especially my sphincter.

"I don't see anyone," Tranq called down from the scaffolding.

"I thought I heard something."

With all the care of a tightrope walker performing without a net, I lifted a foot and swung it slowly in front of the other, then gently set my heel down and rocked my weight forward. I repeated the movement and covered another six inches in the span of a couple of breaths. My goals were simple: keep the tanks between me and them, and make absolutely no noise doing it.

"Probably one of the valves," I heard Tranq say. "A couple of those tanks are almost ready."

I took another slow step, then crouched down. The Brite Tank's bottom was a couple of feet above the ground, supported by four stout legs. Not ideal for hiding, but there was a collection of five-gallon pails strews about that helped provide a bit more cover for my feet and legs. As long as Schnozz didn't drop to his knees and peer under the tanks, I figured I'd be okay.

"Probably," Schnozz agreed. "You ready for the dolly?"

"No. Still have about half the bin to load in."

"Do you mean to be so slow, or can you just not help it?"

The steady sound of dry husks being hoisted into the masher stopped.

"Really?" Tranq said, clearly affronted. "I don't see you up here getting your suit dirty, but you're going to criticize me."

While the two bickered, I took another careful step. The fermentors had those downward pointing cones for bottoms. If I could get to one of those, I could crouch down and peer around with a bit more cover. While I made my slow circuit of the tank, my mind was trying to reassemble a bunch of pieces that I'd obviously stuck together wrong. First, although it broke my heart to admit it, I hadn't discovered a secret brewery. Unless someone had found a way to make beer from corn husks. That didn't seem likely. As far as I knew, husks were only good for holding a cob of corn, or later wrapping up a tamale. That was it. If they were putting corn husks in a masher, it wasn't to make beer.

"Just hurry," I heard Schnozz say. "I'll get the dolly."

I leaned back as I heard footsteps come my way. I had a glimpse of the gaunt man as he passed the space between the tanks, and then Schnozz disappeared from view again. There was a sound like a gym locker being opened, then Tranq called out.

"Hey! Wait. Do you mean to be so careless, or can you just not help it?"

Schnozz cursed. He backtracked, then donned a yellow smock and a face shield.

"Where are the gloves?" he yelled, looking like a helmeted rubber ducky.

"Wherever you left them," Tranq replied.

"I left them right here."

"Obviously not."

I let my knees bend until I could set my palms on the ground, then lowered myself down to my belly. From my new vantage point, I could easily see the angles of Schnozz's shoulders and arms as he cast about in confusion.

"I don't see them" he called out again after straightening and placing his fists on his hips.

"Didn't you pump out tank four yesterday?"

I was used to having pretty shitty luck. It was kind of my thing. Even so, seeing the number four stenciled in black against a bright yellow circle on the tank I was hiding below and a pair of blue rubber gloves on the floor in front of my face seemed a bit much, even by my standards.

I said the word, "Shit," and then Schnozz saw me. He'd just looked toward tank four, and his stork legs were taking annoyed strides in my direction when suddenly his eyes locked onto mine from behind his clear faceplate.

"You!" Schnozz gasped.

"Me!" I agreed.

"What the fuck?" Tranq screamed.

What I heard next wasn't something I was expecting. It was the sound of a body hitting the ground. Tranq had leaped from the scaffolding. The sound of him landing on the cave's floor turned my stomach. What I heard after that was worse. Even though I'd heard it before, it wasn't something you get used to. That sound of a rushing freight train while you're tied to the tracks, a twister coming across the plains, an entire regimen of nightmares on galloping horses. In other words, the voice of the Strach na wróble.

I looked up to the scaffolding and saw a collection of sticks in an old suit emerge from the bottom of the laundry cart Tranq had been emptying. As the Strach na wróble screamed, his arms splayed wide and his threadbare jacket billowed. One bony knee rose to his shoulder, and a foot kicked out and over the cart's lip. A hand braced on the nearby kettle, and the other leg swung up and around. Watching the Strach na wróble was like watching a mantis, a cellar spider, a king crab. That horrible maw in its gunnysack face opened wide, and the rushing sound pushed the decibel meter up a few more ticks.

"Get up!" I heard Schnozz yell. "It's here for the corn spirit!"

Tranq moaned in pain, but got himself upright. He reached inside his suit coat and pulled out that damned gun. Screaming incoherently, the guy swung his arm and started squeezing the trigger. Three loud booms whammed my eardrums. The sound of ricocheting bullets followed.

"Stop, you idiot! Don't shoot the tanks!" Schnozz screamed in a panic.

Whatever bullets might do to the stainless steel tanks, they hadn't done a thing to the Strach na wróble. One leathery hand gripped the railing. Then the thing's limbs and torso were swinging down in a way that told physics and any notion of how joints are supposed to work to just fuck off. Tranq squeezed off one more shot before Schnozz's long strides sent him colliding with his partner. While they briefly wrestled for control of the gun, the Strach na wróble finished its descent.

"Where?" it screamed in its ghastly voice. "Where is the corn spirit?"

"There!" I yelled. Why? I couldn't really say. The smart play would've been to stay very low to avoid any more ricocheting bullets and belly crawl for the exit. Unfortunately, me and smart don't always travel in the same circles. "In that locker over there!"

One thing I can say in my favor: I bring people together in unexpected ways. The two suits immediately stopped their struggles and turned to look at me with shared resolve. Tranq lifted the gun, and Schnozz did nothing to stop him.

"Shit," I managed.

There was another ear-splitting boom, and I felt—actually felt—the bullet go past my head. Past, not into. That realization took a little contemplation. Were there more important things happening? Sure. The Strach na wróble had lunged for Tranq and knocked the hand with the gun. Terrified tears were running down Tranq's face, but to his credit, he was trying to fight back. Schnozz was running toward the office again for reasons he hadn't bothered to yell out loud, meaning I had no idea why he was doing what he was doing. Fleeing through the still-open garage door would've made more sense, but what did I know? I was just the guy trying to process having almost had his head blown off.

"Shit," I said again.

While Tranq flailed his arms at the Strach na wróble, Schnozz reached the office. When he emerged, my addled brain was shaken again by what it was seeing. Why the suit had gone for what looked like a spray paint can was beyond me, but I accepted it. Things had already been weird for a while. A hag's bed-and-breakfast with fake ghosts run by a hidden goblin, and an actual ghost trapped in a spoon. A limestone tunnel that led to an underground brewery where Department of Agriculture operatives weren't brewing beer, but instead were doing something with corn husks and dollies. A living, breathing scarecrow popping out of a laundry bin and fighting with the suits to get its corn dolly back. A shapeshifter lying on his belly under a brew tank after having been visited by his Fetch in what was apparently a portent of impending death. Yeah. Weird was definitely the right word. What difference would it make if someone did a little graffiti in the middle of all that?

Schnozz quickly closed the distance to where his partner struggled with the Strach na wróble.

"Get back!" he yelled.

Why's he going to spray paint the scarecrow? I wondered, and then I saw what Schnozz had in his other hand.

A lighter flicked, and a cone of flame appeared. Tranq dropped and rolled, meaning there was nothing to shield the Strach na wróble from the fiery cloud. A corner of its coat caught flame, and the rushing wind of its cries turned to panicked shrieks. Just like that, the tide of the battle turned. While the scarecrow flapped and staggered backward, Schnozz relentlessly advanced with his improvised blowtorch.

Do something! a foolish part of my brain screamed.

I jumped up and headed for the fight. Tranq was still on the ground, so I gave him a solid kick to the ribs along the way, then dove for Schnozz and tackled the gangly guy to the ground. The can clanked and skittered away, but that wasn't the real threat. While he bucked and squirmed, I tried to grab the lighter from his hands. Meanwhile, the Strach na wróble was making things exponentially worse by running in wide circles. The flames grew to consume more of his coat, and the senseless running was fanning them.

"Stop, drop, and roll!" I yelled, hoping he wasn't too too far gone to hear my words.

Two hands grabbed the collar of my jacket and yank hard. Tranq lifted me from the ground and sent me tumbling with a quick pivot like he was unloading a sack of grain from a cart. I was airborne for a second, then dropped hard onto my belly. My chin hit the floor and jammed my teeth together. Unfortunately, my tongue had been between them, and the taste of blood filled my mouth. I flailed onto my back and reflexively brought my hands to my mouth, eyes squeezed shut to hold back the flood of tears. When they opened again, I saw a curious tableau.

Schnozz had regained his feet and was scrabbling after his lost spray can. Tranq was standing above me with that damned gun and a look of insane fury on his face. The Strach na wróble had extinguished the worst of the flames, but was still busy furiously patting himself. Past him, I saw myself. I was leaning casually against one of the scaffolding's metal legs, black Schott Perfecto jacket hanging open and one leg crossed over the other so that foot's toes rested on the ground. If I'm being honest, I looked more than a bit like the classic James Dean photo. That bright little thought lightened an otherwise shitty moment. I smiled at my Fetch and received a sympathetic grin in response. Then my eyes shifted again to the open garage door, where a woman with a pink mohawk was running down the slope beyond it. Behind Dagmara was...

The sound of the gun going off that close to me was deafening. The feel of a slug hitting my stomach was nothing short of what a red-hot wrecking ball would feel like. I felt my body slide backward a few inches with the impact, and then everything that I used to think mattered was gone. All of it. All the chaos around me. All the chaos inside of me. All my fears and worries. All my hopes and dreams. Gone. Even that volcano of pain in my gut was gone. There was simply nothing. Nothing at all.

Nothing.

CHAPTER 18

"Y OU DIED?" JAY ASKED, aghast.

He and Philo were both on the edge of the liquor store's outside bench. The aspiring warlock was aghast, and the satyr's eyes were full of worried tears.

"I guess? No? Maybe for a minute?" I replied honestly from my lawn chair. "The next bit gets pretty strange, but I'm obviously not dead."

Earlier that morning, I'd made my way into the office. How I'd gotten from Grey Cloud Island to my dingy apartment the night before was a small turn of luck compared to the rest of the story. When I'd arrived at the studio, Jay had waved from his newest artistic endeavor. From the looks of it, it was going to involve a lot of Cream of Wheat. Beyond that, I couldn't say what his brain was cooking up. We'd traded a couple of pleasantries and had decided on a trip to Philo's. I wanted to let the store's proprietor know he wouldn't need to worry about coblynau goons roughing him up again. More importantly, we needed to restock the beer fridge.

It was a nice day, so we broke a few city laws and consumed a few cans outside of the liquor store. Always a good sport—and eager to thumb his pug nose at the city and its ridiculous laws, like no open bottles on the street—Philo had joined us. I'd started the story with me convincing Fannie to give up the spoon, then unfurled the rest: how I'd learned of the ghost of Genevieve McCoy, my night in a not-haunted haunted house, bumping into Snarchurraga, squirming through the limestone tunnel, making a wrong turn, emerging in the underground brewery-not-brewery, meeting my Fetch, getting caught up in the tussle between the suits and the Strach na wróble, and, finally, getting shot.

"Obviously, you're not dead," Jay agreed drolly. "What I think we'd like to hear is how? How are you not dead?"

"You did see your Fetch," Philo added. "Their kind don't tend to make mistakes."

"No, they don't, but I'll get to that. So, anyway. There I was, shot in the gut. There was pain. Lots of pain, and then..."

Nothing.

Nothing at all.

Then a voice. A chipper, congenial, and very Irish voice.

"There we are. Welcome back, lad. Easy, now."

I opened my eyes and cataloged what they showed me. I was still in the cave. The Ag Ops pair were gagged and tied back-to-back a short distance away. Tranq's suit was rumpled and torn. Schnozz was still swathed in his yellow hazmat smock. I wondered if they were thinking, 'We would have gotten away with it, too, if it weren't for you meddling kids,' and laughed an unsteady laugh. To the right of them, Dagmara and the Strach na wróble embraced. Her cheek pressed into his chest beside the blue ribbon on his lapel. One of his arms encircled her shoulders. The other was around her waist, its leathery hand holding a small doll made of woven corn husks. And directly in front of me—his eyes level with mine despite the fact that I was sitting on the floor while he was standing—was a wizened old face with a shocking red beard, a wide smile, and bright, young eyes.

"Top o' the evening to ya, good sir. How's that belly of yours?"

Confused, I told him my gas station hotdog had been fine, thank you very much.

"Ah!" he exclaimed with a laugh. "No. Not the hotdog, lad."

I squinted, then shifted my weight so I could bring a hand to my stomach. I pressed and poked. It was a little bigger and squishier than I'd prefer, but otherwise fine. At least, it was fine until I pressed in one particular spot. That spot hurt. As I hesitantly poked it again, I realized it hurt a lot. I pulled up my shirt and saw a spreading bruise. The surprising discovery led to another one: a hole in my jacket. My baby. My beautiful Schott Perfecto. It was in the middle of the left pocket, and inside the pocket...

I slipped a hand in, and out came a golden coin. Its weight confirmed it was likely the real deal, although the slug smooshed into it was adding its own weight.

"What is this?" I asked with wide eyes.

"A bit o' luck. That's what that is, and it's a grand bit, indeed," the little fella replied as he plucked the coin from my numb fingers.

I raised my voice in response, but it wasn't actually me yelling.

"How is that grand?" my Fetch asked angrily. "None of this is jolly, fine, tip-top, excellent, swell, or nifty, and it sure as hell isn't grand."

The leprechaun turned to look at the other me, and I considered what the leprechaun was seeing. I knew I could sulk and stew, but had never been treated to just how petulant and ridiculous I looked while doing it.

"Lad, I understand your concerns," the leprechaun started.

"Like hell, you do. I had one job. One. And you screwed it up. What am I supposed to do now?"

Red Beard squinted one eye and waggled the plump fingers of a small hand. "For starters, mind your tone, lad. You know who I am."

"Sure. Super important, aren't you? But not so damned important that you get to decide who lives and dies. I'm a Fetch, for cripe's sake. His Fetch. Northern Quorum can do what it needs to do with the likes of those assholes," Fetch-me said as he hooked a thumb at the trussed-up suits, "but you had no business getting involved with me and mine."

I was trying to follow the conversation and getting irritated when I couldn't. There was one question that was getting in the way of pretty much everything else. One detail I wanted cleared up. Who the leprechaun was, why Dagmara was there, how the suits had gone from slinging bullets and blasting fireballs to being tied up like rotten gifts that were sure to disappoint on Christmas morning? Those concerns could all take a number and get in line. What I wanted to know was...

"Did I die?"

"No, you didn't," my Fetch spat. "Were you supposed to? Yes. Did you? No. And why not? Him," he finished while jabbing an accusatory finger at the leprechaun. "Breaks all the rules. Flies in the face of tradition. Completely screws me over, but did anyone bother to ask how I felt about it? No. No one ever cares what I think."

It was so completely something I would say that I laughed.

"No, they don't, do they?" I agreed.

I suppose a fair measure of my good humor had to do with the fact that I wasn't dead. It doesn't matter how terrible your day's been. Discovering you're alive when you are supposed to be otherwise is a brightener, no doubt about it. The leprechaun wasn't as cheery, though. Fetch-me was as annoying as I was, and had obviously gotten under the leprechaun's green-cloaked skin.

"You concerns have been noted. Thank you for your input. Now, I'd suggest you be on your way, lad. This is Quorum business now."

"Where am I supposed to go?" the Fetch practically yelled. "This was supposed to be it. Finally. Do you realize how close this guy has come to dying over and over again? For years, he's teetered on the brink, and there was me, sitting on my thumbs like a worthless jackass because he never did. That was okay, though, because this time, this time," he repeated, "was supposed to be it. End of the line for him, end of the line for me. Now? Fuck. I have no idea what to do."

"Travel. See the sights. Sample the local cuisine. Or don't. Go find a barstool and sulk. I don't care," the leprechaun said dismissively. "Just don't be here."

If someone had told me a little wizened guy with a bushy red beard and tidy green suit could be terrifying, I'd have told them to take another puff of whatever they were smoking. Shows what I knew. My Fetch glared, but beneath it was a distinct apprehension. After a few moments, he turned his eyes to his boots and straightened his leather jacket. I noticed in an off-hand way that his had a bullet hole in the pocket, too.

"Fine. Whatever," he said, doing his best to make it sound nonchalant and failing miserably. Then he turned that glare on me. It was disorienting, to say the least.

"We're not done, though, you and me. Not by a long shot. This will get sorted, then..." he warned as he slid a finger across his neck. "Nothing personal," he added when my eyes widened in shock. "It's just business."

"Uh huh. Business," I agreed, without agreeing at all.

Business was buying a hotdog. Business was getting paid to repo someone's favorite sweater. Seeing myself before I died? That wasn't business. That sucked ass. I was still a little euphoric from being not-dead, though, and I found a silver lining.

"Until then," I said, "no more phone calls, right?"

My Fetch gave me the finger and vanished, leaving me to turn my attention to the leprechaun. If what my Fetch had said was true, I was looking at a member of the Northern Quorum. Not someone you expected to see, and not someone you wanted to see, yet there he was. Me and my luck.

There were four Quorums on the North American continent. Each had a chunk of geography under their purview. The Northern Quorum had the northern portion. I'll let you guess what the other three were called. In a nutshell, they were the overseeing bodies for all serious matters involving paranormals. Since humans outnumbered PNs somewhere on the order of ten to one, we generally lived by their rules and their laws. If a werewolf was speeding to a butcher shop, he'd get a human law traffic ticket. If he knocked off the local butcher shop and stole a bunch of rib-eyes, he'd get jailed for theft. But if that werewolf killed and ate the butcher, the Quorum would step in to mete out its own justice. They didn't just handle the PN-human crimes, either. If that proverbial butcher had been a PN as well, the Quorum would still do its thing, but doubly so. I'd only heard rumors. If they were true, though, punishments for truly egregious paranormal-on-paranormal crimes were severe. Like, majorly severe. The Quorums were the linchpins that kept the human-PN grenade from blowing up and kept the myriad of PNs from tearing each other apart. It was a serious responsibility. As essential—and usually invisible—as gravity. Yet a member of that mysterious body had intervened in my not-to-be-intervened-with death.

"Why didn't I die?" I asked.

The leprechaun winked. "Like I said, lad. Your lucky day."

"Why are you here, though? Like, the Quorum you, not just you you."

"Ah, that," the leprechaun replied, with a return of his earlier joviality. "If memory serves, you're not one who is overly fond of the loquacious leanings of my leprechaun kin. Isn't that so?"

My eyebrows lowered, and I gave my head a slight shake.

"Pity. They say brevity is the soul of wit. I say, sure, for halfwits. To wit, then, I shall be brief. In a word? Her."

He pointed at where Dagmara was folded into the Strach na wróble's long arms.

"She notified us of crimes against the corn spirits. We'd suspected for some time that facilities like this were being set up by ne'er-do-wells like those two. Turning the fair maidens of the field into their chemical fertilizers. Unspeakably awful. Simply not acceptable."

"Fertilizer?" I asked stupidly.

"Fertilizer," the leprechaun agreed somberly. "With these kettles and cauldrons—and a healthy dose of nefarious intent—those poor spirits are being... rendered," he said after searching for the appropriate word. "The resulting liquid is used to fertilize modified seeds for high-yield fields full of unexpectedly strange crops. Imagine someone grinding you up, gristle and bone, then serving you to an orphanage full of hungry tots."

I shuddered, and the leprechaun nodded.

"Exactly. As luck would have it, the Cornflower Wraith found her conscience. Once we knew where to look, it was no trouble finding this location, and here we are!" he finished with a clap of his small hands.

A cold dread settled in my miraculously unshot stomach.

"You know how they got the corn dolly, then?"

Those bright eyes regarded my own.

"Aye, lad. We know."

I looked to where she stood, still wrapped in the Strach na wróble's embrace. Perhaps it was his height or the unusual length of his arms. Perhaps it was my vantage point, looking up from where I sat. Whatever it was, Dagmara looked very small.

"What will happen to her?"

The leprechaun sighed and brushed invisible flecks of dust from the front of his jacket, then tugged at its hem to straighten it. After a brief clearing of a throat, he spoke six words that seared my soul.

"The Quorum will deal with her."

"But the corn spirit," I protested. "It... I mean, she's okay, isn't she? Because Dagmara called you. That has to count for something."

He nodded. "Of a certainty, it does. Absolutely. Your advocacy has also been noted, as has that of the noble Strach na wróble. Battling those two lizards. Nearly sacrificing himself for the sake of the corn spirit. Quite impressive. I'd say there's an award in that fellow's future, but it appears someone's beaten me to that particular punch," he finished with a wink and a tap of his lapel.

"But Dagmara..." I pleaded again.

"Will be dealt with," he repeated, "but fairly, lad. I promise you that. She will be dealt with fairly. Now, I don't think you need to worry yourself about her anymore, do you?"

His tone closed the door on that conversation, and I wasn't dumb enough to push it open again. Instead, I turned to another question.

"Why am I alive, though? Don't say 'luck' again. If I was supposed to die, shouldn't I be, you know, dead?"

The leprechaun put his hands on his knobby knees and leaned in until his nose was mere inches from my own.

"We know you, August Shade. You're trending. Hashtag 'Shady Shifter.' Quite clever. Anyway, we've taken an interest."

"I don't understand," I admitted.

"Nor do you need to. Not tonight. On this fair evening, just know you had a little luck o' the Irish. That's a fine thing, wouldn't you agree?"

The way he spoke was almost hypnotic. That lilt, that cadence, made his words infinitely listenable and eminently sensible.

"I guess," I agreed.

"Grand. Just grand. Now, you'd best be on your way. Let's hope your lucky coin has another turn or two in it, else you'll have a long walk home."

I frowned, put a hand in my jacket pocket, and out came that gold coin again, sans the slug. The leprechaun winked, and I let it fall back into my pocket.

"Can I say goodbye to them?" I asked with a tilt of my head toward Dagmara and the Strach na wróble.

"Of course, lad. Of course. Be quick, though. Luck won't last forever, and it is a long walk home."

The leprechaun dismissed me so completely that I felt like I'd ceased to exist. His short legs and pointy shoes skipped across the cave's floor until he reached the two hogtied suits.

"Hideeleeho and a grand hello, lads! We need to have a little chat. Or rather, you need a talking to, seeing as how you can't talk. I've some words for your masters."

I tuned out the leprechaun and made my careful way to the Cornflower Wraith and the Strach na wróble. That gunnysack face turned and those weird X eyes found mine. Dagmara, though, pressed her face harder into its singed and threadbare lapel.

"I am glad you survived," the scarecrow said, its rough whisper heavy with emotion, "and thank you for trying to save me."

"Yeah, well," I started, but couldn't think of what to say. "You're welcome," I finally managed. "You sure you're okay?"

"The fire was extinguished. Had Dagmara not arrived when she did, it would have been a different matter."

I saw her shoulders convulse and heard a muffled sob.

"Hush, hush," the Strach na wróble said. "It is done."

The Cornflower Wraith pulled back from his embrace. That heavy mascara was a mess.

"It is, isn't it?" she sighed, then turned to me. "August, I. I don't," she tried, then angrily shook her head. "I don't know what to say. Sorry doesn't even come close to cutting it. I had no idea you'd get pulled into this. None of this was supposed to happen."

I shrugged. "It never is. But, thanks, I guess? I mean, for. Uh," I said with a sheepish glance at the Strach na wróble. "For doing the right thing. For what it's worth, the leprechaun said the Quorum will definitely take that into consideration or whatever. You know, when they…"

"Judge me," Dagmara said heavily.

"… Yeah."

The woman untangled herself from her ex's embrace and turned to hug me hard.

"Goodbye, August."

I hugged her back, then felt a tug at my pocket. Surprised, I reached inside and felt a thick fold of bills.

"You deserve that more than the damned bank," she said, "and I don't think I'll need it after this."

I nodded silently, not trusting my voice. When I could speak, I said, "I've got a safe in my office. It will be there. All of it. Because you're going to come and get it."

There was gratitude in her eyes. For the offer to keep her money safe or for the fantasy I'd told, I didn't know.

The garage door led to a sloping ramp. It emerged on the far end of the gravel pit, near where the island's historic limestone kiln stood silhouetted against the pre-dawn sky. As I looked around, I gave a slow whistle. The tunnels I'd crawled through must've been a lot longer than I'd realized. I found the main road, then walked north. There were too many thoughts to hold in my head, so I opted to not think any of them. I put one foot in front of the other and was content to just do that. Maybe a mile or so had passed when I pulled the gold coin from my pocket. A flick of my thumb sent it spinning into the air, then I caught it as it came back down. Again, I sent the coin up, and again caught it on the way down. On the third flick, a car passed me. When I caught the coin again, the car slowed, stopped, and reversed.

"Need a lift?" the driver asked after lowering a window.

"Must be my lucky day," I replied tiredly. "Sure. Why not?"

⚓

I lifted my can and discovered it was empty. A glance at the sidewalk informed me it had been my fourth, which meant it was probably time to hit the pause button. Jay had barely touched his most recent beer, so caught up had he been in my tale. Philo had polished off one bottle of wine and was well on his way to finishing a second.

"The poor woman," he sighed. "She did what she thought was best, knowing all the while that what she was doing was horrible. The Quorum may be fair, but they will not be kind."

"They wouldn't, you know, kill her, though. Right?" Jay asked, looking worriedly from the satyr to me and back. "They wouldn't do that, would they?"

I honestly didn't know and said as much. The Northern Quorum was a mystery to the likes of me.

"I'm certain it won't come to that," Philo said as he reached out to pat Jay's hand. "I'm sure it will all be fine in the end. We're the creatures of folklore and fairy tales, are we not? And don't they always have happy endings?"

Jay took a slow drink, then looked from the satyr to me and back.

"What about those Department of Agriculture guys?" he asked. "Grinding up corn spirits and making fertilizer? They better get what's coming to them. The Northern Quorum can do something about that, right? I mean, I get that they're usually focused on PNs. But when humans do something really awful to your kind, the Quorum can do... something, right?"

When Philo didn't answer, my friend turned his concerned and angry expression my way. I chewed my lip and weighed what I was about to share. I wasn't sure of what I'd seen, and lord knew I didn't want to dump gas on Jay's crazy-fire, but...

"I'm not sure they were human, Jay."

Both his and Philo's eyes went wide.

"They were PNs?" Jay asked. "What were they? You didn't say they were paranormal."

"Maybe they were. Maybe they weren't."

I shared what I thought I'd seen and put a heavy emphasis on the word 'thought.' It had been pretty chaotic down in that cave, and I'd been pretty rattled. What I thought I'd seen, though, was that gigantic schnozz on Schnozz hanging off to the side. Not broken. More like broken off. Beneath it were two slits surrounded by green scales.

"And you said the leprechaun called them lizards," Jay said with growing wonder. "And the butter room. When you were fighting. They were so slow. Oh. My. God. I'm such an idiot."

When Philo and I both cocked our heads in confusion, Jay leveled a serious look at at us.

"Those aliens? They aren't from out there," he said with a vague wave at the afternoon sky. "They're from down there," he proclaimed as he pointed at the ground. "Way down there. How could I have missed that?"

"What is 'that,' exactly?" Philo asked as he looked nervously from my conspiracy-crazed friend to me and back.

"They're reptilians. Hollow Earth theory?" he asked. "No? No, of course not. There are people who believe—and with plenty of evidence, too—that a race of sentient reptiles live deep under the Earth's crust. All the CO2 we're pumping into the atmosphere? Global warming? It's for them. They want to move to the surface."

The satyr flicked me a surreptitious glance, and I returned it with a small shrug. I used to think Jay's conspiracies were a funny quirk. They'd always made for interesting conversations. Silly yarns that passed the time while drinking our beers. That was all. After the past week, though...

"There's really just one thing left," I said, pushing the topic in a new direction. "I have to help Guinevere O'Brien. No clue how. Maybe the leprechaun?" I mused.

Philo shook his head. "The Quorum interceded on your behalf once, August. It wouldn't be wise to beseech them again."

"I didn't beseech anyone," I grumbled.

"Still," he placated. "This is one problem you'd be better fixing on your own."

Against my better judgment, I fished another can out of the case of beer at my feet. Sometimes, drinking too much was a problem. Sometimes, it was the only appropriate thing to do.

"But how?" I complained. "What do I know about getting ghosts out of spoons? Setting spirits free? Nothing, that's what." A heavy sigh slipped out. "It just kills me to know the poor lady has been stuck for over a century, endlessly tormented, and is now a novelty at a hag's all-you-can-eat buffet. Kills me," I said again, then laughed a harsh laugh. "Why does that expression feel different than it used to?"

The three of us drank in silence for a few minutes. Me in my usual pensive state. Philo in a quiet contemplation that was at odds with his usual exuberance and mirth. Jay in a growing state of fidgety nervousness.

"What, Jay? What?" I finally asked. "You obviously have something to say. Just say it before you fidget yourself into a low-earth orbit."

The artist took a breath and released it. Took another, and said, "Um." Finally, on the third attempt, he said, "Don't get mad. I've been doing some research, and I think I know how to help."

CHAPTER 19

ELOUISE'S BED-AND-BREAKFAST LOOMED LARGE in the day's fading light. To my left, Fannie sucked on her gums and looked even more dour than usual. To my right, Jay looked like he had to pee, shifting restlessly from foot to foot. I deliberately didn't consider how I might look. I'd seen more than enough of myself in the recent past.

"You sure you know what you're doing, youngster?" Fannie asked.

Jay shrugged. Not exactly the confidence-inspiring gesture I was looking for, but I told myself that beggars can't be choosers. Of the three of us, he was the closest to an expert we had. I tried to ignore the fact that he'd never actually done what he was going to do. I tried to convince myself that everything would work out fine. Denial was nice and all, but I couldn't sustain it.

"You don't have to do this, Jay," I mumbled. "I mean, it's great that you want to help. But Guinevere has been a ghost for the better part of a hundred and fifty years. A few more weeks, even months, probably won't matter much."

The artist gave me a hurt look. "You don't think I can pull this off?" he asked.

"No! No, it's not that," I hastily lied. "I trust you. We trust you."

When Fannie didn't say anything, I elbowed her in the ribs.

"What's that for?" she spat. "Yah, I trust you. As far as I can throw you," she added. When Jay gaped, the hag laughed. "Stupid human. I can throw you pretty far, and that's a fact."

A look of relief washed over the artist, ahem, warlock-in-training. Just thinking those words darkened my already dark mood. He'd assured me at least thirty times on the drive down to Grey Cloud Island that he was being careful, that spells were more like cooking than anything else, that he wasn't going anywhere near the really bad stuff. After each proclamation, I had nodded, then twisted my bike's throttle a bit to drown out whatever else he might've wanted to say.

"Well, let's get this over with," I said.

The plan, if you could call it that, was simple. Fannie would deal with her sister. I'd deal with Blunder and his cronies. It was a sure thing they were around, too. The coblyn's sedan was parked in the drive. And Jay? Jay would do whatever Jay was going to do. He'd stuffed a backpack with stuff. I hadn't been there for the stuffing, though, so I had no clue what he'd assembled for the chore ahead.

"I said, let's get this over with. So, you know. A little privacy, please?"

Fannie flapped a dismissive hand at me and turned her back. Jay rolled his eyes and turned away as well. We were just past the tree line, which I hoped would protect me from any other prying eyes. If it didn't, well, they were in for a very unexciting show. Unless, of course, they were really into watching a middle-aged guy take his clothes off in public.

A few short moments later, a gorilla hunkered down on all fours next to a pile of clothes topped off with a black leather jacket.

"Gwarr," I said, then chuffed and thudded a fist against my chest. I was ready.

"You sure you don't know where she put my spoon?" the hag asked me.

I shook my big gorilla head, and she sighed in disgust.

"Stupid shifter. You were there for half a night. What were you doing? Wasting time, that's what. Doing nothing. Youngsters. Not a lick of sense in any of you, is there?"

A gorilla fist readied to knock her senseless.

Leave it, I counseled myself. *Just leave it.*

The hag spat one last time, then set her bowed legs in motion and waddled across the bed-and-breakfast's front lawn. I lumbered along behind her, listening to her interminable muttering the whole way. While I waited in the yard, she took the porch steps one at a time. Each step was a clear complaint about the inconvenience the damned things caused. When she reached the front door, she didn't bother with knocking.

"Open up, Elouise. It's your sister. Open this door right now!"

The door opened, but it was Blunder that filled the lower third of its opening, not Elouise.

"Stand aside, you little pipsqueak, or I'll suck you dry."

Blunder feigned hurt incredulity like a pro.

"You wouldn't," he protested. "I've got no quarrel with you, hag."

"You'd be wise to shut your yap," she replied. "You've caused enough trouble already. Fetch my sister, tell her to bring my spoon, and we'll be done with you. Don't," she warned with a tilt of her head in my direction, "and things'll be getting rough."

The coblyn leaned to the side and looked past Fannie's girth. His dark eyes found mine and narrowed.

"It's gonna be like that, is it?"

"It is," she agreed, then hollered, "Elouise! You get down here this minute."

A moment later, the other hag appeared. Despite their similar appearances, the differences were striking. In my short time knowing Fannie, I'd learned quite a bit about her. Was she an irritable, life force-sucking wretch? Sure, but underneath all of that, there was something like a decent person. Elouise, on the other hand, was the pits.

"Have you come to your senses, sister?" Elouise asked. "Or will you be living in squalor and always wondering if you'll have your next meal?"

"You've built a fine house. That you have," Fannie said, "but you did it with this tyrant's coin and on the back of dear Ginny's suffering. That can't be, sister. You know that what you have here isn't worth having. You know it."

Elouise sniffed. "Who doesn't need coin, and who isn't suffering? You and me, sister, haven't we suffered? Why should some lady whose life is long gone be worth more than yours or mine?"

I shifted my weight from fist to fist impatiently. Shifting took a toll. Never mind that the gorilla was probably the easiest one in my repertoire. It wasn't like trying to squish myself into a turkey or a cud-chewing bull. Still, I didn't want to be not-human for any longer than was necessary. Something had to give, or I was going to have to call it a night. No sooner had that thought furrowed my heavy brows over my beady eyes than something gave.

Fannie pleaded again with her sister. Elouise rebuffed her again with her usual sass. Blunder, apparently bored with the whole ordeal, circled a finger, and those goons that I'd known were lurking about appeared. They approached Fannie, menace clear in every step.

"You wouldn't," Fannie whispered, disbelieving, and then one of the coblynau punched her hard in the stomach, and the other tackled her legs.

Cue the pissed-off gorilla, I thought with no small amount of satisfaction, then I waded into the fray.

At the end, it wasn't much of a fight. Coblynau are strong and fast, eager to bite when the need's upon them, and surprisingly resilient. Against a gorilla, though, and without their contraptions? Forget about it. As I knocked them around like a reenactment of Gulliver with an alternate ending—all the while savoring the sweet comeuppance of paying them back for the hurt they'd caused me—I found my mind wandering. For someone that was generally not prone to violence, I'd been in my fair share of recent scraps: rolling in the dirt with a goblin, playing bull fight with a scarecrow, getting shot by a Department of Agriculture operative that maybe lived far underground, and now throwing down with three coblynau.

And I don't have medical insurance, I thought. *Not smart, August.*

Righty pulled his gun. I squeezed his head between one thumb and a forefinger, plucked the pistol from his hand, and sent it sailing over the house's roof. Lefty climbed up my back and onto my shoulder. The jerk was boxing first one ear, then the other. I roared, yanked him free, then sent him flying across the yard. Distraction gone, I let my thoughts drift back to pondering my life. After years of laying low and letting the world pass me by, I was suddenly involved in a bunch of shit that was way too big. It didn't suit me, and I knew it.

Righty had produced a fork and was doing his best to shove its tines into my ass cheek. He wasn't strong enough to do real damage, but getting poked with a fork was still annoying. I kicked a foot back and caught the coblyn in the chest. He swore and stumbled away, fork forgotten, as he clasped his arms around a few badly bruised ribs.

And Jay, I thought worriedly. *He shouldn't be doing this stuff. He shouldn't be involved in any of this.*

Blunder himself had entered the fray. His smoldering eyes held a fury that would've worried me more had I still been human-sized and stuck in his punchy-chair. The gorilla, though, just hunched its massive shoulders. The coblyn's angry eyes flicked nervously from side to side. Ten or fifteen yards away, Lefty was still trying to pick himself up, and Righty was moaning on the ground. I bared my big, pointy gorilla teeth, stood up, and gave my chest a couple of good thumps.

"To hell with this," the loan shark finally spat. "Keep the spoon or not, Elouise. I don't care, but I'll be expecting my payment."

Elouise's spine stiffened, then she crumpled to the ground. Her fancy gown piled around her like a deflated hot-air balloon. Fannie looked down her warty nose and harrumphed in satisfaction. Blunder fired up his pipe and tried to act aloof. The scuffle was apparently over, so I lumbered back to my pile of clothes.

"Is it done?" Jay asked.

"Getting there," I replied after shifting and pulling on my clothes. "Be right back."

I crossed the yard again, stood off to the side while Fannie clacked and Elouise clattered.

"You see?" Fannie said. "Those nasty little coblynau are done. You got no one to help you, sister. Enough of this. Give me my spoon."

"You would, wouldn't you?" Elouise snapped. "Take that spoon right from my mouth. You, so high and mighty now, you'd starve your own sister."

"Oh, for fuck's sake, just shut up," I finally yelled. The post-shifting headache had turned my usually thin patience transparent. "Both of you. Shut up."

Amazingly, they did. Two similar and equally horrible old faces turned my way, and neither one spoke.

Will wonders never cease? I thought.

"Elouise, you don't need Guinevere O'Brien. I know. I was in there, and what you've got is damned impressive."

The truth of my own words surprised me. I'd been scared. Scared witless, until Snarchurraga had her little coughing fit. Before that, though, I had honestly thought the place was haunted.

"Look, I hate to say it, but what Blunder and his coblynau did in there, what Snarchurraga does, it's awesome."

Blunder looked up at me with unbelieving eyes, and Righty bumped fists with Lefty.

"Doesn't matter if it isn't a real haunting," I continued, then inspiration struck. "Have you been to the State Fair?"

"What's that got to do with this?" Elouise asked.

"Stupid shifter," Fannie added. "Did the little cobs rattle your brain, make you dumber than normal? What's this about the Fair?"

I let the insults slide and asked if they knew how many people went to the Great Minnesota Get-Together every year.

"Over two million," I said when they'd shaken their heads. "And one of the biggest attractions is the haunted house. Thousands of people wait in line for the damned thing, and there isn't a real ghost in the place. Just a bunch of teenagers in cheap costumes... and an honest-to-god revenant. You two ever heard of Dieter Saint James?"

The sisters shared a look. "Yeah," Elouise finally said. "Heard that old vampire got tossed in the drink. Took his last dip in the mighty Mississipp'. Why?"

"Well, back when he was among the living, uh... undead. Whatever. He made revenants, and one of them is a buddy of mine. Guy got tossed in a wood chipper, then Saint James stitched him back together. Looks like one of Doctor Frankenstein's whoopsies. Scary as hell. He works at the Fair's haunted house, but that's only for a couple of weeks. He'll be looking for a new job soon, and I bet he'd love to work here. Between what Snarchurraga does and him roaming around and saying, 'Boo!' now and then, this place will be a hit. Oh, and I'll bet his girlfriend will help. She's a revenant, too. Died of cancer. Even so, she's gotta be a better cook than either of you. White toast and coffee? Seriously?"

Fannie turned a skeptical look at her sister. "What's he going on about, Elouise? What's a snarchagar?"

Elouise sniffed. "You've been so busy telling me I'm a dolt and a dullard and a terrible sister that you didn't even come look at what I've done. And it's Snarchurraga, Blunder's niece, thrice removed. Come out here, lass. Let's get a look at you."

A dark face full of pins and bones appeared in the living room window, disappeared, and reappeared at the still-open door. The goblin hunch walked onto the porch and gave what might've been an attempt at a curtsy.

"Uncle. Ma'am," she said. "Other ma'am. August."

I offered a wave, and Fannie wiggled the fingers of a hand in a confused hello.

"There's a goblin in your house, sister," she said.

"You think I don't know that?" Elouise snapped. "She was hanging around that nasty goblin at the end of our lane. He was a worthless lout. Snarchurraga, though, is quite a dear."

Before another argument could erupt, I quickly pointed out that Blunder, despite his general unpleasantness, was a coblyn. He and his kind were skilled and had worked some pretty impressive wonders inside the house.

"And that goblin is the real magic," I said. "She runs all the gears and levers and stuff. Makes the haunting happen."

A blush would never be apparent on the goblin's mottled skin, but I was sure it was there.

"Elouise, Snarcharagga, why don't you give Fannie a tour?"

"Is it over?" a voice called from the distance. "Are you guys still fighting?"

I cupped my hands around my mouth and hollered back to where the artist was still hiding in the trees.

"No one's fighting anymore! Come on up. We're going to tour the haunted house. You'll love it."

While Jay trotted across the wide lawn, I turned back to Elouise. "And when we're done, you're giving Fannie back her spoon."

"You're a crafty one, aren't ya, shifter?" Fannie remarked as she and I joined Jay at the cemetery's edge.

The tour had been great. As Snarchurraga worked her magic, Jay had jumped out of his skin at least ten times, and even old Fannie gave a start once or twice. The fetid wound between the sisters slowly healed as Elouise pointed out this detail and that, showed Fannie how they could slip around in the crawlspaces, how they'd be able to get their fill from the sleeping guests.

"All part of the experience," she'd said proudly. "Their nightmares. That restless, foggy feeling in the morning after we've had our taste. They'll come down for breakfast and scare each other silly all over again as they tell their tales. Then off they go, and a fresh crop of fools shows up that same afternoon."

"And just think," I'd said. "When they look out the window at night, it won't be at some crying lady in the distance. It'll be Leonard and all his stitches and staples lurching about. When they come down for breakfast the next morning, a gaunt walking corpse will poach their eggs. Way scarier."

Of course, I'd still have to convince Leonard and Mona to take the gig, but something told me they'd love it.

The more Jay and Fannie exclaimed over how great the house was, the more Elouise relented. Finally, at the end of the tour, she'd opened a simple display case hanging on a wall, and had retrieved a small, silver spoon.

Fannie calling me crafty felt like a compliment, and it brought a crooked smile to my face. "I get things back after a messy breakup," I said, "and sometimes, those folks get back together. All part of the job, I guess."

"Not so stupid after all," Fannie grudgingly admitted.

"You're welcome. Now, Jay?" I asked. "You ready?"

My friend nodded from where he stood next to Guinevere's gravestone. He'd emptied the contents of his backpack and pointed to each item in turn.

"Sage, to clear the bad energy. White candles to light the way. A white rose to draw in the spirit. Fire," he said with the flick of an old Zippo, "to cleanse the soul. A compass to show the path, and salt to ensure the spirit can't return," he finished while pointing at a compass with an intricately engraved cover and a mason jar full of white crystals.

"You learned all this how, exactly?" I asked.

Jay shrugged. "By studying," he asked with uncharacteristic churlishness. Then, more gently, "A couple of friends online pointed me toward a few places on the dark web."

"The dark web," I repeated, not understanding. "What's the dark web?"

"Geez, you really are out of touch, aren't you?" he replied instead of answering. "Well, I'm all set. All I need is the spoon."

Fannie opened her palm to reveal the small piece of worked silver. As her fingers uncurled, I saw something out of the corner of my eye and heard the echo of an echo of a soft sob.

"She's here," I said.

Jay nodded and started the ritual, or whatever it was, while I crossed my arms and watched. First, he lit the sage and waved it in a few wide circles. Plumes of cloying smoke hung in the late summer eve's still air. Satisfied, he extinguished the smoldering clump of herbs and then smudged a few strange markings on Genevieve's gravestone. Next, the Zippo lit the white candles, five in all, which he then set at the points of an invisible pentagram around the grave. The roses were next. He set them gently on top of the grave, then stepped back.

"The spoon," he said in a low voice.

Fannie held out her hand, but curled her fingers reflexively when Jay reached out. After a moment, she relented.

"Wow..." he sighed, carefully pinching its silver handle between his fingers. "Oh, wow."

The flicker of white that had been just past the edge of my sight moved. It was over there, then over there, and then—suddenly—directly across the grave from us. Guinevere O'Brien hollow eyes pleaded and her fingers clawed at the air. In response, Jay bent to set the spoon down next to the roses, then picked up the compass. He opened its lid, and I saw the needle spinning madly inside its housing. The artist held a hand open over the compass, palm down and fingers splayed. His lips moved silently, and the needle ceased its crazed spinning and pointed directly at his chest.

My arms were still crossed, and my hands squeezed my biceps. Jay and the ghost stared at one another, her with open agony and him with steely resolve.

"I'm sorry," Fannie suddenly blurted out. "I'm so sorry, and you have to know it. I'm sorry for what I done. I'm sorry for that little baby boy."

Jay's eyes narrowed, and his hand moved. A subtle tilting, and the needle in the compass moved. No longer did it point at the artist's chest. Now it pointed at the hag.

"What's happening?" I asked.

"She could have another chance," he said. "Guinevere. I could bring her back."

My jaw dropped. "What? What are you talking about?"

The ghost turned her sightless pits to face Fannie. The furtive grasping of her hands intensified and her mouth stretched wide. That distant wail took on a new timbre; less sad, more angry.

"Her. The hag," Jay said. "She doesn't deserve that body. Not after what she did. I can give it to Guinevere." His voice had an edge of wonder to it. "I can bring her back."

Fannie held her hands out and took a step back. Before she could turn and flee, Jay grabbed her wrist. His other hand thrust the compass toward the terrified hag.

"Jay…" I begged. "Think about it. How does that help? Guinevere O'Brien living here, now? Her boy's still gone. What would there be for her?"

The artist blinked in confusion. "But… But I could do it. I can do it."

"Can or can't isn't the question, Jay. Should or shouldn't. That's the question, right? Don't you think you should set the poor woman free? After all this time, all the long years that she's suffered."

When he turned to look at me, there was comprehension in his eyes, but also a hunger. A hint of madness. I saw my friend, my only friend, teeter on the brink of a high cliff. At its base was a deep and unrelenting darkness.

"Jay," I pleaded again. "C'mon, Jay. What are you doing? This isn't you. You aren't Tony or Dieter."

"You don't know who I am," he said in a low, harsh whisper, "or who I can become."

I took a cautious step forward.

"Yes, I do. And I know you aren't someone that kills people. You aren't like them," I said, with heavy emphasis on the 'them.' "You're one of the good guys, right?"

There was a long moment where the only sounds I could hear were Fannie's pathetic pleas, Jay's heavy breathing, and the pounding of my own terrified heart.

"Yes," he finally—thankfully—agreed. "Of course. Of course."

His fingers released Fannie's wrist, and the hag fell hard on her rump. Jay swung the compass around and angled his arm downward so it made a straight line to the white roses on the grave.

"There," he whispered.

I felt a gust of wind and heard a woman's forlorn sigh. While I watched, the shape of Guinevere came apart in wisps and tendrils. A moment later, the roses bloomed, then withered and faded. When the petals were little more than translucent echoes of their former glory, Jay stepped onto the grave. First, he took the spoon and shoved it into the mason jar of salt. Next, he took the Zippo and held its flame to the roses' stems. They caught like a fuse. Fire raced up, obliterating stem and thorn and leaf, then finally, the faded blossoms. As the fire consumed the flowers, there was a bright flash. All five of the candles flared, and then extinguished. While the light they'd cast had been meager, the darkness without them was startling.

"So, that was it?" I asked carefully.

Fannie looked up at the sound of my voice. "Say it's so, warlock. Say it's over. Say that she's at peace."

Jay had fallen to his knees, hands on the ground and head hanging down.

"I'll say no such thing," he said in a voice that couldn't have been his. "Your punishment isn't over. You'll never know if she's at peace. You'll only know that you aren't. Go."

Fannie scrabbled backward, then rolled to her knees, found her feet, and ran for her sister's house. I didn't dare move. I could hardly breathe. I stood, a statue among the gravestones, until Jay gasped and looked up.

"August? August. Holy shit. I did it. She's free. Guinevere O'Brien is free! I did it," he exclaimed, then laughed. "I knew it. Wait. Where's Fannie? Did she see? Where'd she go?"

I kept myself still, inside and out.

"She saw, and she's gone home to her sister. You, uh, don't remember that?"

The smile faltered. "Yes? Maybe? Oh, I don't know," he admitted with a fresh smile to replace the one that had dimmed. "But it's done. That sure was something, wasn't it?"

I nodded, then helped Jay to his feet.

"That sure was," I agreed. "That was definitely something."

CHAPTER 20

"Farmers only worry during the growing season, but townspeople worry all the time."
- Edgar Watson Howe

J AY TOOK HIS CHANGE from Philo and offered a wave of thanks.

"I'll tell you more about it next time," he promised, "as long as you're still wearing pants."

"As you must, young warlock," the satyr replied. "Pants or no, I must hear the tale."

I had the case of beer and hoisted it up to a shoulder to make carrying it easier. The world beyond Philo's Liquors seemed completely normal. How that could be, I didn't know. All I'd learned, all that I'd experienced, made that normalcy feel like a thin shroud over much stranger things. With a start, I realized it was how the conspiracy theorist must feel damn near all the time.

"Young warlock," Jay repeated as we walked. "I don't know about all that, but I gotta admit that it sounds pretty cool."

I grunted, earning me an eye-roll from my friend.

"I know you don't approve, but I'm not like Tony. Or Dieter Saint James. You know that."

I grunted again, but softened it with a smile. "Well, you're not a douchebag, and you're not orange."

Another block had passed when Jay asked if Leonard and Mona had taken the gig. When I replied that yes, the revenants were going to help a couple of old hags haunt a bed-and-breakfast, Jay clapped his hands in delight.

"Awesome. We'll have to go visit."

Another grunt passed my lips. If Jay wanted to be a hag's midnight snack, more power to him. I had other plans. We reached the old casket factory-turned-art-studios, and I paused by the front door.

"Hang on a sec," I said. "Don't make it obvious, but do you see that dark blue minivan across the street?"

Jay looked at me curiously, then let his eyes expertly flick over my shoulder and back to my face. "Yeah? So?"

"I think it's been following me," I whispered as I headed inside and started to climb the stairs.

Jay stopped a step below, then took the next few two at a time to catch up. "Seriously? You're sounding like me, August. In a good way, though. I like what I'm seeing here."

I waited while he unlocked the studio's door, then followed him inside. While he loaded the fridge, I checked my answering machine. There were a couple of messages. I jotted down the names and numbers so I could call them later and break the bad news. Then I spun the dials on each of the four safes that lined the back of my office. One after another, I opened the safes for stupid stuff, sappy stuff, valuable stuff, and dangerous stuff. All but one was empty. The money Dagmara had given me sat in neat stacks of bills. I hoped that someday she'd stop by and we'd reminisce about the bizarre adventures we'd endured. I told myself that day would come and ignored how unlikely it felt.

The phone was next. I gently disconnected its curly cord, then unplugged the answering machine. I watched its red digital zero fade to black and nodded.

"Where you at?" Jay called from the other room. "It's beer o'clock."

I gave my office one last look, then pulled the chain on the lightbulb dangling down from the ceiling. The door swung shut, handle already locked, and I walked as casually as possible to my customary bean bag on the studio's floor.

"Thanks," I said as I accepted a beer.

"You bet," Jay replied, then scooted a camping chair closer to where I sat. "Okay. Let's talk about that van. Who do you think it is? Department of Agriculture? Blunder?"

I had no clue because I'd made that bit about the van up. I'd seen it on the street a few moments prior, and inspiration had struck. My decision to get out of town for a while—or, more specifically, to get away from Jay for a while—had been made. All I had needed was an excuse.

"I don't know, and I don't really want to find out," I said while thinking that at least those words were all true. "I'm worried about that damned video online, too. That 'shady shifter' hashtag or whatever. I've spent years trying to be as hard to find as possible, then some damned nix splashes me all over the interwebs."

Jay nodded sympathetically. He didn't know the half of my past, but I'd shared enough tidbits over the years for him to get the idea. As a conspiracy-minded sort by nature, all I'd had to say were things like, 'secret hospital,' 'experiments,' and, 'escaped.' He had quickly filled in the rest with his supercharged imagination.

While my mind had been wandering, Jay had been talking.

"What's that?" I asked.

"I said, do you want me to go shake them up a bit? Hit 'em with a little vortex? Or I could make it really hot inside the van so they have to come out, then rumble the ground a bit and really give 'em a scare?"

My mouth hung open, speechless, souring Jay's enthusiasm.

"What? They've been messing with our lives for years. Decades. Centuries. Hell, they're not even human. Or paranormal," he added quickly when I gave him a look. "You said you saw scales. August, I know you don't want to believe this, but the Hollow Earthers know what they're talking about. The reptilians have lived underground for millennia, closer to the planet's core. It was fine until Hiroshima. When we started dropping nukes, they got mad and have been working their way into our ranks ever since. We outnumber them, so they're slipping into places of power—like the Department of Agriculture—and pulling levers from the inside. Geoengineering the climate so they can survive up here. Altering our DNA so our future kids are more like them than us. And you're going to give me attitude because I want to give them a little dose of their own medicine? Actually fight back?"

As Jay's tirade had increased in intensity, a breeze began to swirl in the studio. It tugged at my unkempt hair and ruffled the old newspapers Jay kept strewn about.

"Easy," I said as I held out my hands. "Calm down, man. No need to get so worked up."

"Isn't there?" he shot back, but at least I could see his blood pressure coming down.

"No, there isn't," I said as I shifted my weight in the beanbag. A familiar farty sound followed, and we both chuckled. Forced chuckles, sure, but better than nothing. "You might be right, Jay," I placated. "About all of it. But messing with them isn't going to help."

And it would absolutely terrify the poor guy in that van, whoever he is, I thought with a twinge of guilt.

I got up, went to the window, and peeled back a corner of tinfoil. Thankfully, the van was gone.

"Anyway, it's a moot point now. They've gone. False alarm."

The artist leaned back in his camping chair, defeat clear in every line of his body.

"You just don't get it, do you?" he said sadly. "They're never gone. Ever. They are always out there."

I seized the moment. "Well, that's why I've been thinking. I'm going to get out of town for a bit. Lie low. Let the internet thing and the Ag Ops thing and... well, everything just cool down a bit."

Jay's head nodded absently, then tilted. His eyes narrowed as they looked at me. Really looked at me.

"Wait. You're leaving?"

"Just for a little while," I soothed. "Like I said, let things cool down a bit."

The artist chewed on his thumbnail for a moment.

"Yeah, I guess. I mean, that makes sense. Sure. Where are you going to go?"

I turned my palms up and shrugged. "Maybe north? Duluth? Two Harbors? Or further inland to the Iron Range? Not sure."

He went back to worrying his thumbnail, then asked if I had a place to stay.

"No, but I've got enough cash to cover a cheap room for a while."

He nodded reluctantly. "So, that's it. Wow. When are you leaving?"

My throat closed up for a minute, then I said, "Uh, today. Now, I guess."

"Now?" Jay exclaimed. "You jerk. Fine. Just... One more beer first."

I laughed. "Before I ride a motorcycle up the highway? I'm dumb, not stupid."

"Lunch, then?" he asked. "We could go to Uncle Sid's."

My head shook slowly from side to side. "Sorry, but I kinda feel like the noose is tightening, you know? All this stuff from the past few months. It's a lot to process. Hey, chin up, little fella," I joked as Jay stuck out his lower lip. "You'll be okay."

"I'm not worried about me," he said.

But I am, I thought sadly. *That's why I have to go.*

* * *

The drive north offered a couple of options. Highway Thirty-Five was the most direct route to Duluth, a smallish city perched on the rocky shores of Lake Superior. I could be there in two, maybe two and a half hours if I didn't dawdle. Here's the thing, though. I didn't have to be there by a certain time. I didn't have to be there at all. I didn't have to be anywhere. If I wanted, I could go as far as Sandstone, another small town along the way, and veer off onto Highway Twenty-Three. The smaller road would offer a little more scenery. Or I could cut across the Minnesota-Wisconsin border and head up on the Sconnie side. Hell, if I wanted, I could go south on Highway Thirty-Five all the way to Mexico's border, then turn around and go back to Duluth. It didn't matter. It just didn't matter. The only thing that did was leaving.

I sat on my bike and considered my options, then finally settled on a meandering drive north. I'd already run through my mental checklist. I'd slipped two months' rent under my landlord's door with a note saying I was going to visit some friends out of state. All the lights were off in my dingy basement apartment. My only appliances, a toaster and a coffee pot, were both unplugged. I'd splurged on a timer for one lamp so it'd flick on and off of its own accord. Why, I didn't know. It wasn't like I cared whether someone broke in. Hell, if they did, they'd be hard pressed to leave things worse than they already were. Mail wasn't an issue. I didn't get any, besides the junk variety addressed to 'resident.' If the mailman couldn't fit it all in the box, he was welcome to drop it on the lobby's floor. At least that way the mice could get at it for their nests and create some value out of the worthless ads and coupons. I glanced at the duffel bag in my sidecar and mentally ran through its contents.

Underwear, socks, jeans, shirts, I cataloged. *Rain gear. Deodorant. Toothbrush. Crap, forgot toothpaste. Fuck it. I'll grab some along the way.*

I had everything I needed. Well, not everything. October was creeping up, and northern Minnesota could tilt from summer to winter in the blink of an eye. I'd spent time in

Duluth, though, and already knew of a few good secondhand stores. Once I found a place to hunker, I could add a few essentials. For now, though?

Good enough, I thought.

With a kick, I convinced my Moto Guzzi to live another day and rolled away from my apartment building. I took a winding route rather than going straight for the freeway's on-ramp. Past Uncle Sid's. Past my local bar where Betty and a regular or two like Ted would maybe pause and wonder why I hadn't stopped by. Past the Broadway Bridge where I hoped the old troll, Canute, was enjoying whatever it was trolls did for fun that didn't involve killing and eating people. Now that I knew beyond a doubt that the Northern Quorum really was a thing, I hoped they continued to turn a blind eye. I also hoped old Canute stuck to crispy douchebags. As I passed place after place, I realized more and more that I loved Nord'east and was reluctant to leave.

Oh, knock it off, a part of my brain complained. *You aren't moving to France, for Pete's sake.*

It's an option, though, an unexpected part of my brain pointed out. *What do I have here? Why stay?*

Hotdogs. Beer. Jay.

Jay. My best and only friend. Sure, I had picked up a few acquaintances. Leonard was a great guy, once you got past his multitude of scars and mopey attitude. Betty and I weren't exactly friends, but it was hard to deny that we had some sort of connection. Despite our many differences, I liked her and knew I would miss her. Then there were the other familiar faces: Ted, Philo, that guy that worked most days at Uncle Sid's. Fine people, all, but not friends. Not really. It was just Jay. The guy that had pretty much saved me when I'd rolled into town all those years ago, penniless and afraid. The guy that had accepted me—secrets and surliness and all—without question.

The guy who's now a warlock with a twitchy magic finger, I added. *The guy that's starting to scare the shit out of me.*

Annoyed, I revved the engine and put an end to my nostalgic toodle. I just needed a little space, a little time. Not everything I'd said to Jay had been a lie. I was worried about that damned video of me online. I was worried about Blunder. I was even a little worried about the possible walking, talking reptiles that may or may not exist, and may or may not be working for a certain government agency. I was worried about my Fetch. We all know we're going to die someday. It was different having a very familiar face telling you when your day had come.

So many worries, and I didn't want to deal with any of them. A stoplight turned green, and I pointed my bike down an on-ramp, picking up speed all the while. With a little luck, the wind would push all that worry from my head. I flicked on my signal and checked my side view mirror for cars. I turned my head back to the highway, then did a double-take in the mirror. A few cars back was what looked like a blue minivan.

"There are lots of blue minivans," I reminded myself. "Don't go down that rabbit hole, August. Don't you dare."

I hunched my shoulders, leaned into the wind, and headed north. And that worry I'd so desperately wanted to leave behind?

It followed.

<hr>

AUTHOR'S NOTE

Thanks for reading! Poor August. If it weren't for bad luck, he'd have no luck at all. Except that isn't quite the case, is it? Our favorite curmudgeonly shapeshifter gets knocked down, sure, but something—call it fate, call it luck, call it good, old-fashioned stubbornness—gets him back on his feet every time. Unfortunately, getting back on your feet means you're primed to get knocked down again.

The misadventures continue in **A Siren Sings Her Heart Out**. *A chance encounter with a siren sends August into the deep end of a very big lake. Will plumbing its depths reveal a world-changing discovery, or send him to a watery grave? For a guy that's tried to not make waves, life is getting pretty choppy. It's sink or swim for the poor repo man. If he's going down, though, August will make sure he goes down singing.*

<hr>

If you like paranormal comedy, sign up for my once-a-month newsletter, **The Paranomedy Pint**, *and get a FREE short story! Each month, I share a great book to read, a fun show to watch, a tasty drink to drink, and a little paranormal weirdness, too.*

<hr>

THE END

Did you have fun?

I HAD A HECK of a good time writing this book. If you enjoyed reading it, I hope you'll take a moment to share a rating or even a review! Ratings and reviews for authors are like tips for bartenders. We love 'em. They also help others who stumble across the book decide if they should give it a try.

Use these QR codes to easily post a review on your preferred site(s):

Amazon

Goodreads

BookBub

A Strach na wróble by Any Other Name...

We've all had that moment.

You're at the store, and you see a shirt. It's a good-looking shirt. The cut, the style, the pattern or print, the buttons or collar. Whatever it is—one particular detail or the sum of its parts—you suddenly image it on you and realize it is you. One-hundred percent. Just like that, you start to think about how good you'll look when you're wearing it. How many heads you'll turn. You take it off the rack and run for the dressing room. That other shirt, the one you're wearing, the one you can't believe you thought was a good shirt before this moment, slides off your back. With barely contained excitement, you slip first one arm, then the other, into those fresh new threads. You tug at the hem, pull at the shoulders, wriggle a bit to help the fabric smooth out. Then you look in the mirror... and hot damn. You look good. Great. Fan-flipping-tastic.

The whole drive home, all you can think about is wearing your new shirt. You're going to roll up in that shirt and you are going to steal the show. Everyone is going to look at you, and they are going to love what they see.

The moment arrives. You pull on that shirt and head out to wherever you're going to debut your snazzy new look. You walk into the room feeling like fate has made you six inches taller and a few IQ points smarter. And then...

And then...

Yup. Someone else is rocking your shirt. The exact same one.

Yeah.

Welp, I had that moment with this book. My 'shirt' was a funny word I'd stumbled across when doing a little brainstorming early in my first draft. The seeds of *Scarecrow* had been planted (pun intended). I knew August would be heading to farm country because I wanted to pull him out of his element. I'd already settled on the corn dolly story, and was kicking around various monsters and supernatural creatures for him to encounter. The idea of a scarecrow as a character had a lot of appeal, but I wanted to make my scarecrow unique. Somewhere in my search for inspiration, I stumbled across the word 'tatterdemalion.' It's an adjective, and a damned good one at that. It means ragged or disreputable in appearance, being in a decayed state or condition, and dilapidated. Nice, right? Now try it as a noun. Say, "The Tatterdemalion." Wow. Pretty awesome, right?

Fast forward to a few weeks before the book's release. I'd received great feedback from my beta readers and was working through some final revisions. My wife was hard at work on my cover. The book's formatting was nearly finished. Soon, so soon, my new book would be in the world. Why I decided to do a quick internet search for 'tatterdemalion,' I don't know. All I know is that I did. This time, though, I added one more word to my search. Instead of just searching for 'tatterdemalion,' I added the word 'folklore.'

Whoopsies. Turns out I wasn't the first genius to use an adjective as a noun.

My search results turned up a vampire-like creature from Ozark folklore and a Marvel villain. How I'd missed that way back in the beginning, I don't know. The important part is that I had.

I won't profess to be an expert on cryptids and creatures and myths and folklore. When I put monsters and the like in my stories, I do a little research and then make them my own. That said, I try not to stray too far from the collective consciousness. Doing so risks confusing—or worse, upsetting—you: my reader. You are the most important person in my writerly world. The last thing I want to do is trip you up or piss you off. That, and I also don't want to get sued by Marvel. When I realized that a quick search online would turn up very different Tatterdemalions from my own, I knew mine had to go.

I loved the Cornflower Wraith. A Polish demon that punishes farm workers. Feared and despised for centuries while just wanting to be loved. She and my scarecrow needed a lot of history for her betrayal and his decision to have the impact I wanted. Originally, their history started with them meeting in Minnesota. When it occurred to me that their relationship could stretch back a lot further than that, I decided to make the Tatterdemalion Polish, too. The next question was whether there was a Polish myth about a scarecrow-like creature. I dug a bit more, but nothing I found quite fit. I didn't want to borrow another myth. I wanted to have the origin of all the myths. The very first creature that inspired all the scary scarecrow tales that followed. In short, I didn't want *a* scarecrow. I wanted *the* scarecrow.

So I translated the word 'scarecrow' to Polish, and the Strach na wróble was born.

Near as I can tell, I'm the first guy at the party wearing this particular shirt. I hope you like it as much as I do!

A Bit About Scott

People say you should write what you know. That's damned good advice, so Scott writes about ordinary Midwesterners making an extraordinary mess of things. Hey, if the flannel fits...

Oh, one more thing. "Ordinary" totally includes vampires, werewolves, zombies, witches, shapeshifters, aliens and more!

Find Scott on:
    www.swbauthorblog.wordpress.com
    www.facebook.com/swbuthor
    www.instagram.com/swbauthor
    www.goodreads.com/swbauthor
    www.bookbub.com/authors/scott-burtness
... and in bars and bowling alleys up in the Midwest.

FREE Short Story

Get *Five Stars,* a FREE demonic horror comedy short story, when you sign up for **The Paranomedy Pint**, Scott's once-a-month email featuring a great book to read, a fun show to watch, something terrific to drink, and a little paranormal weirdness to enjoy!!

BEER-FUELED URBAN FANTASY BY SCOTT BURTNESS

THE MISADVENTURES OF A PARANORMAL
POST-RELATIONSHIP PERSONAL EFFECTS
REPOSSESSION SPECIALIST
An Oracle Walks into a Bar
A Scarecrow Wins an Award
A Siren Sings Her Heart Out

MONSTERS IN THE MIDWEST
Wisconsin Vamp
Northwoods Wolfman
Undead Cheesehead
Monsters in the Midwest: The Complete Trilogy
Bjørn Again: A Monsters in the Midwest short story

ODDS 'n' ENDS
A is for All the Monsters We Can't Stand: A Hilarious Monster-Themed Coloring Book for
Grownups
Story and poems by Scott Burtness | Illustrations by Harold Torres